Robert Holdstock was born in Kent in 1948, and holds a degree in Medical Zoology. His first novel was published in 1976, and he has been a full-time writer ever since. He lives in London.

By the same author

Eye Among the Blind
Earthwind
Necromancer
Where Time Winds Blow
In the Valley of the Statues
The Fetch

Mythago Wood
Lavondyss

The Bone Forest

Robert Holdstock

Grafton
An Imprint of HarperCollinsPublishers

Grafton
An Imprint of HarperCollins*Publishers*
77–85 Fulham Palace Road,
Hammersmith, London W6 8JB

Published by Grafton 1992
9 8 7 6 5 4 3 2 1

First published in Great Britain by
GraftonBooks 1991

Copyright © Robert Holdstock 1976, 1984, 1986, 1987,
1989, 1991

Magic Man first appeared in *Frighteners 2*, 1976; *The Time Beyond Age* first appeared in *Supernova*, 1976; *The Boy who Jumped the Rapids* first appeared in *Beyond the Lands of Never*, 1984; *Thorn* first appeared in *The Magazine of Fantasy and Science Fiction*, 1986; *Scarrowfell* first appeared in *Other Edens*, 1987; *The Shapechanger* first appeared in *GM Magazine*, 1989; *Time of the Tree* first appeared in *Zenith*, 1989.

The Author asserts the moral right to
be identified as the author of this work

Illustrations by Geoff Taylor

ISBN 0 586 21292 2

Set in Times

Printed in Great Britain by
HarperCollinsManufacturing Glasgow

All rights reserved. No part of this publication may be reproduced, stored in a retrieval system, or transmitted, in any form or by any means, electronic, mechanical, photocopying, recording or otherwise, without the prior permission of the publishers.

This book is sold subject to the condition that it shall not, by way of trade or otherwise, be lent, re-sold, hired out or otherwise circulated without the publisher's prior consent in any form of binding or cover other than that in which it is published and without a similar condition including this condition being imposed on the subsequent purchaser.

CONTENTS

The Bone Forest	7
Thorn	97
The Shapechanger	121
The Boy who Jumped the Rapids	149
Time of the Tree	177
Magic Man	193
Scarrowfell	211
The Time Beyond Age	237

The Bone Forest

Time past and time future
Allow but a little consciousness.

T. S. Eliot

ONE

The sound of his sons' excited shouting woke Huxley abruptly at three in the morning. His breath frosting in the freezing room, he shivered his way into his dressing gown, tugged on slippers, and walked darkly and swiftly to the boys' room.

'What the devil – ?'

They were standing at the window, two small, excited shapes, their breath misting the glass. Steven turned and said excitedly, 'A snow woman. In the garden. We saw a snow woman!'

Rubbing the glass for clarity, Huxley peered down at the thick snow that covered the lawn and gardens, and extended, without break, into the field and to the nearby wood. He could just see the fence, a thin dark line in the moongrey landscape. The night was still, heavy with the muffling silence of the snow. He could see clearly enough that a set of deep tracks led from the gate, towards the house, then round to the side.

'What do you mean? A snow woman?'

'All white,' Christian breathed. 'She stopped and looked at us. She had a sack on her shoulder, like Father Christmas.'

Huxley smiled and ruffled the boy's hair. 'You think she's bringing presents?'

'Hope so,' said Steven. In the dark room his eyes glittered. He had just turned eight years old, a precocious and energetic child, and Huxley was conscious of the extent to which he neglected the lad. Steven was forever soliciting instruction, or games, or walks, but there was so much to do, and Huxley rarely had time for frivolity.

The wood. There was so much to map. So much to discover . . .

He found the torch and went down to the back door, opening it wide (pushing against the drifted snow) and shining the beam across the silent yards. Steven huddled by him. His elder brother Christian had returned to bed, cold, teeth chattering.

'What did she look like, this woman? Was she young? Old?'

'Not very old,' Steven whispered. He was holding on to his father's dressing gown. 'I think she was looking for somewhere to sleep. She was going towards the sheds.'

'Dressed in white. Not very old. Carrying a bag. Did she wave at you?'

'She smiled. I think . . .'

By the light of the torch he could see the tracks. He listened hard but there was no sound. Nothing in the chicken hut was being disturbed. He closed the back door, looked out of the front, shining the torch around the wide drive and the garages.

Bolting the door closed he chased his son up to bed, then tucked himself down below the covers, taking ages to get the circulation back into his frozen hands and feet. Jennifer slept soundly next to him, a hunched, curled lump below the eiderdown.

Not even wild horses could wake her when the weather was as cold as this.

4 January 1935

What had woken the boys? Did she call to them? They say not. They were aware of her in some secret way. Steven especially is attuned to the woodland. And it is he who has called this latest visitor from the edge 'Snow Woman'. It may be that she is nothing more than a traveller, using the shelter of Oak Lodge as she makes her way towards Shadoxhurst, or Grimley, one of the towns around. But I am increasingly aware that the wood sheds its mythagos in the night, and that they journey into the unreal world of our reality, before decaying and fading, like the leaf and woodland matter that they are. There have been too many glimpses of these creatures, and insufficient contact. But in the spring, with Wynne-Jones, I shall make the longest journey yet. If we can succeed in passing the Wolf Glen and entering more deeply, then with luck we should begin to make a firmer contact with the products of our own 'mythago-genesis'.

He closed the book and locked it with the small key he kept hidden in his desk, then stood and stretched, yawning fiercely as he tried to wake up a little more. A tall, lean man of forty-five, he was inclined to stoop, especially when writing, and he suffered agonies of back pain. He took little exercise, apart from the long treks into Ryhope Wood, and, as happened every winter, he was allowing himself to become unkempt. His hair was long, hanging over his collar slightly, and with its burden of grey in the oak brown, he was beginning to look older than he was, especially now that he had a winter's growth of grizzled beard (to be removed before he started teaching again, in a week's time).

The diary in which he had just written was not his regular journal, the scientific record of his discoveries and experiments with Wynne-Jones. This was a more private book in which he was keeping a log of 'uncertainties'. He didn't want Steven or Christian reading accounts of his study of *them*. Nor Jennifer. Nor did he want his dreams read, but the dreams he recorded, after visiting the wood, were sometimes so appalling that even he had difficulty in confronting them. These were private thoughts, a private record, for analysis in quieter times.

He kept this second log hidden behind the bookcase where his journals were shelved. He placed the book there now, then tugged on his wellington boots and overcoat.

It was just after dawn, seven thirty or so, and he was aware of two things: the odd silence of the day outside (no clamour from the chicken house), and the second set of tracks through the snow.

These led back, almost in parallel with the first. He could see, now, as he followed them at a distance, that a coat or cloak had trailed between the prints. The right step dragged slightly, as if the woman had been limping.

At the gate, which opened to a track and then a field, there was a crush of snow where the visitor had climbed over and fallen, or struggled upright. Beyond the gate the tracks led down towards the winter wood, and Huxley stood there for a while, staring at the tall, black trees, and the dense infill of bright green holly. Even in winter Ryhope Wood was impossible to enter. Even in winter it was not possible to see inwards more than fifty yards. Even in winter it could work its magic, and dissolve perception in an instant, spinning the visitor round and confusing him utterly.

There was such wonder in there. So much to learn. So much to find. So much 'legend' still living. He had only just begun!

Steven appeared in the doorway, wrapped up warmly in muffler, school overcoat and boots. He sank in snow up to his knees and had to wade with great difficulty towards his father, his cheeks red, his face alive with pleasure.

'You're up early,' Huxley called to his son. Steven bent down and scooped up a snowball. He flung it and missed, laughing, and Huxley thought about returning fire, but was too intrigued by what he might find in the chicken hut. He was aware of the look of disappointment on Steven's face, but blanked it.

Steven followed him at a distance.

There was no sound from the ramshackle chicken house. This was unnerving.

When he opened the door he smelled death at once, and half gagged. He was used to the smell of a fox-attacked hut, but often the scent of the fox itself was the odour that was most prominent. There was only the smell of raw meat, now, and he stepped into the slaughter-house and his mind failed to comprehend what he could see.

Whoever had been here had made a bed of the chickens. There had been twenty birds and they had been torn into fragments, and the fragments, featherside up, had been spread about to make a mattress.

The heads had been threaded onto a length of primitive flax, which was looped across the hut from one shelf to another.

A small patch of burning, with charred bones, told of the fire and the meal that 'Snow Woman' had created for herself.

Expecting mayhem, finding such order in the slaughter, such ritual, Huxley backed out of the hut and closed the door, puzzled and perturbed. The sound of such slaughter should have been deafening. He had heard nothing. And yet he had lain awake for most of the night, after the boys had disturbed him.

The chickens had made no sound as they'd died, and the smoke from the fire had not reached the house.

Aware that Steven was standing by him, looking anxiously at the chicken house, Huxley led the boy away, hand on his shoulder.

'Are they all right?'

'A fox,' Huxley said bluntly, and felt a moment's irritation as he realised that his tone was callous. 'It's sad, but it happens.'

Steven had not failed to understand the meaning of his

father's words. He looked shocked and pained. 'Are they *all* dead? Like in the story?'

'They're all dead. Old Foxy's got them all.' Huxley rested a comforting hand on the boy's shoulder. 'We'll go to the farm later and buy some more, shall we? I'm sorry, Steve. Who'd be a chicken, eh?'

The boy was disconsolate, but remained obedient, looking back over his shoulder, but stepping away through the snow at his father's urging, to walk down to the gate again.

There were tears in his son's eyes as Huxley rounded up a snowball and tossed it in a shallow curve. The snowball impacted on the lad's shoulder, and after a moment of sad blankness, Steven grinned, and threw a snowball back.

Christian was up at the bedroom window, banging on the glass, calling something that Huxley couldn't hear. Probably: wait for me!

It was then that Huxley found the 'gift', if gift it was. It was by the gate, a piece of rough cloth wrapped around two inch-long twigs of wood and a yellowing bone from some small creature, a fox, perhaps a small dog. The pieces had holes bored through them. The package had sunk slightly into the snow, but he spotted it, rescued it, and opened it before the boy's fascinated gaze.

'She *did* leave you a present,' Huxley said to his son. 'Not much of one. But it must be a lucky charm. Do you think?'

'Don't know,' Steven said, but he reached for the cloth and its contents and clutched them into his grasp, rubbing his fingers over the three objects. He looked more puzzled than disappointed. Huxley teased the gift back for one moment in order to examine the shards carefully. The wood looked like thorn, that smooth, thin bark. The bone was a neck vertebra.

'Look after these little things, won't you, Steve?'

'Yes.'

'I expect there's a magic word to say with them. It'll come to you suddenly . . .'

He straightened up and started to walk indoors. Jennifer appeared in the kitchen door, a sleepy, pretty figure, arms wrapped tightly around her against the cold. 'What's all the activity?'

'That old Drummer Fox,' said Steven gloomily. Jennifer woke up fast. 'Oh no! A fox? Really?'

''Fraid so,' Huxley said quietly. 'Got the lot.'

As Jennifer led the frozen boy inside to breakfast, Huxley turned again and watched Ryhope Wood. A sudden flight of crows, loud in the still air, drew his attention to the stand of holly close to the ruined gate where the sticklebrook entered the wood. This was his way into the deeper zones of the woodland, and he fancied he saw movement there, now, but it was too far away to be sure.

Two pieces of twig and a bone were small payment for twenty chickens. But whoever had been here, last night, had wanted Huxley to know that they had visited. There was, he felt, an unsubtle invitation in the shadowy encounter.

TWO

Ryhope Wood is unquestionably a stand of *primordial forest*, a fragment of the wildwood which developed after the last Ice Age, and which – using a power which remains obscure – has erected its own defences against destruction. It is impossible to enter too far. I can at last penetrate further than the eerie glade in which a *shrine to horses* is to be found. I am not the only visitor to this site of worship, but of course my fellow 'worshippers' come from *inside* the wood, from the zones and hidden world that I cannot reach.

I have coined the word *mythago* to describe these creatures of forgotten legend. This is from 'myth imago', or the *image of the myth*. They are formed, these varied heroes of old, from the unheard, unseen communication between our common human *unconscious* and the vibrant, almost tangible sylvan mind of the wood itself. The wood watches, it listens, and it draws out our dreams . . .

After the thaw came a time of rain, a monotonous and seemingly endless downpour that lasted for days, and depressed not just the land around Oak Lodge, but the life within that land, so that everything moved slowly, and sullenly, and seemed devoid of spirit. But when the rain eased, when the last storm cloud passed away to the east, a fresh and vibrant spring set new colour to the wood and the fields, and as if coming out of hibernation, Edward Wynne-Jones made a new appearance on the scene, driving to the Huxleys' from Oxford, and arriving in enthusiastic mood one afternoon in early April.

Wynne-Jones was also in his forties and lectured, and researched, in historical anthropology at Oxford University. He was a fussy man, with odd and irritating habits, the most obvious and annoying of which was his smoking of a prodigious pipe, a calabash that belched reeking smoke from its bowl, and did little to improve the aura around the smoker. With his weasel looks, a certain sourness of expression that Jennifer Huxley had at once taken against, and which did nothing to relax the children of the house, he seemed incongruous as he sat, puffing on the 'billy', as it had been nicknamed by the Huxley boys, and holding forth in lecturer's tones about his ideas.

He caused a strain in Oak Lodge, and Huxley was always glad to be able to shunt his compatriot and valued fellow researcher into the haven of the study, at the farther end of the house. Here, with the french windows opened, they could converse about mythagos, Ryhope Wood, and the processes of the unconscious mind that were at work in the sylvan realm beyond the field.

A map was spread out over the desk, and Wynne-Jones pored over the details, stabbing with his pipe handle as he made points, brushing at the pencil-covered paper. They had detected several 'zones' in the wood, areas where the wood's character changed, where the dominant tree form was different and where the season felt different from that which existed on the outside of the stand. The Oak–Ash Zone was particularly intriguing, and there was a Thorn Zone, a winding, spiralling forest of tangled blackthorn that ran close to a river, but which kept that water source hidden from view.

It would be Wynne-Jones's task, this trip, to try to break through the thorn and photograph the river.

Huxley would strike deeply into the wood from the Horse Shrine which both men had discovered two years before.

They assessed their route, and listed provisions necessary.

Then Huxley displayed the artefacts he had gathered over the winter months, while Wynne-Jones had been in Oxford.

'Not a great haul. These are the most recent,' he indicated the wood and bone from the gate, 'left by the first mythago to actually enter the garden. She returned – '

'She?'

'The boys say it was a female figure. They called her Snow Woman. She slaughtered the chickens – in silence, I might add – stayed the night in the coop, then returned to the wood. I followed the trail: she had emerged and returned at the same point. I have no idea what her purpose was, unless it was to make a tentative contact.'

'But nothing since?'

'Nothing.'

'Do you have any sense of her status as a "heroine"? What legend she represents?'

'None at all.'

Other finds included a head-piece of rusted, battered iron, a circlet wound round with briar, the thorns trimmed on the inside, and a gorgeous, luxuriantly coloured amulet, the stones not precious, the metal work merely filigreed with gold on a bronze plate. But it was unlike anything that Huxley could find listed or depicted in the pages of his books of previous finds and ancient treasures. It had been suspended from the branch of a beech, two hundred yards inwards, just before the first barrier in the wood where orientation was affected. Wynne-Jones handled the amulet appreciatively.

'A talisman, I'd say. Magic.'

'You think everything's a talisman,' Huxley laughed. 'But on this occasion I'm inclined to agree. But who would have worn this, do you think?'

He placed the cold, crushed circlet on his head. It fitted well, uncomfortably so, and he removed it at once.

Wynne-Jones did not volunteer an opinion.

'And figures?' the younger man prompted after a while. 'Encounters?'

'Apart from Snow Woman, and I didn't see her . . . just the Crow Ghost, as I call him . . . the feathers are mostly black, but I noticed this time that his face is painted and that he *sings*. I'm intrigued by that aspect of him. But he's just as aggressive as before, and so *fast* in his movement through the wood. So, the Crow Ghost. Who else . . . let me think . . . oh yes, the wretched "Robin Hood" form, of course. This one seemed advanced, perhaps thirteenth century.'

'Lincoln Green?' Wynne-Jones said.

'Mud brown, but with some fancy weavework on arms and breast. Slightly bearded. Very large in build. Took the usual shot at me, before merging – '

He placed a broken arrow on the table. The head was a thin point of steel, flanged. The shaft was ash, the flights goosefeather, no decoration. 'The "Hoods" and "Green Jacks" worry me. They've already shot me once. One day one of them is going to strike me in the heart. And the way they just appear – '

He used the word 'merge' deliberately. It was as if the forms of the Hunter – the Robin Hoods, or Jack o' the Greens – *oozed* from the trees, then slipped back into them, merging with the bark and the hardwood and becoming invisible. Too frightened to investigate further, because of the threat to his life, Huxley had no idea whether he was dealing with a phenomenon of the supernatural, or superb camouflage.

'And of the Urscumug?'

Huxley laughed dryly. But it was less of a joke, these days, more a fixation, a belief, bordering on the obsessive. The first hero, the primal form, ancient, probably malevolent. Huxley had heard *references* to it, found *signs* of it, but he could not get deeply enough into Ryhope Wood to come close to it – to see it. He was convinced it was there, however. *Urscumug*. The almost incomprehensible hero of the first spoken legends, held in the common unconscious of all humankind and almost certainly being generated in Ryhope Wood, somewhere in the glades of this primal, unspoiled stretch of forest.

The Urscumug. The beginning.

But Huxley was beginning to think that he was fated *never* to engage with it.

Standing by the open windows, watching the woodland across the neat garden, with its trimmed cherry trees and clipped hedges, he felt suddenly very old. It was a sensation that had begun to concern him: all his adult life he had felt like a man in his thirties, but it had been a vigorous feeling; now that he was in his middle forties he felt stooped, sagging, a fatigue that he had expected to encounter in his sixties, not for many many years. And it was a feeling of being too old to *see*, to see the wood for what it was, to see out of the corner of his eyes — those frustrating, tantalising glimpses of movement, of creatures, of colour, of the *ancient* that hovered at peripheral vision, and which vanished when he turned towards them.

The boys, though. They seemed to see *everything*.

'Have you brought the bridges?'

Wynne-Jones unpacked the odd electrical equipment, the headsets with their terminals, wires and odd face-pieces that formed electric linkages across the brain. The voltage was low, but effective. After an hour of electrical stimulation, 'peripheral view awareness' perked up remarkably. And it was in the peripheral vision that glimpses of mythagos were mainly to be experienced: Huxley called them the 'pre-mythago' form, and imagined these to be gradually emerging memories of the past, the passage of memory from mind to wood.

Huxley picked up the apparatus. 'We are old, Father Edward, we are too old. Oh God for youth again, for that far sight . . . The boys see so much. And so often with full fore-vision.'

'What could they see if we enhanced them, I wonder?' Wynne-Jones said softly.

Huxley was alarmed. This was the second time that the Oxford man had suggested experimenting on Steven and Christian, and whilst the idea tantalised Huxley, he felt a strong, moral repellence at the notion. 'No. It wouldn't be fair.'

'With their consent?'

'We may be damaging ourselves, Edward. I couldn't inflict that risk on my boys. Besides, Jennifer would have something to say about it. She'd forbid it outright.'

'But with the *boys*' consent? Steven especially. You said he was a dreamer. You said he could call the wood.'

'He doesn't know he's doing it. He dreams, yes. Neither boy knows what we know. They just know we go exploring, not that time runs differently, not that we encounter dangers. They don't even know about the mythagos. They think they see "gypsies". Tramps.'

But Wynne-Jones wrestled with the idea of enhancing Steven's perception of the wood. 'One experiment. One low voltage, high colour stimulation. It surely would do no harm . . .'

Huxley shook his head, staring hard at the other man. 'It would be wrong. It's wrong to even think about it. Fascinating though the results would be, Edward . . . I *must* say no. Please don't insist any more. Set the equipment up for ourselves. We'll enter the wood the first moment after dawn.'

'Very well.'

'One other thing,' Huxley added, as the scientist busied himself. 'In case anything should ever happen to me – and I'm disturbed by being shot at by the Merry Man, the Hood figure – in case something unfortunate should occur, I keep a second journal. It's in a wall safe behind these books. You are the only other person who knows about it, and I shall trust you to secure it, should it become necessary, and to use it without revealing it. I don't want Jennifer to know what it contains.'

'And what *does* it contain?'

'Things I can't account for. Dreams, feelings, experiences that seem less related to me than they do to . . .' he searched for appropriate words. 'To the animal realm.'

Huxley knew that he was frowning hard, and that his mood had become dark. Wynne-Jones sat quietly, watching his friend, clearly not comprehending the depth of despair and fear that Huxley was trying to impart without detail. He said only, 'In the wood ... in parts of the wood ... I have been very disturbed ... As if a more primordial aspect of my behaviour had been let out, dusted off, and set loose.'

'Good God, man, you sound like that character of Stevenson's.'

'Mr Hyde and Mr Jekyll?' Huxley laughed.

'*Dr* Jekyll, I believe.'

'Whatever. I remember reading that whimsy at school. It hadn't occurred to me to see any connection, but yes, my dreams certainly reflect a more violent and instinctual creature than I'm accustomed to greeting every morning in the shaving mirror.'

'And these observations and records are in the second journal?'

'Yes. And accounts, too, of what the boys are experiencing. I really don't want them to know that I've been watching them. But if our ideas about the mythago-genesis of heroes in the wood are right, then all of us in this house, even you, Edward, are having an effect upon the process. At any one time, the phenomena we witness might be the product of one of five minds. And then there are the farm hands, and the people at the Manor. Our moods, our personalities, shape the manifestations —'

'You've begun to agree with me, then. I made this point a year ago.'

'I *do* agree with you. That Hood form ... it was strange. It echoed a mind different to my own. Yes. I do agree with you. And this is an area we should study more assiduously, and more vigorously. So let's prepare.'

'I shall say nothing about the second journal.'

'I trust you.'

'I still think we should talk about Steven, and enhancing his perception.'

'If we talk about it, let's talk about it after this excursion.'

'I agree.'

Relieved, Huxley reached into his desk drawer for his watch, a small, brass-encased mechanism that showed date as well as time of day. 'Let's get ourselves ready,' he said, and Wynne-Jones grunted his agreement.

THREE

'Your son is watching you,' Wynne-Jones said quietly, as they walked away from the house, still shivering in the crisp and fresh dawn. All around them the world was coming alive. The light was sharp to the east, and the wood was dark, shadowy, yet becoming distinct with that peculiar clarity which accompanies the first light of a new day.

Huxley stopped and shrugged his pack from his shoulders, turning to look back at the house.

Sure enough, Steven was pressed against the window of his bedroom, a small, anxious shape, mouthing words and waving.

Huxley stepped a few paces back, and cupped his ear. Chickens clattered close by, and the old dog growled and worried in the hedges. Rooks called loudly, and their flight, in and among the branches of Ryhope Wood, made the day seem somehow more desolate and silent than it was.

Steven pulled the sash window up.

'Where are you going?' he called down, and Huxley said, 'Exploring.'

'Can I come?'

'Scientific research, Steve. We'll only be gone today.'

'Take me with you?'

'I can't. I'm sorry, lad. I'll be back tonight and tell you all about it.'

'Can't I come?'

The dawn seemed to lengthen, and the early spring cold made his breath frost as he stood and stared at the anxious, pale-faced boy in the window, high in the house. 'I'll be back tonight. We have some readings to take, some mapping, some samples to take . . . I'll tell you all about it later.'

'You went away for three days last time. We were worried . . .'

'One day only, Steve. Now be a good boy.'

As he hefted his pack onto his back again, he saw Jennifer standing in the doorway, her face glistening with tears. 'I'll be back tonight,' he said to her.

'No you won't,' she whispered, and turned into the house, closing the kitchen door behind her.

FOUR

. . . poor Jennifer is already deeply depressed by my behaviour. Cannot explain it to her, though I dearly want to. Do not want the children involved in this, and it worries me that they have now twice seen a mythago. I have invented magic forest creatures – stories for them. Hope they will associate what they see with products of their own imaginations. But must be careful.

There is a time before wakening, an instant only, when the real and the unreal play games with the sleeper, when everything is right, yet nothing is real. In this moment of surfacing from the sleep of days, Huxley sensed the flow of water, and the passing of riders, the shouts and curses of a troop on the move, and the anguish and excitement of pursuit.

Something bigger than a man was moving through the wood, following the pack of men that ran before its lumbering assault.

And there was a woman, too, who came to the river, and touched her hand to the face of the sleeping/waking man. She dropped a twig and a bone on him, then left with a laugh and swirl of perfumed body, the sweat of her skin and her soul, sour and sexual in the nostrils of the recumbent form that slowly . . .

Came to waking . . .

Came alive again.

Huxley sat up and began to choke. He was frozen, and icy water ran from his face.

He was deafened by the sound of the river, and his sense of smell was offended by the stink of his own faeces, cool and firm, accumulated in the loose cotton of his underclothes.

'Dear God! What's happened to me . . . ?'

He cleaned himself quickly, crouching in the river, gasping with the cold. From previous experience he knew to bring a change of clothing and he searched gratefully in his pack, now, finding the gardening trousers and a thick, cotton shirt.

He fumbled with shaking fingers for his watch and closed his eyes as he saw that it had been four days since he had reached this place, dazed and confused, and lain down on the shore with his head on his arms.

Four days asleep!

'Edward! Edward . . . ?'

His voice, a loud, urgent cry, was lost in the rush and swirl of this river; he was about to shout again, when the first piece of memory returned, and he realised that Wynne-Jones was long gone. They had parted days before, the Oxford man to find, if he could, the river beyond the thornwoods, Huxley himself to document the edges of the zones that were Ryhope Wood's first true level of defence.

How perverse, then, that Huxley should find himself by the expanded flow of the tiny sticklebrook. Had Wynne-Jones been here too? He could see no sign of the other man.

There were the ashes of a small fire, away from the water, in the shelter of a grey sarsen, whose mossy green stump seemed almost to thrust from the tangle of root and ragged earth. Huxley had seen enough failed fires, built by Wynne-Jones, to notice that this was not of the other man's making.

He gathered his things together. Starving, he wolfed down a bar of chocolate from his pack.

Memory raced back, and the disorientation resulting from his sudden waking after another of the long dreams began to fade.

He stared hard at the patch of thorn through which he had entered this place. He fixed, in his mind, the image of the woman who had caressed him as he slept in a half slumber, semi-aware of her presence, but unable to rise beyond the semi-conscious state. Not young, not old, filthy, sexual, warm ... she had pressed her mouth to his and her tongue had been a sharp, wet presence against his own. Her laughter was low. Had he put a hand on her leg? He had the sensation of less than firm flesh, the broad smoothness of a thigh below his fingers and palm, but this might have been his dream.

Who, then, had the riders been? And that creature that had stalked them across the river?

'Urscumug,' he murmured as he checked for spoor. There were no tracks, beyond the shallow imprint of an unshod horse.

'Urscumug ... ?'

He was not sure. He remembered a previous encounter.

The Urscumug has formed in my mind in the clearest form I have ever seen him . . . face smeared with white clay . . . hair a mass of stiff and spiky points . . . so old, this primary image, that he is fading from the human mind . . . Wynne-Jones thinks Urscumug may predate even the neolithic . . .

He wanted his journal. He scrawled notes in the rough pad he carried with him, but the pad was wet, and writing was difficult. Around him the wood was vibrant, shifting, watching. He felt intensely ill at ease, and after a few minutes shrugged on the pack and began to retrace his steps, away from the river.

Half a day later he had reached the Wolf Glen, the shallow valley, with its open sky, where he and Wynne-Jones had separated several days before. This was an eerie place, with its smell of sharp pine, its constant, cool breeze, and the sound of wolves in the darkness. Huxley had seen the creatures several times, fleet shadows in the dense underbrush, rising onto their hind limbs to peer around, their faces half human, of course, for these creatures were no ordinary wolves.

They moved in threes, not in packs; and never — as far as he could see — in solitary. Their barking resolved into language, though of course the language was incomprehensible to the Englishman. Huxley carried a pistol, and two flares, well wrapped in oilskin, but ready to be lit if the wolves came too close.

But in the three visits he had made to the Wolf Glen, the beasts had shown curiosity, irritation, and then a lack of interest. They had approached, gabbled at him, then slunk away, running half on hind limbs, to hunt beyond the edge of the conifer forest, beyond the low defining ridge of the Wolf Glen itself.

If Wynne-Jones had returned here he would have left the prearranged mark on one of the tall stones at the top of the

Glen. No such mark was in evidence. Huxley used chalk to create his own message, gathered the necessary wood for a fire, later in the day, and went exploring.

At dusk, still Wynne-Jones had not returned. Huxley called for him, his voice echoing in the Glen, carrying on the wind. No hail or hello came back, and a night passed.

In the morning Huxley decided that he could wait no longer. He had no real idea of the passage of time, this far into Ryhope Wood, but imagined that he had now been absent the better part of a day and a night, longer than he had intended. He had a precise idea of how distorted time became as far in as the Horse Shrine, but he had never tested the relativity of these deeper zones. A sudden anguish made him strike hard along the poor trails, cutting through deep mossy dells, drawn always outwards to the edge.

It was always easier to leave the wood than to enter it.

He was exhausted by the time he reached the area of the Horse Shrine. He was hungry, too. He had brought insufficient supplies. And his hunger was increased by the sudden smell of burning meat.

He dropped to a crouch, peering ahead through the tangle of briar and holly, seeking the clearing with its odd temple. There was movement there. Wynne-Jones, perhaps? Had his colleague come straight to this place, to wait for Huxley? Was he roasting him a pigeon, as he waited, with a flagon of chilled local cider to accompany it? Huxley smiled at himself, laughed at the way his baser drives began to fantasise for him. He walked cautiously through the trees, and peered into the glade.

Whoever had been there had heard him. They had backed away, hugging the shadows and the greenery on the opposite side. Huxley was sufficiently attuned to the sounds, smells and shifting of the wood to be aware of the human-like presence that stared back at him.

Between them, close to the bizarre shrine, a fire burned and a bird, plucked and spitted, was blackening slowly.

FIVE

The Horse Shrine, in its oak glade, is my main point of contact with the mythic creatures of the wood. The trees here are overpoweringly immense organisms, storm-damaged and twisted. The trunks are hollow, their bark overrun with massive ropes of ivy. Their huge, heavy branches reach out across the clearing and form a roof; when the sun is bright, and the summer is silent, to enter the glade is like entering a cathedral. The greying bones of the odd statues that fill the shrine reflect the changing shades of green and are entrancing and enticing to the eye; the horse that is central to the shrine seems to move; it is a massive structure, twice the height of a man, bones strapped together to form gigantic legs, fragments of skull shaped and wedged to create a monstrous head. It could be some dinosaur, reconstructed out of madness by an impressionist. Shapeless but essentially manlike structures stand guard beside it, again all long-bone and skull, lashed together with thick strips of leather, impaled by wood, some of which is returning to leaf. They seem to watch me as I crouch in the shifting, dancing luminosity of this eerie place.

Here I have seen human forms from the palaeolithic, the neolithic and the Age of Bronze. They come here and watch the greening of the spirit of the horse. To the earliest forms of Man, this silent respect is for a wild, untamed creature, a source of nourishment rather than burden. To later forms, it is a closer need that is reflected. Some visitors to the shrine leave brilliant trappings and harnessing, invocations to their primaeval form of Epona, or Diana, or any other *Goddess of the Steed*. These I have collected. Many of them are fascinating.

I have watched and recorded many of these visitors, but failed to communicate with any of them. All this now changed as I encountered the woman. She was in the glade, tending a small fire, and staring up at the decaying statues. Alarmed by my sudden arrival, she stood and drew back into the edgewood, watching me. The sun was high, and she was drenched in shadow and green light, blending with the background. The fire crackled slightly, and on the still air I could smell not just burning wood, but the charred smell of some meat or other.

I waited cautiously, also within the scrub that lined the glade. Soon she re-emerged into the cathedral, and crouched by the fire, spreading her skirts. She began to sing, rocking forwards in rhythm, prodding at the smouldering wood. She was very aware of me, glancing at me continually. I gained the impression that she was . . . disappointed. She frowned and shook her head.

Eventually she smiled, and there was an invitation to approach in that simple gesture. As I stepped through the tangled grass and fern of the glade, her lank hair fell forward. It was copper-hued, magnificent, but full of leaf-litter, nature's decoration. She occasionally pushed it back with her free hand, watching me through eyes that were enchanting. Her clothing was of wool, a skirt dyed a dull shade of brown, a faded green shawl. She wore a necklace of carved and painted shapes, bone talismans, I thought, and many of these were strikingly bright. Rolled beside her was a cloak, fur side hidden for a while. Then she unfurled the garment to fetch out a thin knife, and I saw white fur – fox fur, I think – and knew at once that this creature was the 'Snow Woman' that the boys had seen last Christmas.

We sat in silence for a while. She cooked and picked at the small bird she had snared, a wood pigeon, I believe. Around us, the dense wood seemed alive with eyes, but this is the life of Ryhope Wood, the sylvan-awareness drawing out human dreams and fashioning forgotten memories into living organisms. When I am in the oak and ash zones, deeper than the Horse Shrine, I can often *feel* the presence of the wood in my unconscious mind; images at the edge of vision seem to slip past me: out of mind, into the forest, to become shaped, then no doubt to return to haunt me.

Was this woman one of my own *mythagos*, I wondered?

She carried an ash stick, and when she had finished eating she lay this across her lap before flicking earth onto the smouldering wood of her fire. She smiled at me. There was grease on her lips and she licked at it. Below the grime she was truly lovely, and her smile, and her laughter, were enchanting. I mentioned my name and she grasped what I was trying to do, referring to herself in some incomprehensible tongue. Then, seeing my puzzlement, she held up the stick and pointed to herself. She was called Ash, then, but this reference meant nothing to me.

Who or what was she? What aspect of legend was embodied here? By sign and smile, by gesture, by the tracing of shapes in the air, by exaggerated communication with fingers, we began to understand each other. I showed her a rag effigy that I had gathered from near this shrine on the inward journey, and she stared at this bounty with puzzlement (at first) and then with an odd, searching look. When I dangled a bronze, leaf-like necklet – found by a stream – she touched the piece, then shook her head as if to say 'don't be so childish'. But when I showed her an ochre-painted amulet that I had found in the Horse Shrine itself, she exhaled sharply, looked at me with murderous, then pitying eyes. She would not touch the object and I ran it through my fingers, wondering what message reached from this crafted bone to the mind of the woman. The uneasiness lasted a little while, then – by sign – I asked her about herself.

She returned to me, a bird returning from a flight of fancy, a mind returning to the reality of a woodland glade. In a moment or two she seemed to understand that I was questioning her about her own history. She frowned, watching me as if wondering what to reveal. I noticed distinctly, but took no warning from the observation, that she looked afraid and angry suddenly.

Then, with the merest shrug, she reached into her rolled cloak and drew out two leather bags which she shook. One of them rattled, the sound of bone shards.

By gesture, she had made certain strange comments during the previous hour, and now she compounded my confusion. First she shook out the contents of the larger bag, dozens of short fragments of wood, strips of bark, some dark, some silver, some green, some mottled, all gouged with a small hole. I formed the idea that she had something, here, from every type of tree. With her eyes on the amulet that I had shown her, she picked out two of these pieces of wood, held them in her left hand. She sang something softly and the glade seemed to shiver. A coolish breeze whipped quickly through the foliage, then danced up and away; an elemental life-form, perhaps, summoned then dismissed.

From the second bag she poured out the bone, forty or fifty shards of ivory. From these she picked a single piece. Holding wood and bone in her hand she shook the three fragments, before threading a loop of thin, worn leather through the holes and passing the necklet to me. I accepted it, remembering, with no clear understanding, the gift she had left by the gate during the winter. I put the necklet on.

She sat back and replaced the rest of the wood and ivory into their respective bags. Then she stood and gathered her fox-fur cloak, and with a knowing smile, stepped out of the glade and into the silence and darkness of the forest. Her last gesture before departing was to rattle a tiny wrist-drum, a double sided cylinder of skin, beaten by small stones attached to thongs.

I had no idea what to do next. She had seemed to dismiss me, so I rose, intending to leave the glade and return to Oak Lodge.

SIX

Huxley got no further than the first overpowering oak. As he ducked below its heavy branch, heading towards the narrow track outwards, his world — the wood itself — turned inside out!

From the warm and musty odour of summer, suddenly the air was sharp and autumnal. The light from the foliage was stark, brilliant; the drowsy green luminosity had gone. Trees, dense and dark, rose straight and bleak around him. These were birches, not oaks; thickets of holly shimmered in the lancing silver light. He stumbled through this unknown world, scratched and torn in his panic to orientate himself. Above him, birds screeched and took to wing. A cold wind swept through the upper branches. Unfamiliar smells struck at random, damp leaf mould, pungent vegetation, then the crystal sharpness of autumn. The light from above was startling in its brightness, and if he glanced up, then looked around him, the trees showed as black pillars, without feature, almost formless.

He suddenly heard horses crashing through the forest, their lungs straining as they ran, their whinnying screams telling of the burden of pain and bruising inflicted by this tangled, ancient wood. Huxley glimpsed them as they struggled past, immense creatures, each impaled on its back with what he assumed quickly were the signs of *taming*: one carried flaring torches, spears with burning heads that had been stuck deeply through its thick skin; another was decorated with stems of corn or wheat; a third with tight bundles of greenery and thorn, blood seeping from where the sharpened stalks of some of these plants had been pushed too deep. The fourth carried in its flesh the slim, quivering shafts of a pale wood — *ash* perhaps —

that were arrows, each trailing rags of the skin of creatures, the grey, white, brown and black of furry hides.

What had sounded like the frantic passage of a *herd* of these wonderful creatures was in fact the furious bolting of four horses only.

One came close enough to show Huxley the grey and bloodied hide of its flanks. This was the creature 'decorated' with burning and smouldering torches. It towered over him, its mane full, flowing and lank; it reeked richly of dung. The horse turned briefly to stare at him and its eyes were filled with a feral panic. Huxley pressed himself against one of the great birches, which shuddered as the beast kicked at the trunk, turning to expose huge, cracked teeth that were the colour of summer-ripened wheat; it moved on, then, working its way inwards, escaping its tormentors.

The tormentors, following close behind the horses, were humans, of course. And Huxley was soon to realise what Ash had done.

There were four men, dark haired and heavily cloaked. They moved through the forest, uttering shrill cries, or gruff barks, or resonating song fragments that increased in pitch until they became an ululating echo. Sometimes they screeched *words*, but these were frightening and alien sounds. Each of the men wore his hair in a different, elaborate plaited style. Each was bedecked with stone or bone or shells or wood. Each had a colour on his face: red, green, yellow, blue. They passed by Huxley, sometimes running, sometimes laughing, all of them torn by thorn and holly, the leaf and wood impaling their crude clothing, so that they seemed no less than extensions of the birch and thorn forest itself.

Crying out and celebrating their vigorous pursuit of horses!

It was, Huxley chose to think at that moment, their way of controlling the horses. How many myths of the *secret language* of horses had come down to modern times, he wondered briefly? Many, he imagined, and here were men who *knew* those secrets! He was watching an early herding, the horses pushed into the tangle of the wood, the best way to trap them, in fact, a *wonderful* way to trap them, in a time before corrals or stables! Run the horse into the thicket, and the sheer difference in size between *chaser* and *chased* would have marked the difference between *eaten* and *eater*.

For he had no doubt at that moment – this being a pre-neolithic event – that these beasts were being herded for food, rather than as creatures of burden.

Striking at the underbrush with long, flint-edged sticks, the four men strode past. And the hindmost of them, looking as broad in his heavy furs as he was tall, turned suddenly to stare at the hooded intruder, green-grey light glittering in pale eyes. On his chest he wore an identical amulet to that which Huxley had found in the Horse Shrine. He touched it, almost nervously, a gesture of luck, perhaps, or courage.

His companions called to him, shrill sounds, almost musical in their rhythm and pitch, that sent birds whirring from the tree tops. He turned and was gone, consumed by the thickets of holly, and the confusing patterns of light and shade of the birchwood. Nervously, Huxley tugged the green hood of his oilskin lower over his face.

I followed, of course. Of course! I wished to see this ritual herding through to its final, awful conclusion. For I had now begun to imagine that a *sacrifice of horses* would be the outcome of the pursuit to which Ash, by her magic, had despatched me.

Yet, in substance I was wrong. It was not to be the oddly bedecked stallions that were sent on to the afterlife, encouraged there by flint and by flax rope. Not immediately, anyway. In the wide clearing, with its tall, crudely fashioned wood-gods, the horses were disturbed by the smells and the cries of extinguished life. The gathering of winter-clad men calmed the beasts. The glade in the birchwood echoed to the thumping of wood drums and the chanting of ancient hymns. There was laughter within the cacophony of sacrifice, and throughout all, the whooping cries of other herders, the music of magic, punctuating the confusion, serving to bring peace to the restless horses as they were held by their harnessings, and loaded with their first real burden.

Towards dusk, the horses were sent into the world again, running, slapped to encourage them, back along the broken tracks, towards the edge of the wood, wherever that lay. On their backs, tied firmly to cradles of wood, the horrific shapes of their pale riders watched the gloom, dulled eyes seeing darker worlds than even this darkening forest. The first to depart was a chalk-white corpse, grotesquely garrotted. Then a man, still living, swathed in thorns, screaming. After that, a ragged creature, stinking of blood and acrid smoke from the part-burned but newly skinned pelts that were wrapped around him.

Finally came a figure decked and dressed in rush and reed, so that only his arms were visible, extended on the crucifix-like frame that was tied about the giant horse. He was on fire; the blaze taking swiftly. Flame streamed into the night, shedding light and heat in eerie streamers as the great stallion galloped in panic towards me.

I thought I had moved quickly enough to take avoiding action, but before I knew it the beast had collided with me, one front leg striking me a blow to the side, then its shoulder pitching me down. I curled up to protect myself, but my body seemed to disobey and struggled to stand . . .

For one eerie moment I sensed I was *behind* the flaming figure, feeling the heat on my body, the wind and fire on my face, the rough movement of the horse below me.

The illusion lasted a second only before I was pitched

backwards again, stunned and disorientated as I lay on the ground, stifled as if hands were pressing down on my mouth, neck and lungs.

I recovered swiftly.

I cannot record the full detail of what I saw in that clearing – so much has faded from memory, perhaps because of the blow from the stampeding horse. I am still shocked by the nature of the sacrifices and the awareness that the murdered men seemed *willing participants* in this early form of acknowledgement of the *power of the horse*.

Such wonderful creatures, and yet they would be both friend of Man and carrier of his destruction . . .

All of this was passing through my mind as a freezing night fell upon the primaeval world, and other thoughts too: by horse would come war, and plague, and the populations to overrun and overwhelm the food available from the land. By horse would come the fire that clears, and kills, and cleanses.

But this forest, this event, reflected something that had occurred *tens of thousands of years before the present*! Was I witnessing one of the first true *intuitions* of early humankind? That the beast could be both friend and foe to a tribe that increasingly looked for control over nature itself? Sacrifice was made to new gods: the assuaging of fears. And it entertained me to think that later, much later, John the Divine would remember these early fears, and talk of the four horsemen, in fact describing his deep-rooted memories of an ancient understanding . . .

But with darkness came silence, and with the freezing silence of night came my helpless abandonment to sleep.

I awoke from the dream to the wet nuzzling of a dog. I was at the edge of Ryhope Wood – God alone knows how I had got there – in the scrub that overlooks the fields of the Manor House. The dog was a springer, being walked by an alarmed and determined woman, who strode away from what she presumably believed to be a tramp. She called for her hound, which bounded after her, not without a regretful and hungry glance towards me.

SEVEN

When he opened the back door to Oak Lodge, Jennifer screamed and dropped the mug of tea that she was holding. She looked at her husband through wide, frightened eyes, then collapsed back with relief against the table, laughing and brushing at the tea which had spilled over her dressing gown.

'I didn't realise you'd gone out again . . .'

Her words were meaningless, but he was too tired to think. He said, 'I must look terrible. I should bath at once.'

He was dog tired. He drank the fresh tea she made, and wolfed down a slice of buttered bread. Steven came and watched him as he undressed, stripping off his stinking clothes, drawing hot water from the tank to make a deep bath. Jennifer picked up the clothes, frowning as she watched her husband.

'Why did you put these on again?'

'Again? I don't know what you mean . . . I'm sorry . . . to have been away so long . . .'

He sank into the water, groaning and sighing with pleasure. Steven and Christian giggled on the landing outside. They had seen their father's naked body, something they had never witnessed before, and like all children this glimpse of the forbidden had amused and shocked them.

When he had washed himself, and dried off, he went to Jennifer and tried to explain. She was distant. He had already noted from the calendar that his absence, this time, had been two days. For himself, the passage of time had been much greater, but even so, Jennifer was rightly anguished, and had suffered an intense day of concern.

'I hadn't intended to be away so long.'

She had made him breakfast. She sat opposite him at the table in the dining room, and leafed through *The Times*. 'How could you get so dirty in so few hours?' she said, and he frowned as he forked slices of sausage into his mouth. Her words were confusing, but he himself was confused, now. He was oddly disorientated.

When he went to his study he found that his desk drawer had been disturbed. Angry, he almost confronted Jennifer, but decided against it. The key to his private journal was lying on the desk top. And yet the last time he had written in the journal he had — he was sure — replaced the key carefully in its hidden position, pressed to the underside of the desk top.

He wrote an official entry in his research journal, and then fetched the personal diary from its hiding place, entering an account of his encounter with Ash. His hand shook and he had to make many corrections to the text. When he had finished he blotted the ink dry, sat back, and turned back through the journal's pages.

He read through what he had written shortly before the last trip with Wynne-Jones.

And he suddenly realised that there were six additional lines to the text!

Six lines that he had no recollection of writing at all.

'Good God, who's been at my journal?'

Again, he stopped himself going to Jennifer, or confronting the boys, but he was shocked, truly shocked. He bent over the pages, his hands shaking as he ran a finger word by word along the entry.

It was in his own handwriting. There was no question of it. His own handwriting, or a brilliant forgery thereof.

The entry was simple, and had about it that haste with which he was familiar, the scrawled notes that he managed when his encounters were intense, his life hectic, and his need to be in the wood more important than his need to keep a careful record of his discoveries.

She is not what she seems. Her name is Ash. Yes. You know that. It is a dark world for me. I will acknowledge terror. But there is
  I cannot be sure
She is more dangerous, and she has done this. Edward is dead. No. Perhaps not. But it is a poss
  The time with the horses. I can't be sure. Something was watching

'I didn't write this. Dear God. Am I going mad? I *didn't* write this. Did I?'

Jennifer was reading and listening to the radio. He stood in the doorway, uncertain at first, his mind not clear. 'Has anyone been to my desk?' he asked at length.

Jennifer looked up. 'Apart from you yourself, no. Why?'

'Someone's tampered with my journal.'

'What do you mean "tampered" with it?'

'Written in it. Copying my own hand. Has anybody been here during my excursion?'

'Nobody. And I don't allow the boys into the study when you're not here. Perhaps you were sleepwalking last night.'

Now her words began to fidget him. 'How could I have done that? I didn't get home until dawn.'

'You came home at midnight,' she said, a smile touching her pale features. She closed the book, keeping a finger at the page. 'You went out again before dawn.'

'I didn't come back last night,' Huxley whispered. 'You must have been dreaming.'

She was silent for a long time, her breathing shallow. She looked at him solemnly. The smile had vanished, replaced by an expression of sadness and weariness. 'I wasn't dreaming. I was glad of you. I was in bed, quite asleep, when you woke me. I was disappointed to find you gone in the morning. I suppose I should have expected it . . .'

How long had he slept at the edge of the wood, before the woman and her dog had woken him? Had he indeed come home, unconscious, unaware, to spend an hour or two in bed, to write a confused and shattered message in his own journal, then to return to the woodland edge, to wait for dawn?

Suddenly alarmed, he began to wonder what other magic Ash had worked on him.

Where was Wynne-Jones? He had been gone over a week, now, and Huxley was increasingly disturbed, very concerned for his friend. Each day he ventured as far into the wood as the Horse Shrine, seeking a sign of the man, seeking, too, for Ash, but she had disappeared. Four days after returning home Huxley trekked more deeply, through a mile or so of intensely silent oakwood, emerging in unfamiliar terrain, not at the Wolf Glen at all.

Panicked, feeling himself to be losing touch with his own frail perception of the wood, he returned to Oak Lodge. He had been gone nearly twenty hours by his own reckoning, but only five hours had passed in the house, and Jennifer and the boys were not at home. His wife, no doubt, was in Grimley, or had perhaps taken the car to Gloucester for the day.

So it startled him to enter his study through the locked main door and to see his french windows opened wide, and the cat nestling in his leather chair. He shooed the animal away from the room, and examined the doors. There was no sign of them having been forced. No footprints. No sign of disturbance in the room. The study door had been locked from the outside.

When he opened his desk drawer he recoiled with shock from the bloody, fresh bone that lay there, on top of his papers. The bone was in part charred, a joint of some medium-sized animal, perhaps a pig, that had been partially cooked, so that raw and bleeding flesh remained at the bone itself. It was chewed, cracked and worried, as if a dog had been at it.

Gingerly, Huxley removed the offending item and placed it on a sheet of paper on the floor. The key to his private journal was not in its place, and shakily he fetched the opened book from its hole behind the shelves.

Bloody fingerprints accompanied the scrawled entry. This one was hastier than before, but unmistakably a copy of his own hand.

A form of dreaming. Moments of lucidity, but am functioning in unconscious.

No sign of WJ. Time has interfered.

These entries seem so controlled, the others. No recollection of writing them. I have so little time, and feel tug of woodland. Have linked somehow with sylvan time, and everything is inverted.

So hungry. So little chance to eat. I am covered with the blood of a fawn, hunted by a mythago. I grabbed part of carcase. Ate with ferocious need.

Pangs strong. Flesh! Satiation! Blood is on fire, and night is a peaceful time, and I can emerge more strongly. But no way of entering those moments when I am clearly myself.

So controlled, the other entries. Cannot remember writing them.

I am a ghost in my own body.

Huxley looked at his own hands, smelled the fingers. There was no blood in evidence, not under the nails, no sign of charcoal. He examined his clothes. There was mud on the trouser legs, but nothing that suggested he had torn and wrenched at a half-cooked carcase. He ran his tongue around his teeth. He checked his pillow in the bedroom.

If *he* had written this entry, if he himself had come into the study, in a moment of unconscious separation, eating the raw bone, he would surely have left some trace.

The words were odd, had an odd feel. It was as if the writer genuinely believed that he *was* Huxley, and that Huxley's own entries in the journal were being made during times of unconscious calm. Reality, for the bloody-fingered journalist, was a time of 'lucidity'.

But Huxley, keeping a rational and clear mind now, was certain that two different men were entering notes in the private journal.

It astonished him, though, that the other writer knew about the key.

He picked up his pen and wrote:

Today I went in search of Wynne-Jones. I didn't sleep, and I am convinced that I remained alert and aware for the full twenty hours that I was away. I am concerned for Wynne-Jones. I fear he is lost, and it grieves me deeply to anticipate the fact that he might never return. In my absence, someone else is making entries in this journal. The entry above was not written by me. But I believe that whoever has entered this place believes themself to be George Huxley. You are not. But whoever you are, you should tell me more about yourself. And if you wish to know more about me, then simply ask. It would be preferable for you to show yourself, perhaps at the edgewood. I am quite used to strange encounters. We have much that we need to talk about.

EIGHT

He had just finished writing when the car pulled into the drive. Doors slammed and he heard the sound of Jennifer's voice, and Steven's. Jennifer sounded angry.

She came into the house and a few seconds later he heard Steven go into the garden and run down to the gate. He stood from his desk and watched the boy, and was disturbed by the way his son glanced suddenly towards him, frowned, seemed to stifle back a tear or two, then went to hide among the sheds.

'Why do you neglect the boy so much? It wouldn't hurt you to talk to him once in a while.'

Huxley was startled by Jennifer's calm, controlled, yet angry tones speaking to him from the entrance to his study. She was pale, her lips pinched, her eyes hollow with fatigue and irritation. She was dressed in a dark suit and had her hair tied back into a tight bun, exposing all of her narrow face.

She entered the room the moment he turned and crossed to the desk, opening the book that was there, touching the pens, shaking her head. When she saw the bone she grimaced and kicked at it.

'Another little trophy, George? Something to frame?'

'Why are you angry?'

'I'm not angry,' she said wearily. 'I'm upset. So's Steven.'

'I don't understand why.'

Her laugh was brief and sourly pointed. 'Of course you don't. Well, think back, George. You must have said something to him this morning. I've never known the boy in such a state. I took him to Shadoxhurst, to the toy shop and the tea shop. But what he really wants – ' She bit her lip in exasperation, letting the statement lie uncompleted.

Huxley sighed, scratching his face as he watched and listened to something that simply wasn't possible.

'What time was this?'

'What time was what?'

'That . . . that I said something to Steven, to upset the boy . . .'

'Mid-morning.'

'Did you come and see me? Afterwards?'

'No.'

'Why not? Why didn't you come and see me?'

'You'd left the study. You'd gone back to the woods, no doubt. A-hunting and adventuring . . . down in dingly dell . . .' Again she looked at the grim and bloody souvenir. 'I was going to suggest tea, but I see you've eaten . . .'

Before he could speak further she had turned abruptly, taking off her suit jacket, and walked upstairs to freshen up.

'I wasn't here this morning,' Huxley said quietly, turning back to the garden, and stepping out into the dying sunlight. 'I wasn't here. So who *was*?'

Steven was sitting, slumped forward on the wall that bounded the rockery. He was reading a book, but hastily closed it when he heard his father approaching.

'Come to my study, Steve. There's something I want to show you.'

The boy followed in silence, tucking the book into his school blazer. Huxley thought it might have been a penny-dreadful western, but decided not to pursue the matter.

'I went deep into Ryhope Wood this morning,' he said, sitting down behind the desk and picking up his small pack. Steven stood on the other side, back to the window, hands by his sides. His face was a sad combination of uncertainty and distress, and Huxley felt like saying, 'Cheer up, lad,' but he refrained from doing so.

Instead he tipped out the small collection of oddities he had found at the Horse Shrine, and beyond: an iron torque, a small wooden idol, its face blank, its arms and legs just the stumps of twigs that had once grown from the central branch; a fragment of torn, green linen, found on a hawthorn bush.

Picking up the doll, Huxley said, 'I've often seen these talisman dolls, but never touched them. They usually hang in the trees. This one was on the ground and I felt it fair game.'

'Who hangs them in the trees?' Steven asked softly, his eyes, now, registering interest rather than sadness.

Huxley came close to telling the boy a little about the mythogenetic processes occurring within the wood, and the life forms that existed there. Instead he fell back on the old standby. 'Travelling folk. Tinkers. Romanies. Some of these bits and bobs might be years old, generations. All sorts of people have lived in and around the edge of our wood.'

The boy stepped forward and tentatively picked up the wooden figure, holding it, turning it over, then grimly placing it down again.

Huxley said, 'Did I upset you this morning?'

Oddly, the boy shook his head.

'But you came to the study. You saw me . . . ?'

'I heard you shouting by the wood. I was frightened.'

'Why were you frightened?'

'I thought . . . I thought someone was attacking you . . .'

'*Was* someone attacking me?'

The boy's gaze dropped. He fidgeted, biting his lip, then looked up again, and there was fear in his eyes.

'It's all right, Steven. Just tell me what you saw . . .'

'You were all grey and green. You were very angry . . .'

'What do you mean, I was all grey and green?'

'Funny colours, like light on water. I couldn't see you properly. You were so fast. You were shouting. There was an awful smell of blood, like when Fonce kills the chickens.'

Alphonsus Jeffries, the farm manager for the Manor. Steven had been taken round the farm several times, and had witnessed the natural life of the domestic animals, and their unnatural death with knife and cleaver.

'Where were you when you saw this, did you say?'

'By the woods . . .' Steven whispered. His lips trembled and tears filled his eyes. Huxley remained seated, leaning forward, holding his son's gaze hard and firm. 'Grow up, boy. You've seen something very strange. I'm asking you about it. You want to be a scientist, don't you?'

Steven hesitated, then nodded.

'Then tell me everything. You were by the woods . . .'

'I thought you called me.'

'From the woods . . .'

'You called me.'

'And then?'

'I went over the field and you were all grey and green. You ran past me. I was frightened. I could hardly see you. Just a little bit. You were all grey and green. I was frightened . . .'

'How fast did I pass you?'

'Daddy . . . ? I'm frightened . . .'

'Be quiet, Steven. Stand still. Stop crying. How fast did I pass you?'

'Very fast. I couldn't see you.'

'Faster than our car?'

'I think so. You ran up to here. I followed you and heard you shouting.'

'What was I shouting?'

'Rude things.' The boy squirmed beneath his father's gaze. 'Rude things. About Mummy.'

Stunned and sickened, Huxley bit back the question he longed to ask, stood up from his desk and walked past the wan-faced lad, into the garden.

Rude things about Mummy . . .

'How do you know the man you saw was me?' he murmured.

Steven ran past him, distressed and suddenly angry. The boy turned sharply, eyes blazing, but said nothing.

Huxley said, 'Steven. The man you saw . . . whoever it was . . . it only *looked* like me. Do you understand that? It wasn't me at all. It only *looked* like me.'

The answer was a growl, a shaking, feverish, feral growl, in which the words were dimly discernible from the furious face, the dark face of the boy as he backed slowly away, sinking into himself, lowering his body, eyes on his father. Angry.

'It . . . *was* . . . you . . . It . . . *was* . . . you . . .'

And then Steven had fled, running to the gate. He left the garden and crossed the field almost frantically, plunging into the nearby woods.

Huxley hesitated for a moment, half thinking that it would be better for the boy to calm down first before pursuing the matter further. But he was too intrigued by Steven's glimpse of the ghost.

He picked up one of Wynne-Jones's frontal-lobe bridges and trotted after his son.

NINE

As I had imagined he would, the boy became intrigued when I told him about the frontal-lobe bridges (I called them 'electrical crowns'). He was hovering in the edgewoods, shaking, by the time I reached him. I have never seen Steven so distressed, not even after he and Christian glimpsed the Twigling, and were given a great fright. I said that WJ and myself had been experimenting on seeing ghosts more clearly. Would he like to try one on? Oh the delight! I felt smaller than the smallest creature in so tricking Steven, but by now there was an overwhelming compulsion in me to know who or what this 'grey-green figure' had been.

As we returned to the house Steven glanced backwards and frowned. Was it the figure? I could see wind stirring the trees and scrubby bush that borders the denser zones of the wood, but no sign of human life. Can you see anything, I asked the boy, but after a moment he shook his head.

We returned to the study and after a few minutes I tentatively placed a crown on Steven's head. He was trembling with excitement, poor little lad. I should have remembered WJ's instructions of two years ago, when first he had started to tinker with this electrical device. Always use with a calm mind. We had had our greatest successes under such conditions, perking up the peripheral vision, sharpening the focus of the pre-mythago forms that could be glimpsed when within the swell and grasp of the sylvan net. It was wrong of me to go ahead with Steven without first checking the notebooks. I have no excuse, just shame. The effect on the boy was devastating. I have learned a severe and sobering lesson.

TEN

Steven remembers nothing of the incident with the frontal bridge. It is as if the electrical surge that sent him into such hysteria has blanked the last five days from him. His most recent memory is of school, on Tuesday. He remembers eating his lunch, and walking to a class, and then nothing. He is happy again, and the fever has died down. He didn't wake last night, and has no memory of the grey-green man. I walked with him by the edge of the wood, then ventured in through the gate, down by the thin stream with its slippery banks. Inside the wood I sensed the pre-mythagos at once and asked Steven what he could see.

His answer: Funny things.

He smiled as he said this. I questioned him further, but that is all he would say. 'Funny things.' He looked quite blank when I asked him to look for the grey-green man.

I have destroyed something in him. I have warped him in some way. I am frightened by this since I do not understand even remotely what I have done. Wynne-Jones might know better, but he remains lost. And I cannot bring myself to explain in full just what I did to Steven. This act of cowardice will destroy me. But until I understand what has happened, who is writing in my journal, I must keep as free as possible of domestic difficulty. I am denying something in myself for the sake of a sanity that will collapse as soon as I am free of mystery. This is limbo!

Jennifer treats me harshly. I am spending as much time as I can with the two boys. But I must find Wynne-Jones. I must find out what has happened to bring this haunting upon myself.

ELEVEN

So tired he could hardly walk, Huxley walked across the night field, glad of a moonglow behind clouds that showed him the stark outline of Oak Lodge. Using this as a marker he stepped slowly towards his home, the sickness in his stomach still a jarring pain and a nauseous surge. Whatever he had eaten, he should have been more careful.

This excursion had been short, again, but he had hoped to have returned before nightfall. As it was, he imagined dawn was just an hour or so away.

The sound of Jennifer's cry stopped him in his tracks. He listened carefully, close to the gate, and again he heard her voice, a slightly strangled, then increasingly intense evocation of pain. She was gasping, he realised. The sound of her voice stopped quite suddenly, and then there was a laugh. The sound was eerily loud in the night, in the still night, this solitude of sound and sensation that was so close to dawn.

'Oh my God. Jennifer . . . Jennifer!'

He began to walk more swiftly. An image of his wife being attacked in the night was insisting its superiority over the obvious.

The doors of his study were shattered abruptly. Glass crashed and the doors flung wide. Something moved with incredible speed across the lawns, through the trees, causing leaves and apples to fall. Whatever it was stopped suddenly close to the hedges, then crashed through them, passing Huxley like a storm wind.

And stopped. And moved in the moonlight.

Grey-green man . . . ?

There was nothing there. There was moon-shadow only. And yet Huxley could sense the outline of a man, a naked man, a man still hot from exertion, the smell of the man, the heat of the man, the pulse of heart and head, the shaking of the limbs of the man . . .

Grey-green . . .

'Come back. Come and talk.'

The garden was aflow with movement. Everything was bending, twisting, writhing in a wind that circled the motionless shadow. And the shadow moved, towards Huxley, then away, and there was no glimpse, no sight, no feeling of reality, just the sense of something that had watched him and had returned to the wood.

Huxley ran back to the broken gate, tripping on the shattered wood. He had not even heard the breaking of the gate, but he followed the wind with his ears and night vision, and saw the scrubwood thrash with life, then die again into the steadiness of night, as whatever it was passed through it and beyond, into the timeless realm of the wood.

'Jennifer . . . oh no . . .'

She was not in the room. The bed was still warm, disturbed and dishevelled in an obvious way. He walked quickly out onto the landing, then downstairs again, following the slightest of sounds to the smallest of rooms. She was seated on the toilet, and pulled the door shut abruptly as he opened it.

'George! Please! A *little* privacy . . .'

'Are you all right?'

'I'm very all right. But I thought you were going to have a heart attack.'

She laughed, then pulled the chain. When she emerged into the dark corridor she reached for him and put her arms around his neck. She seemed startled to discover him wearing his jacket. 'You've not got dressed again! Good *grief*, George. There really is very little hope for you.' She hesitated, half amused, half anguished. 'Well . . . perhaps there's *some* hope . . .' Her sudden kiss was deep, moist and passionate.

Her breath was strong, a sexual smell.

'I'm going back to bed. I rather hoped you'd be there too . . .'

'I have to think.'

In the darkness he couldn't see her face, but he sensed the smile, the weary smile. 'Yes, George. Of course. You go and think. Write in your journal.' She walked away from him, towards the stairs. 'There are fresh bones in the pantry should you get peckish.'

But her voice gave away her sadness. He heard the moment's crying, and intuited instantly and painfully that something she had thought renewed she now realised was not.

So he *had* been here again. The encounter in the garden, in the darkness . . . that *had* been the grey-green man. And he had seduced Jennifer!

Huxley drew the journal from its hiding place, and with shaking hands opened it, switching on the lamp.

The same? You and I? No. No! It feels wrong. I am no ghost.

Am I a ghost? Perhaps. Yes. When I read your words. Yes. Perhaps right.

I am confused. I live in brief moments, and the dreams are strong and powerful. I am dreaming a life. But I belong in Oak Lodge. When I am there I feel warmth. But the wood pulls me back. You are right. You other writer. I am your dream and I am free, but not free. Oh confused! And ill. Always so ill. The blood is so hot.

The dreams, the urging. I am such a hunter. I run them down and use my hands. I am plastered with detritus from the forest.

My son Steven. You have tampered with my son. This was wrong. Such fury in me. If I see you I fear to control my anger. Leave Steven alone. I am aware of him in the wood. He is here. Something has, or will happen, and he is everywhere. Something will happen to him. Do not interfere with him. An immense event is shaping around him, not yet happened, but already changing the wood, and time is recoiling and refashioning. I watch seasons in frantic change, in full, seconds-long flight. I hear sounds from all times. This is Ash's doing.

The horses, the time of horses. Something happened there, something small. Something to you/me to cause this you/me, this wild split. What happened? I see it only in dreams. I am too wild, too base, when I am free of dreams I am wild and running, the merest scent of blood is an enragement, the scent of flesh sends me surging, Jennifer is not safe from me, guard her guard her, even though you recognise that passion

Find Ash and find where she sent you. Why did she

send you there? The horse, the fire in that wood. All a dream

Guard Jennifer from the ghost and the bloody obsessions of the ghost

I am so close to this earth, so much matter of rock and wood and silent night that lives, claws, crawls, devours, desires, surges and comes into all life that interferes and crosses paths and tracks

Kill me?

How?

Join again, return me to you. Ash. The key. The wood is tugging, a root around me. It draws me tight. The smell of must and rotten wood. The stink. Each a chain around me. Each a tug. I am a prisoner

Steven will be lost to us. He will never

But with this tantalising and terrifying half sentence, the entry ended.

TWELVE

What *had* happened in that living dream of the cold wood, and the running horses? He had been run down by one of the creatures. He had tried to see the face of the corpse on its back, but had failed. He had, when he thought about it clearly, felt himself torn spiritually apart: there had been that moment of wild riding, of moving with horse and cadaver through the trees . . .

Had that been the moment of division?

Had that been when Green-grey man had split from him?

He wrote in his journal:

To my shadow: What do you know of Ash? What do you remember of the moment when the horse collided with you in

THE BONE FOREST

the birchwood glade? How shall I contact Ash again? Why do you think Wynne-Jones is dead? Why do you think Steven will be lost? What is the great event that you feel forming? Is there any way that we can talk? Or must we continue to correspond through the pages of this journal?

He placed the book behind the shelves, then went out into the rising dawn. Wisps of what looked like smoke, funnels of greyish smog, rose, from over Ryhope Wood. As the light increased, the odd vortices vanished. The last thing he saw before returning to the house was the shimmering movement of leaves and green, running, it seemed, for several yards along the edgewood. He could not quite focus upon it, although the sensation of movement was strongest when he looked away, catching it from the corner of his eye.

The new day was a Saturday and both boys were at home. By mid-morning the sound of their antics and play had begun to irritate Huxley as he tried to concentrate his mind — his tired mind — on thinking through the experience with Ash. He watched the boys from his study window. Christian, the more rumbustious of the two, was swinging from every branch he could find during a game of some form of chase. Steven seemed to become aware of his father, watching him, and froze for a moment, his face anxious. Only when Huxley moved away did he hear the sound of the game restart.

They are both afraid of me. No: they are both missing closeness with me. They hear their friends talk about fathers . . . they think of their father . . . I feel so helpless. I am not interested in them as boys, only in the men, the minds, the thoughts and explorations of deeper thought that they will become . . . they bore me . . .

The moment he had written these lines, he inked them through, so strongly, so savagely, that none would ever read this terrible and sickening moment of self honesty.

No. I am envious of them. They 'see' in a way that is beyond my ability. Their fantasy games include glimpses of pre-mythago forms that I would give *anything* to witness. They are attuned more deeply to the wood. I hear it in their stories, their fantasies, their games. But if they were too aware of what was happening to them . . . might that not diminish their spontaneous 'seeing'? These thoughts seem irrational, and yet I feel that they must be kept in ignorance for their talents to be pure.

Later in the day the boys left the garden. The sudden cessation of their noise attracted Huxley and when he went to see where they'd gone he noticed them, distantly, tearing round the edge of the wood, in the direction of the railway tracks.

He knew where they'd be going, and out of curiosity followed them, taking his stick and his panama hat. The day was bright, if not hot, and there was a brisk, moist-smelling breeze, heralding rain later.

They had gone to the mill pond, of course. Christian was sitting on the old jetty, where the boat had once been tethered. The pond was wide, curving round between dense, overhanging trees, to end in a sprawling patch of rushes out of sight. The oaks at that far end were like a solid wall, great thick trunks, the spaces between them a clutter of willow and spreading holly. It was as if the wall had been deliberately built to stop the wood being entered at that point.

Once, there had been fish in abundance in this pool, but at some time in the twenties the life had faded. A pike or two still could be seen, gliding below the water. But there was little point in fishing, now, and the old boat was rapidly rotting.

Huxley had warned both boys *never* to take that boat out, but he could see that Christian was contemplating such an act, as he dangled his feet in the water. Such a headstrong boy. So wilful.

Steven was beating through the reeds with a stick. No, not beating: cutting. He gathered a thick armful and carried them back around the pond's edge, and Huxley drew back into the concealing undergrowth.

The exchange of conversation between his sons confirmed that they were planning to make a reed boat, and float it on the pond.

He smiled, and was about to withdraw and walk silently back along the short path that led from open land to this pond, when he realised that the boys were alarmed.

Christian was running over the decaying piles of the boathouse, pointing into the thick woods. Steven followed him, and they dropped to a crouch, peering into the gloom.

From his lurking place, Huxley followed the direction of their interest. He realised that a wide, strange face was watching from high in the branches of a tree. He was reminded of the Cheshire Cat from Alice, and smiled. But the face wasn't smiling.

It withdrew abruptly from the light. Something crashed noisily to the ground, startling and scattering birds from the tree tops. It moved with great speed through the woodland, round the pondside, was silent for a moment, then crashed noisily into the deep wood, finally vanishing from earshot.

Huxley remained where he was. The excited lads passed by him, talking about the 'monkey face', and sharing the burden of reeds for the hull of their reed ship, which they intended to build in the woodshed. As soon as they were gone Huxley went round to the boathouse, and struck into the tangle of undergrowth behind. There was no path, and his trousers were snagged and torn by the screen of briar rose and blackberry bramble. He found that the simple barrier of this untamed wood would not allow him in, but after a while he found a patch of nettles, stamped them down, laid his jacket over them, and sat, screened from sight, surrounded by the heavy silence and air of the wood, watching through the shifting light for any further sign of 'monkey face', a mythago that he had not yet observed himself at quarters close enough for him to make a judgement upon its mythological nature.

It was a fruitless wait, and he returned to Oak Lodge a disappointed man. There were no further entries in his private journal, and he made a short entry in his research journal, defining the mythago as far as he was able. He asked Steven and Christian about their day, and teased their perception of the creature from them, affecting idle interest. But neither boy could add more to what he himself had seen, save to say that the face was wide, high-browed and painted. It was perhaps, then, an early manifestation of Cro-Magnon belief? Its appearance was too modern for it to be associated with the culture that had given rise to the man from Piltdown, the nature of whose belief systems constantly exercised Huxley's imagination and interest.

At eleven o'clock Jennifer announced that she was retiring for the night, and as she walked past him paused, held out her hand. 'Are you coming?'

It horrified Huxley to feel such shock, such fear of accepting his wife's invitation. A cold sweat tingled on his neck and hairline, and he said casually, 'I do need to read a little further.'

'I see,' she breathed with resignation, and went to bed.

How could he feel like this? He noticed that his hands

were shaking. The intimacy that had characterised their first years together more by its regularity than its passion, had certainly, in recent years, changed to a self-conscious routine of tentative suggestion, almost unknowing touch, and brief encounter by darkness. And yet he had accepted this change for the worse – it always occurred to him that Jennifer might have been accepting the status with far less complacency – without really conscious thought. It had taken the sound of her pleasure to remind him of their early years, and to make him aware, now, of the avoidance that he had been practising.

He nearly cried as he thought of how much he had denied the closeness of their life that Jennifer so needed.

He stared hard at the ceiling, thinking of her in bed, thinking of holding her. And gradually he forced himself to his feet, and walked upstairs, and entered the bedroom where she slept softly, half exposed from below the summer sheet, her body faintly illuminated by moonlight from the bright summer night.

She was naked, he realised, and the shock made him catch his breath. He was almost embarrassed to look at her, at the leg that lay outside the covers, the soft breast that was crushed in the bend of her arm, as she slept, her head turned half towards him.

He undressed and pulled on pyjamas. In bed beside her he watched her for a long time, long enough to bite all skin from the inside of his lower lip, so that he tasted blood, and his lip was sore.

He almost woke her once, his hand out to her, the fingers hovering just above her tousled hair.

But he didn't. He closed his eyes, sank a little lower, and thought of the primal mythological form of humankind, his great quest: The Urscumug . . .

Somewhere in the woods, the creature lives. It must have formed many times. But it is deep. It is in the heart. How to find it? How to find? I must devise a way of calling it to the edge...

He was still thinking about his quest when he heard the sound of movement downstairs. It startled him at first, but then he lay quietly, listening hard.

Yes. It was in the study. There was a long time of silence, then again the sound of furniture being moved, drawers opened, cabinets opened as perhaps his souvenirs were examined.

Then a sudden sound on the stairs, someone coming up the stairs at great speed.

Again, silence.

It was on the landing. It moved along the landing to the door of the bedroom and again stopped; then the door was opened and something sped into the room, a fleet shadow crossing the floor to the window in an instant, and closing the curtains. A deeper darkness descended, but in the moment of dim light Huxley had seen the man shape, the deep shadow shape that was unquestionably a naked human male. The shoulders were broad, the body hard and lean, and the creature's member was distended and almost vertical. A strong odour filled the room, something of undergrowth, something of the sharp smell of an unwashed man.

Slowly Huxley sat up in bed. He sensed the movement of the figure, short darting movements that carried it from one side of the room to the other, then back again.

It was waiting for him to go!

In its last journal entry it had written 'protect Jennifer against me. Protect her against the ghost...'

'Go away,' Huxley breathed. 'I won't let you come near her. You told me not to...'

It raced up to him in the darkness and hovered there, its eyes dimly reflecting, showing how wide they were, how intense. It was hard to define shape; he sensed shadows shifting, a depthlessness to the figure, but yet it was solid. The heat and the smell that came off it were overpowering.

In a voice that sounded like the restless stirring of a breeze, it whispered 'journal'.

It had written in the journal!

It towered over him, and Jennifer suddenly stirred. 'George . . . ?'

She tossed her head slightly, and her arm extended towards him, but before the hand could touch him it was intercepted. The creature had her, and Huxley felt willed to leave the bed.

'Journal,' breathed the grey-green man, and there was the hint of a laugh, of a smile as the word was said for the second time.

'George?' Jennifer murmured, coming more awake.

His heart pounding, the sense of the grey-green man's mocking laughter teasing at his conscience, Huxley swung out of bed and left the room.

Half way down the stairs he heard Jennifer's cry of surprise as she woke fully. Then her sudden, splendid laugh.

He blocked his ears against the sounds that came next, and went into his study, tears streaming down his face as he fumbled behind the books for his private journal.

THIRTEEN

Will try to speak. But you move slowly, ghostly. Perhaps I am the same to you. I observe the house and Jenny, the boys, and they are real, although they seem to be a dream. But you are slow, the me part, the me factor, too ghostly, and it is hard to speak.

Steven is in the wood, Chris too. Something huge in the wood, some event, some rebirth or regeneration. I sense it. I hear it from mouths, from tales. I have been here so long, and the world of the mythago is my world.

This is puzzling. Why have you not been in the wood, in the same way, in the same wood? Confused. My mind does not focus. But I have had encounters. You have not had the same encounters.

I can't answer about Steven. As a man, he will come here. Or as a boy and grow to a man. Somehow. It has to do with the Urscumaga. Pursuit. Quest. I cannot say more. I know NO more! Be gentle with Steven. Be careful of him. Be watchful. Love him. LOVE HIM!

Wynne-Jones was in the horse temple. You saw him. You MUST have seen. I think he was killed. He was trapped.

You should know this. Why not? Why do you not?

Perhaps you have forgotten. Perhaps some memory is stripped from you and exists in me. Memory in you is denied me. No. Not true. Your account of Ash is my account. Almost. You describe the amulet as dull. The amulet was bright. You say a green stone. Yes. You say a leather thong. No. Horse hair. Twined horse hair. Can you have made such a mistake?

I see now that you make no mention of Ash previously. Not my journal then, though so many entries are the same. Yes. Snow Woman, Steven's word, was the same as Ash. I remember her visit, that winter. But Wynne-Jones made contact in February. No mention in the journal of that. But I wrote an account. He understood the basic nature of Ash. But no mention in either journal. Yet it was written.

Are we the same?

Ash: She carries the memory of wood. She is the guardian of ancient forest and can summon from them and send to them. She uses the techniques of the shaman to do this. By casting her charms of wood and bone she can create — and destroy, too, if she wishes — forests of lime and spruce, or oak and ash, or alder and beech. She can send hunters to find pigs, or stags, or bears, or horses. Other things! Forgotten creatures. Forgotten woods. Her skills are legion. She can send the curious to find curiosities. She can even send a stealer of talismans to find ... well, what can I say to you? To find a little humility, perhaps. I am certain that she was telling me to leave alone things I did not understand.

The hunters of the land have always believed in her, knowing that she can control all the woods of the world. In her mind, and in her skills, forests are waiting to be born, ancient forests are waiting for the return of the hunters. Through Ash there is a strange continuity. No matter what has been destroyed, it lives in her, and one day can be summoned back.

She sent us to the horse sacrifice for a reason.

We must ask: what reason?

I was riding the horse when it collided with the hooded man. I remember nearly falling. The horse was bolting. It had two bodies on its back. One alive (me) beginning to burn badly. One dead. The hooded man was struck. I fell, the horse ran on. Then I came home. But I am a ghost.

Find Ash! Return us to the horses! Something happened!

He had walked quietly to the landing, tiptoeing up the stairs, shaking badly, but with a rage, now, and not with fear. He stripped off his pyjamas and felt the cool touch of night air on his naked skin. Then he banged loudly on the banister.

As he expected, the door to his bedroom opened and something moved, with blurring speed, into the darkness.

Grey-green man stood at the far end of the landing, and Huxley sensed the way it watched, the way it suddenly grinned.

Jennifer was hissing, 'What *is* it?'

Huxley moved along the landing. Grey-green came at

him and there was static in the air where they almost touched.

'Go to the study,' Huxley hissed stiffly. 'Wait for me . . .'

There was hesitation in the ghost, then that mocking smile again, and yet . . . it acceded to the instruction. It passed Huxley, and went downstairs, lurking in the grim darkness.

Jennifer ran out onto the landing, dragging her housecoat around her. There was no sound of disturbance from the boys' room, and Huxley was glad.

She sounded anxious.

'Is there someone in the house?'

'I don't know,' he said. 'I'd better look around.'

Her hand touched his bare back as she peered over the banister into the gloom below. She seemed slightly startled. 'You're so cool, now.'

And a lot flabbier, he thought to himself.

And Jennifer added, 'You smell fresher.'

'Fresher?'

'You needed a good bath. But you smell . . . cleaner, suddenly . . .'

'I'm sorry if I smelled strong before.'

'I quite liked it,' she said quietly, and Huxley closed his eyes for a moment.

'But perhaps it's the sheets,' Jennifer said. 'I'll change them first thing in the morning.'

'I'll investigate downstairs.'

The french windows were open, the study light off. Huxley switched on the desk lamp and peered down at the open page of the journal.

Grey-green man had scrawled the words: *then how do I get back? Must think. Will go to Horse Shrine and stay there. But the blood is hot. You must understand. I am not in control.*

This entry occurred below the response that Huxley

had penned to his alter ego's earlier, substantial account of Ash, and his questions about the nature of their dual existence.

Huxley had written:

We are clearly not the same, but only similar. We are aspects of two versions of George Huxley. If I am incomplete then it is in a way that is different from the incompleteness of you. You seem to be the most isolated. Perhaps your existence in this world, my world, is wrong for you. Perhaps there is a part of me that is running, fearful and dying, in a world that is more familiar to you.

If I had no other reason for concluding these things it is this: I have never called Jennifer 'Jenny'. Not ever. It is not possible for me to even contemplate writing that nickname. She is J. in my journals, or Jennifer. Never the shorter form.

Your Jennifer is not my Jennifer. I have let you loose upon the woman I love, and you have taught me one thing, about how callous I have become, and I accept that lesson. But you will not enter this house again, not beyond the study. If you do, I shall endeavour to destroy you, rather than help you. Even if it means losing Wynne-Jones forever, I shall certainly find a way to disseminate the bestial spirit that you are.

I should prefer to return you to the body from which you have gone missing: *my* body, albeit in another location, another time, some other space and time that has somehow become confused with my own world.

Yes, other things give away the fact that we are living parallel lives, closely linked, yet subtly different. I refer to the 'Urscumug', not 'Urscumaga'. You know more about Ash than I do. Wynne-Jones, in your world, has raced ahead of my own, pipe-reeking friend. The talisman most definitely was hung with leather, not horse hair. Clearly *I* am the hooded man over whom you ran, in your mad canter from the forest glade. My oilskin hood was torn, quite beyond repair!

And so you must propose a way for us to meet, to engage, to communicate.

But I repeat, you are not to enter my house beyond this desk.

If you doubt that I have the skill to destroy you, then look into your own bestial heart: remember what I/you have achieved in the past. Remember what happened to you/I in the Wolf Glen, when we discovered a certain magic of our own, destructive to mythagos!

And below this entry, Grey-green man had scrawled *then how do I get back?*

Huxley closed and concealed the journal. He walked out into the garden, and stepped carefully across the lawn to the bushes. The ground was wet with dew, the air scented with raw, rich night perfume of soil and leaf. Everything was very still.

Huxley stepped among the moist bushes of rhododendron and fuchsia. He pressed the wet leaves and flowers against his torso, and found, to his mild surprise, that he was excited by the touch of nature upon his dry, cool body. He rubbed leaves between his fingers, crushed fuchsia flowers, reached down and rubbed his hands over the dewy soil. He drew breath in through his nostrils, filling his lungs, and as he stood so he smeared his hands over his shoulders and belly . . .

A blur of night-lit movement, the earth vibrating, the undergrowth shaking, and Grey-green man was there, shimmering and shadowy, watching him.

They stood in silence, man and ghost, and then Huxley laughed. 'You frightened me once, but no longer. And yet, I feel sympathy for you, and will try to send you back. By doing that I believe I can release Wynne-Jones.'

Grey-green man took a slow step forward, reaching to Huxley.

Huxley stepped forward too, but ripped up a branch of bush, and swept it at the ghost.

'Go to the Horse Shrine! I'll meet you there tomorrow.'

Grey-green man didn't cower, but there was something about it, something less triumphant than before. It hovered, then withdrew, then turned (or so Huxley thought) to stare again at its alter ego. It seemed to be questioning.

Huxley squeezed sap from the torn branch and rubbed it on his face.

'She liked the smell,' he said, and laughed as he tossed the branch aside, before turning and entering the house.

Locking the french windows behind him.

Jennifer was sitting up in bed, the covers round her knees. She stared at Huxley by lamplight, her face puzzled, anguished.

'I want you to tell me what's going on,' she said quietly, firmly. She was looking at him, staring at him, taking in his nakedness. He imagined he knew what she was thinking: he did not look like the body she had so recently felt against her. He was broader, chubbier, less fit.

'It will take some time.'

'Then take time.'

He climbed into bed beside her and on a new and strong impulse turned towards her, putting his arm across her to turn out the lamp.

'I would like to kiss you first,' he said. 'And then I'll tell you everything.'

'One kiss, then. But I'm angry, George. And I want to know what's happening . . .'

FOURTEEN

The boys were at school. Huxley entered their room and stood, for a moment, surveying the truly appalling mess that the lads had left after a weekend of playing, pillow fighting, and reading. They had been making a model boat, and against their father's instructions had brought the model up to their bedroom. The floor, the surfaces, the bed itself, were covered with bits of reed.

He reached down and picked up several sheets of white paper with pencil drawings. They were the blueprints for the model: crude, but skilful, and he recognised Christian's imagination at work here. He was impressed. Plan view, side view, rear elevation, cross section . . .

Of the ship itself there was no sign. It was an ambitious project. They usually contented themselves with smaller, wooden models.

The room was quiet and he closed his eyes for a moment, summoning the imaginations at work here. He banished from his mind the smell of unwashed socks that instantly struck his consciousness. What he wanted was to feel the *fantasies* of the boys, their dreams, and in this room he might be able to touch the edge of those dreams.

It was an odd thought, and yet: he was convinced that one of the boys had created the Ash mythago.

He went through their drawers, where clothes were crushed and crumpled, apple-cores rotted, penny dreadfuls were concealed, and rock hard ends of sandwiches – made for midnight feasts – nestled side by side with pictures torn from magazines.

Eventually he found the fragments of wood and bone that Ash had left. They were still in their leather container. Huxley placed them on the desk, rolled them over the surface, remembered the time last winter when Snow Woman had left these items at the gate.

Then he went over to the bed and sat down, staring at the magic from across the room.

Why did you leave these pieces? Why? Why did you come to Oak Lodge? Why did you destroy the chickens? Why did you ensure that Steven would see you?

Why?

Steven and his passion for presents, his need for gifts. Had he created a mythago that was designed to fulfil that need in him?

Give me something. Bring me something. Bring me a gift. Give me something that makes me feel . . . wanted . . .

Was she Steven's mythago, then? Gift-bringing Ash. But what sort of gift was implied in two fragments of thorn, and a piece of wild cat?

Perhaps Steven was intended to wear them. Perhaps then he would journey, in the same way that Huxley had journeyed. These bits of wood represented a different forest, though.

Why did you come out of the wood? Why did you leave these fragments? Why the chickens? What did you hope to achieve?

He thought back to the time in the Horse Shrine. Ash had watched him closely and carefully for a long while, and perhaps there *had* been disappointment in her face? Was she expecting someone else?

She had been waiting for someone. She had been at the Horse Shrine since the winter, if the evidence of the waste spoils was to be believed. She had been trying to make contact with the Huxleys, and yet all she had done was send George Huxley on a nightmarish trip to a freezing wood, long in the past . . .

If she had wanted Steven, what had she wanted to do with him?

And if Wynne-Jones *had* been present in the same ancient mythago-realm — and the grey-green man suggested that perhaps he had — what had Ash wanted with *him*?

How had he come to play a part in the same ancient sequence?

Why had he played any part at all, if Ash had wanted *Steven* . . . ?

Huxley prowled the room, drinking in the disorder, tapping the imagination that reverberated here.

Steven and Ash . . . a shocking visitation to the henhouse . . . a bed of dead hens . . . *just like in the story* . . .

He went quickly to the window, staring down at the yard, the spring sunshine. He tried to replay the whole of that snow-deadened encounter, after Christmas.

What had Steven said to his mother? 'Got them all . . . just like in the story . . .'

What story?

Steven hadn't seen inside the shed, but Huxley had told him that all the hens had been killed. A fox had done it, he said, and Steven had seemed to accept that statement, despite the fact that Ash had clearly been to the henhouse herself.

What story?

Steven had said, 'That old drummer fox . . .'

Huxley had taken no notice, and Jennifer had simply responded to the shock of losing all their hens.

Who was that 'old drummer fox'?

He looked at the scattered books, searched among them, but found nothing. He called for Jennifer and she came into the room, frowning at the mess. She looked as tired as she felt. It had been a long night, and a long talk, and Huxley had told her much that she should have known before, and explained about the supernatural event that was occurring.

Not unsurprisingly, Jennifer was shocked, and was still shocked, and had spent an hour on her own, fighting a feeling of nausea. He had left her alone. It had seemed inappropriate to try to explain that in a way she had slept only with her husband, that no man from this, the real world, had touched her apart from Huxley. But that was not how she saw it, and there were other considerations too, no doubt.

'Drummer Fox and Boy Ralph? That was Steven's favourite story for years, when he was much younger. He was obsessed with it . . .'

'I've never heard of it.'

'Of course,' she said acidly. 'You never read *anything* to the boys. I did all the reading.'

'Rebuke accepted,' Huxley said quickly. 'Can you find the book? I must see that story.'

She searched the shelves, and the scatter of books on the floor, opened the wardrobe where albums, school books, and magazines were stored, but couldn't find the volume of tales that included Drummer Fox.

Huxley felt impatient and anxious. 'I must know the story.'

'Why?'

'I think it may be the key to what is happening. What can you remember of it? You said you'd read it to him – '

'Hundreds of times. But a long time ago.'

'Tell me the story.'

She leaned back against one of the desks and gathered her thoughts. 'Oh Lord, George. It's *so* long ago. And I read so many stories to them, Christian especially . . .'

'Try. Please try.'

'He was a sort of gypsy fox. Very old, older than any human alive. He'd been wandering Europe for centuries, with a drum, which he beat every dawn and dusk, and a sack of tricks. He either played tricks on people to escape from them, or entertained them for his supper. He also had a charge, an infant boy.'

'Boy Ralph.'

'That's right. Boy Ralph was the son of a Chief, a warrior of the olden days. But the boy was born on a highly auspicious day and his father was jealous and decided to kill the infant by smothering him. He was planning to use the carcase of a chicken for the vile deed.

'Drummer Fox lived at the edge of the village, entertaining people with his tricks and sometimes giving them prophecies. He liked the boy and seeing him in danger stole him and ran away with him. The King sent a giant of a warrior after the fox, with instructions to hunt him down and kill them both. So Drummer Fox found himself running for his life.

'Wherever Drummer Fox went he found that humans were tricky and destructive. He didn't trust them. Some were kind and he left them alone. He always paid a small price for whatever he had taken from them. But others were hunters and tried to kill him. At night he would make his bed in their chicken sheds, making mattresses and blankets from the dead chicks – '

Huxley slapped his knees as he heard this. 'Go on . . .'

'He used to say [and here, Jennifer put on a silly country voice], "Nothing against the chicks but their clucking. They'd give me away. Give me away. So better a feather bed than a nice egg in the morning. Sorry chicks . . ."'

'And then he'd silently kill the lot of them.'

'Of course. This *is* a story for children.' Huxley shared Jennifer's smile. 'Anyway, that isn't all. Drummer Fox made the infant Ralph a plaything of the heads of the chickens, threaded on a piece of string.'

Huxley was astonished and delighted. 'Good God! That's exactly what had happened in the chicken house. And Steven never saw inside! He didn't know about that particularly gruesome piece of Ash's game. Go on. Go on!'

'That's more or less it, really. The fox is on the run. He gets what he can from the human folk he meets, but if in danger he tricks the humans into the forest where they invariably get crushed under the hooves of the Hunter who's following the fox. It's quite murderous stuff. The boys lapped it up.'

'And how is it resolved? Is it resolved?'

Jennifer had to think for a moment, then she remembered. 'Drummer Fox gets cornered in a deep, wooded valley. The Hunter is almost on him. So the fox makes a mask and puts it on and goes up to greet the giant warrior.'

'What mask?'

'That's the clever part. For a child, at least. He puts on a *fox* mask. He tells the Hunter that he's a local man who has tricked Drummer Fox by pretending to be a renegade fox as well. Drummer Fox has revealed his weakness to him. To destroy the fox all the Hunter needs to do is to disguise himself on horseback with dry rushes and reeds.'

'Aha. The ending loometh.'

'The Hunter duly ties reeds all over his body and – '

'Drummer Fox sets light to him!'

'And away he gallops, trailing flame and cursing the Fox. The nice or nasty little coda is that one day Drummer Fox and Boy Ralph are making their way back through a dark wood when they hear a hunting horn and the smell of burning.'

'The stuff of nightmares,' Huxley said, pacing about the room, thinking hard. 'No wonder the boy is afraid of horses. Good God, we've probably traumatised him for life.'

'It's only a story. The stories the boys tell each other are far more gruesome. But then they've leafed extensively through the copy of *Gray's Anatomy* on your shelf.'

'Have they! Have they indeed! Then at least their stories will be colourful.'

'Does it help? Drummer Fox, I mean?'

Huxley swung round and walked up to Jennifer, gathering her into his arms and hugging her. 'Yes. Oh yes. Very much indeed.' She seemed startled, then drew back, smiling.

'Thank you for letting me know about your madness,' she said quietly. 'Whatever I can do . . .'

'I know. I don't know *what* you can do for the moment. But I feel deeply relieved to have told you what is happening. The grey-green figure frightens me, even though I know it is an aspect of *me*.'

Jennifer went pale and looked away. 'I don't wish to think about that any more. I just want you to be safe. And to be near me more often . . .' The look in her eye as she glanced at him made Huxley smile. They touched hands, and then went downstairs.

FIFTEEN

A wonderful example of convergence, or perhaps *merging*: Steven's imagination is inculcated with the legend and image of the fox: but *Drummer Fox* is just a corruption of a more powerful mythological cycle concerning Ash. Ash *herself* is a 'story' reflecting an ancient event, perhaps an incident from the first migrations and movements of a warrior elite of Indo-Europeans, from central Europe.

Ash, the inherited memory, is present in Steven's mind, and the corrupted form of the folk-tale/fable is also strongly present. So Ash – *created by Steven* – emerges from the wood with associations of Drummer Fox: hence the killing of chickens, the necklace of hen heads.

But this Ash has no child!

Drummer Fox: shaman? The drum, the classic instrument of shamanic trance. And Fox's bag of tricks. The same as Ash's bone and wood bag, her magic.

And Ash carries a tiny wrist-drum!

The story of Ash, then, has been shaped by a time nearer to her own origination as a *legendary tale*. Later, as the tale corrupts further into Drummer Fox and other tales of that ilk, so certain shaman trappings return.

Steven summoned Ash. Ash came, half myth, half folklore,

and called to Steven. Her gift at the gate – the bone and wood pieces – is part attraction to Steven, part the price she pays for her night's stay on the carcases of the hens.

She wants Steven, then. But why? To replace the lost child? Drummer Fox protects Infant Ralph. In one story – the Ash story – has she, I wonder, *lost* the child? Does she then seek to replace the lost child with another, perhaps so that she can pretend that the true 'prince' is still alive?

How I wish I knew more of the Ash legend.

Wynne-Jones and myself are seen as 'intruders, not to be trusted' and sent to the 'hooves of the horses' by Ash. But she selects a key moment, a primary event in mythological time, when images occur that will last into the corrupted form: the burning man, the horses riding wild, the crushing of men below hooves.

So is it Steven who has directed this aspect of Ash? Or is it Ash conforming to the *older* ritual?

And how do I convince Ash to return me to that moment? And once there, how do I return Wynne-Jones safely?

And how did my alter ego slip into this world from his own?

A primary moment, a focus, may be the meeting point of many worlds simply because of its importance . . .

I *must* return to that moment. Something happened there, something was there, that will explain the complication!

You will have to offer her Steven. You fool! Don't you see? You will have to offer her the boy. And then trust her. Can you trust her? Can WE trust her? She will not perform her magic without the gift she seeks. Fool!

But I came *back*. She cast me away, into a landscape both remote in time and place; but it was not a permanent dislocation. She is Steven's mythago. This has tempered the fury that might otherwise be present within her. I still have the necklet of wood and bones with which she dispatched me before; now I will hope to reason with her.

He left the journal open on his desk and went through the house to begin to collect his supplies and equipment for the trek. At some point during the next ten minutes he was aware of the wafting smell of undergrowth in the house, and the sound of movement from his office. The visit was brief, and he caught sight of the shadow as it ran with uncanny speed back across the field to the woodland edge.

A brief response, then, and without much interest Huxley returned to read what had been written.

'Damnation!'

He ran to the garden, dropping the journal as he went. 'Come back!' he shouted. 'You're wrong. I'm sure! Damn!'

Now he was frightened. He swept up the journal, turned again to the scrawled line: *Steven is not safe from Ash. She must be destroyed*, and then flung the book into its hiding place.

Now there was no time to lose. He roughly packed his sack, crammed whatever food lay to hand – bread, cheese, a piece of cold mutton – and almost demolished Jennifer as he ran to the garden.

'Wait until dawn at least . . .' she said, recovering from the impact and helping him gather the spilled items from his sack.

'I can't.'

'You're in a lather, George . . .'

Furious, eyes blazing with panic, he hissed, 'He's going to kill her! That will undo everything. Wynne-Jones, gone forever. Maybe . . .' He hesitated, and bit back the words, 'Steven too.

'I have to follow him,' he went on, 'and fast. God, he's so fast . . .'

Jennifer sighed, seemed sad, then kissed her husband.

'Off you go then. Be careful. For the boys' sake, and for mine.'

He made a feeble attempt at humour. 'I'll return *with* Wynne-Jones, or on him . . .'

'But lose his pipe, if you can,' she added, then turned quickly away as her voice began to break.

SIXTEEN

It took Huxley over four hours to locate the Horse Shrine, the longest search ever. He had been confident of the route, but became distracted by the sudden change in the wood from a stifling, chirruping zoo of green light and intense shade, to a silent, gloomy dell, where the overpowering smell of decay set his heart racing and his senses pounding. By moving too fast through this deadly glade he disorientated himself, and took hours to find some part of Ryhope Wood that prompted memory.

At one point a blur of movement swept past him, noisily disappearing into the deep wood. At first he thought that it might be the grey-green man, overtaking him on his passage inwards, but then remembered that his shadow was far ahead of him. More likely, then, the movement was one of the various forms of the Green Jack. As such he took precautionary manoeuvres and measures against attack, keeping his leather flying jacket firmly buttoned to the throat, despite the humidity, and holding a small wooden shield on the side of his face nearest the disturbance.

It was maddening to be so lost, and to be so desperate to find a shrine that, over the years, he had found with no difficulty.

By a stream he washed his face and cleaned his boots, which were heavy with clay from a tree-crowded mire into which he had stumbled. His lungs were tight with pollen and the damp, heavy air. His mouth was foul. His eyes stung with dust, tiny seeds, and the endless slanting, slashing light from above the dense foliage cover.

The stream was a blessing. He didn't recognise it, although the ruins of a building on its far bank, a building in Norman style, high earth defences, compact and economic use of stone, reminded him of a place he had seen three years before. He knew from experience that the mythagoscapes changed subtly, and that they could be brought into existence by different minds and therefore with slightly different features. If this building was a corrupting form of the river station – from a story-cycle told in the courts of William Rufus – which he had recorded before, then the Horse Shrine lay behind him.

He had come too far.

There was no use in using a compass in this wood. All magnetic poles shifted and changed, and north could be seen to turn a full three hundred and sixty degrees in the stepping of four paces in a straight line. Nor was there any guarantee that the perspective of the wood had not changed; hour by hour the primal landscape altered its relationship with its own internal architecture. It was as if the whole forest was turning, a whirlpool, a spinning galaxy, turning around the voyager, confusing senses, direction and time. And the further inwards one journeyed, the more that place laughed, played tricks, like old Drummer Fox, casting a glamour upon the eyes of the naive beholder.

No. There was no guarantee of anything, here. All Huxley knew was that he was lost. And being lost, yet being comforted by this encounter with the river-station of the piratical *Gylla*, from the eleventh-century story, he felt suddenly confident. He had nothing to use but his judgement. And he had something of great value to lose: his friend of many years standing ...

So he summoned his courage and returned along the trail.

The sound of a horse screaming finally allowed me to locate the shrine, but on arrival at the wide glade I found only desertion and shambles. Something has been here and almost utterly destroyed the place. The monstrous bone effigy of a horse, with its attendant skeletal drivers, is shattered, the bone parts spread throughout the glade and the wood around. They are overgrown, some even moss-covered, as if they have lain like this for many years. Yet I know this place was intact just a few days ago.

The stone temple remains. There are withered leather sacks inside it, some decayed form of food offering, fragments of clay, two wristlets of carved, yellowing ivory pieces resembling crude equines, and carved, I imagine, from horses' teeth. There is also a fresh painting on the grey stone of the outside of the place, a mark, like no animal or hieroglyph that I have encountered. It is complex, of course symbolic, and utterly meaningless. Depicted in a mixture of charcoal and orange ochre, it is tantalising. My sketch, over the page, does not do it justice.

No sign of the horse that screamed.

Light going, night coming. No sign of Ash, and no movement around. This place is dead. Eerie. I shall make a single foray in a wide circle, then return here for the night.

He finished writing and packed the book away in his rucksack. With a nervous glance around he entered the dense woodland again, and ducked below the branches, hesitating as he orientated himself, then striking away from the glade by measured paces, constantly stopping and listening.

He had intended to walk a wide circle, but after a few minutes the abrupt and noisy flight of dark birds, behind him, caught his attention and induced in him a state of frozen silence. He hugged the dark trunk of a tree, peering through the light-shattered gloom for any substantial movement.

When, after a minute or so, he had seen nothing, he began a hesitant return to the glade.

The sound of a scream, a woman's angry, fearful cry, shocked him, then set him running.

A small fire was burning, close to the stone walls of the shrine. The intensity of the flame, the sharp crackle of wood, told Huxley instantly that the fire was new. He was tantalised by the thought that Ash had been near the clearing all the time, watching him, waiting for him to leave.

He approached, now, crouched low in the cover. Ash was a running shape, a twisting, struggling form, caught darkly in the light from her own fire. Something was grappling with her, hitting at her. He could hear the blows. Her cries of anger became groans of pain, but she fought back with vigour, rough skirts swirling, arms swinging.

Huxley dropped his pack and stepped quickly into the clearing. The process of murder was interrupted and Ash looked at him angrily, then with puzzlement. Behind her, the wood shimmered and the grey-green shape of a man moved swiftly to the right. He still had hold of Ash and the startled woman stumbled as her head was wrenched back, dragging her over.

'Let her go! Let go of her at once!'

Huxley snatched a piece of burning wood from the small fire. He dropped it at once and yelled as flame curled round his fingers, singeing the hair on his skin. More carefully he selected a fragment of branch that was burning only at the end –

And grimaced as he realised that the whole of the wood was at what felt like red heat!

– And charged at the shadow of his alter ego.

Ash was being throttled. Her body had pitched back, her naked legs thrashing. Her head and upper torso were hidden by the brush. Her cries were stifled, choking.

Huxley leapt through the undergrowth and thrust the burning brand at the shadow.

'Get away from her! I won't have this, do you understand me? Stop at once!'

The fire at the end of the brand went out. He shook the wood vigorously, hoping to restart the flame, but the life had gone from it.

Then his face erupted with pain and he felt himself flung back into the clearing. He moaned with genuine discomfort and struggled to stand, but all strength had evaporated from his legs, and he fell back, onto one elbow, reached to hold his face, now numbed and oddly loose around the jaw.

Distantly he heard a sharp crack, a half cry, fading quickly, a woman's cry, dying.

'Oh Dear God, he's killed her . . . I've killed her . . .'

Fire burned into his eyes and he shrieked and struck against the brand. A foot crushed down upon his belly, and when he doubled so he felt a further blow, by foot or hand it was hard to tell, against his eyes, striking him flat again. The fire waved down, the flames took on his shirt, and he patted a hand at them, before again fingers closed around his wrist and wrenched him up, to a sitting position, half blinded by flickering yellow fire, and –

Rope around his neck!

Tightening!

He snatched and scrabbled at the thong, managed to cry out. 'Stop this! You have no right! Stop this at once . . . !'

He was lifted, turned, swung. He struggled to retain a degree of dignity, but felt his feet leave the ground and his stomach turn over as he was dragged around by the creature, swinging him with astonishing strength, finally flinging him against the stone of the shrine.

He looked up, then felt burning and realised he was half in the fire. He scrabbled away from the heat, but had the presence of mind to fling gleaming shards and hot ashes against the blurry shadow that had come to tower over him. Where they impacted he caught the grim outline of a naked man, leaning down, and he could tell the smile, and the glitter of menace in the eyes that watched.

A voice like bubbling water hissed, 'Let her die . . .'

'Animal!' Huxley spat. 'You sicken me. To think that you are a part of *me*. Dear God, I hope I never live to see the day that – '

'Steee-vaaaan . . .'

It was an animal howl. It shattered Huxley's concentration. It rattled his nerves. There was such desperation in the cry, such need, such fury. The grey-green shadow bent to its task of killing, but on its lips, on the green-shadow gates of hell that were the exit from its heart, on that invisible, yet tangible mouth was his son's name, and love for his son, *love*, and compassion too, a misguided, misdirected shadow that fought and killed to save the life of

'Steee-vaaaan . . .'

Again the howl of anguish, and then the creature went to work; and with what energy, what power it began to rend the prone and failing body of the man, the human creature that lay before it!

Huxley experienced the scientific process of his death with abstract, disconnected ease . . .

He had no strength left. There was nothing he could do.

That he witnessed the leather thong that suddenly appeared around the shadow's neck was more a testimony to the strength of the scientific curiosity that inhabited the man than any strength of will, or need to survive. He had documented the punishment to his body, and thought only of how this grey-green shadow, this dissection of his mind, his personality, loose in an alien world, could summon the forces of nature such that it could be tangible, whole, and sexual . . .

It was a beast at large, a creature formed from mind, myth and manhood, substance crowning the power of its thoughts, its needs, its desires, its baser hungers. And within that hunger lurked the higher mind that Huxley was proud to call his own, the awareness of love, the curiosity that formed the exploring nature of a man like Wynne-Jones, or young Christian Huxley, or George himself. Poor George. Poor old George.

On the strangling leather, two pieces of wood and a sharp shard of bone showed up clearly by the scattered light of the scattered fire, and the grey-green man shrieked and drew back, swung on his own noose, caught by his own animalistic arrogance as Ash, one arm hanging quite limp, the other wrapped around the thong, dragged the shadow backwards. The eerie sound of his cry was suddenly drowned by the violent flight of birds from all around, a massive flight that filled the glade of the Horse Shrine with leaves and feathers, and the darkening sky with a streaming blur of circling shapes.

There were horses in the wood. They snorted, stamped and shook their manes, with a rustling of woodland and a rattle and clatter of crude stone and bone trappings, slung on hair twine and stretched and softened leather . . . They were everywhere, all around, and Huxley groped his way to his knees, watching the dark woods.

Movement everywhere. And sound, like chanting: and the rapid beating of drums, the rhythmic rattle of bone and shell . . . It was all so familiar. He could hear the cries of tortured men, and the shrieking laughter that had so unnerved him in a recent encounter. All of this was taking place deeper in the wood, almost out of sight.

Ash had let go of Grey-green man and now stood shakily at the edge of the glade, her good arm flexing as she used the wrist drum to beat out a frantic tattoo. And behind her, light . . . *fire* light . . .

And passing quickly across that light, as it came nearer, a stooped, running shape, a man's shape, swathed in cloak and hood. Which vanished into darkness.

In the centre of the glade the grey-green shadow rose from where it had fallen, tall, frightened, arms reaching out from its sides, head turning this way and that. Again, Huxley watched its sleek, virile form, the hard musculature, the animal litheness as it stepped swiftly to one side, then prowled, half crouched, back across the glade.

The woods were on fire. Flame began to streak into the darkening night. The grey-green man rose from his cowering position, darted to Huxley, bent close.

'Wrong . . .' he breathed.

Huxley backed away, still frightened of the raw power that emanated from the creature. 'What is wrong?'

'I . . .'

Huxley tried to understand, but his mind was befuddled by beating and fear. He said, 'Don't kill Ash . . .'

But the creature seemed to ignore him. It said simply, 'Return.'

'What do you mean? What do you mean *return*? Who?' Huxley struggled to sit. 'Who do you mean? Me? You?'

'I . . .' said the grey-green man, and the hand that reached suddenly to the flinching Huxley merely touched a finger to his lips, closed Huxley's mouth, lingered, then was gone.

And with it, the grey-green shadow, fleeing towards the flame-horse, which burst into the glade, a mass of burning rushes, wrapped around the stiff corpse strapped to the horse's back.

The horse screamed. It was huge. It was higher at the back than a tall man, a giant of a beast, burning, to be sacrificed along with the flaming cadaver that rode it to hell and beyond.

The grey-green shadow seemed to fall beneath its hooves, but then a blur of colour, of light and darkness, moved effortlessly up behind the flaming corpse, and reached around almost to hug the flames. The horse reared, scattering burning strands of rush, fire that filled the noisy glade. The animal turned, struggling through pain and panic, then kicked forward again, the body shifting and shaking on its back, streams of fire like flags, rising and waving in the night wind.

And Grey-green man followed it, and went out of the Horse Shrine, riding to hell, riding home, riding through the breach in whatever fabric between the worlds had been rended in that earlier and near fatal encounter with the horses, and the time of sacrifice.

I felt sure that my shadow had been taken back to its rightful body, that version of me that had unwittingly and unwillingly shed its darker aspect.

With the departure of the shadow there was, in myself at least, a sense of inordinate relief. I saw Ash across the glade, a bruised and battered woman, the wrist drum in her hand being flexed with almost urgent need.

I understood that she had helped me. And I suppose she helped me because she had recognised that I had helped her, that the two forms of Huxley with which she had come into contact were not the same at all, and that I was a friend, whereas the violent *anima* was not.

All was not finished. I had underestimated (I probably always shall) the subtle power of this mythago form, this Ash, this shaman, this worker of magic within the *frame* of weirdness that is Ryhope Wood.

She had not sent me to the time of horses. She had – perhaps through gratitude – brought the time of horses to the shrine . . .

She had located the event further away from the shrine itself, so that as I wrestled with the primogenetic manifestation of the grey-green man so I was also watching the sacrifice at some way distant. That hooded shape, passing before the flames . . . myself, perhaps, of the earlier encounter. The flame-horse had ridden on to recapture the errant part of the personality that had played truant from my alternative presence in the wood . . .

It makes me shudder to think of it, but surely *I* was the corpse in the flames; in that other world, from which Grey-green man had come, Ash's banishment of me to the past had ended in cruel murder.

Grey-green man had written: *I was riding the horse when it collided with the hooded man. I remember falling. The horse was bolting. It had two bodies on its back. One alive (me) beginning to burn badly. One dead. The hooded man was struck. I fell, the horse ran on.*

But there had been only one body, flaming, and only the animal survival of the dying, screaming man within the rushes allowed one part of its *anima* to escape, to cling to me, to haunt me.

Poor George. Poor old George.

These sinister thoughts fled rapidly when, with a feeling of joy almost childlike in its power and its simplicity, I saw Wynne-Jones again . . .

Three giant horses, their riders strapped to their backs, encased in an armour made from nature: already rush and reed, flaming, had fled the glade. Now the chalk-white corpse rode around the stone shrine, white rider on a black steed, limbs pinned and positioned by the frame of wood that held the victim upright on the crude cloth saddle. Then came the rider all decked out in thorns, a weave, a suit of branches and berries that allowed only the face to show, a face as dead, as barren as the chalk escarpments of the downs.

But the fourth of the horses carried the man of animal rags, the skins and limbs and heads of the creatures of field, forest and wood, the gaping heads of fox, cat and pig, the hides of grey, brown and winter-white creatures, all draped, bloodily and savagely, around the wild rider.

Crucified in the saddle, but alert and alive, the ragman was ridden round the glade on the back of a stallion whose face showed its pain, its torture, and whose snorting scream told of its fury. It stamped as it waited, pawed the ground, kicked back against the stones of the shrine, and eyed the wood, listening to the whooping calls of the herders, the men who chased the sacrifices through the woodland.

Around its neck dangled a necklace of wood and bone – three pieces!

'Edward! Dear God, Edward!'

The eyes of the man swathed in the rags of creatures widened, but no sound escaped the lips of the face that suddenly flexed with recognition and hope.

As the horse bolted towards Huxley, intending to again penetrate the forest, Huxley flung himself in front of the creature, watched it rear and stamp against him. He backed away, then darted to its side, reached up and *tore* the crucifix from the great beast's back, bringing the wood down upon him, Wynne-Jones and the stink and slime of freshly cut pelts with it, so that the two men tumbled in blood and rot, while the horse entered the wood and was lost.

Huxley unbound his friend. Ash hastened to them, grabbed at Huxley's sleeve and drew them swiftly away into cover. She also tugged the necklet from his chest, indicating that Wynne-Jones should do the same.

When Huxley glanced backwards he saw the tall herders enter the glade, dark shapes in the dying fire, beating at the space with flint tipped weapons, calling for their mares and stallions. But rapidly, as if fading into a sudden distance, the sound of chanting and drumming drifted away, became a mere hint of sound, then was gone completely.

At some time during the night, as Huxley huddled in half sleep against the shivering body of his friend, Ash slipped away into the darkness, abandoning the men. She took with her the necklet of wood and bone that had earlier transported Huxley to the ancient version of the Horse Shrine. But she left the small wrist drum, and Huxley reached for it and twirled it, watching the small stones strike the taut hide on each side of the decorated box.

A gift for Steven, he wondered? Or something for himself, something with a hidden power? He decided not to beat the drum, not in these woods.

They found a stream during their walk in the raw dawn, and Wynne-Jones washed the blood and filth from his body, drawing on Huxley's spare clothes gratefully.

'I've lost my pipe,' he murmured sadly, as they began the long trek back to Oak Lodge.

'Someone, or something, will use it as a talisman,' Huxley said. Wynne-Jones laughed.

CODA

Steven came running across the thistle meadow, kicking with skinny legs through the high grass. One flap of his white school shirt was hanging loose over the belt of his short grey-flannel trousers. He looked upset, hair unkempt, shirt buttons undone.

He was calling for his father.

Huxley crouched down, huddled back behind the ruined gate that almost blocked the access at the woodland edge to the muddy stream that wound so deeply into Ryhope Wood. He hunched up, hugging the undergrowth in the dark, slippery area where the stream widened and dropped a few inches to weave its way inwards. The trees here were like sentries, reaching inwards, outwards, towering over the ramshackle gate, their roots a twisting snake-like mass that made entry all the more difficult.

Brightness entered this gloomy gateway to hell from the summer's afternoon beyond, and Steven at last came to the high bank that dropped to the stream. Here he called for his father yet again.

Behind him, Wynne-Jones and Jennifer were crossing the field more slowly. Huxley rose slightly, peered at them, and beyond them at the house . . .

Wrong! There was something wrong . . .

'Dear God in Heaven . . . What has happened?'

'Daddy!'

The boy was in earnest. Huxley looked at him again, out on the open land. All he could see, now, was Steven's silhouette. It disturbed him. Steven was standing on the rise of ground just beyond the brambles, the thorns, and the old gate that had been tied across the channel to stop animals entering this dangerous stretch of wood. The boy's body was bent to one side as he peered into the impenetrable gloom of the forest. Huxley watched him, sensing his concern, and the anguish. Steven's whole posture was that of a sad and earnest young man, desperate to make contact with his father.

Motionless. Peering anxiously into the realm that perhaps he suddenly feared.

'Daddy?'

'Steve. I'm here. Wait there, I'm coming out.'

The boy hugged him delightedly. The house in the distance was a dark shape, bare of ivy. The great beech outside the boys' bedroom was as he remembered it. The field, the overgrown field, was four weeks advanced from when he had left it.

Something was wrong.

'How long have I been gone, Steven?'

The boy was only too glad to talk. 'Two days. We were worried. Mummy's been crying a lot.'

'I'm home now, lad.'

'Mummy says it *wasn't* you who shouted at me ...'

'No. It wasn't. It was a ghost.'

'A ghost!'

(Said with delight.)

'A ghost. But the ghost has gone back to hell, now. And I'm home too.'

Jennifer was calling to him. From his crouching position Huxley watched her as she walked quickly towards him, her face pale, but her lips smiling. Edward Wynne-Jones staggered along behind her, a man exhausted by his ordeal, and confused by Huxley's sudden terror as he had reached the edgewoods and refused to emerge into open land.

There was so little time, Huxley thought, and took Steven by the shoulders. The boy gaped at his father, then shut his mouth as he realised that he was about to be addressed in earnest.

'Steven ... don't go into the woods. Do you promise me?'

'Why?'

'No questions, lad! Promise me ... for God's sake ... *promise* me, Steven ... *don't* go into Ryhope Wood. Not now, not ever, not even when I'm dead. Do you understand me?'

Of course he understood his father. What he couldn't understand was the why. He gulped and nodded, glancing nervously at the dense wood.

Huxley shook him. 'For your own sake, Steve ... *I beg you* ... don't ever again play in the woods. Never!'

'I promise,' the boy said meekly, frightened.

'I don't want to lose you – '

From close by Jennifer called, 'George. Are you all right?'

Steven was crying, tears on his cheeks, his face fixed in a brave look, not sobbing or breaking up: just crying.

'I don't want to lose you,' Huxley whispered, and gathered the boy to him, holding him so very tightly. Steven's hands remained draped by his sides.

'When did the farmer last mow this meadow?' he asked his son, and he felt Steven's shrug.

'I don't know. About a month ago? We came and gathered hay. Like we always do.'

'Yes. Like we always do.'

Jennifer ran up to him and quickly hugged him, a full embrace. 'George! Thank God you're safe. Come back to the house and get washed and freshened up. I'll make us all some food . . .'

He stood and let Jennifer take him home.

Edward has read the entire account of the Bone Forest and is much exercised by its detail and implications. He was puzzled by my reference to having 'destroyed mythagos in the Wolf Glen', a statement I made when warning the grey-green man away from Jennifer. He seemed bemused when I explained that this had merely been a bluff to win the fight: after all, Grey-green man – myself of an alternative reality – was fully aware that our experiences in the mythago-realm of Ryhope were subtly different, so how could he be sure that at a time when he – Huxley – had failed to destroy an aggressive mythago, I – Huxley – had not succeeded? It was a sufficient bluff, I believe. Grey-green man was discouraged from the house and held to the wood, although in retrospect my decision came close to being fatal for Ash.

WJ agrees with me that Ash – the *original* mythic tale of Ash – is closely related to horses, perhaps to the Horse Shrine itself, and that in her original form she was a female *shaman* who exercised particular power over the untamed horses of the valley of her origin.

My regret is that I did not communicate with her on the subject of the primal myth, the core legend: I wonder if she might have had –

'Daddy?'

Huxley looked up sharply from his desk, the words in his mind flowing and becoming confused.

'What the devil is it?'

He turned in his chair, furious at the interruption to his train of thought. Steven stood in the doorway, in his dressing gown, looking shocked, nervous. He was holding a mug of hot chocolate.

'What is it, boy? I'm working!'

'Will you tell me the story?'

'What story?'

Huxley glanced back at his journal, laid his finger on the last line, trying to summon the words that were fading from mind so fast.

Steven had faltered. He was torn, it seemed, between running upstairs, or standing his ground. His eyes were wide, but there was a frown on his face. 'You said as soon as you came back you'd tell me a story about Romans.'

'I said no such thing!'

'But you *did* . . . !'

'Don't argue with me, Steven. Get to bed with you!'

Meekly, Steven stepped away. His mouth was tight as he whispered, 'Goodnight.'

Huxley turned back to the journal, scratched his head, inked his pen and continued. He had written – concerning Ash – that she might have had:

some awareness of what I believe was called the *Urscumug*? But probably she dates from a time considerably later than this primal myth.

The mythago that is Ash can *manipulate* time. This is an incredible discovery, should it be confirmed by later study. So Ryhope Wood is not just a repository of legendary creatures created in the present day ... its defensive nature, its warping of time, its playing with time and space ... these physical conditions can be imparted to the mythago forms themselves: Ash's magic – perhaps legendary in her own time – seems to become *real* in this wood. WJ and myself *have* travelled through time. We were sent, separately, to an event that had occurred in the cold, ancient past, an event of such power (for the minds of the day) that it has drawn to it not just *our* space and time, but others too, similar times, alternatives, the stuff of fantasy, the stuff of wilder dreams.

For one brief instant, the wood was opened to dimensions inconceivable. Grey-green man came through, returned. And for my part, my memory was affected, a dream, perhaps, like many dreams ... I had thought the meadow to be newly cropped, but clearly this had been a dream, and I had mis-remembered.

Ryhope Wood plays tricks more subtle than I had previously imagined.

I am safely home, however, and WJ too. He talks of 'gates', pathways and passages to mythic forms of hell. He is becoming obsessed with this idea, and claims to have found such a gateway in the wood itself.

So: two old men (no! I don't feel old. Just a little tired!), two tired men, each with an obsession. And a wealth of wonder to explore, given time, energy, and the freedom from those concerns that can so interfere with the process of intellectualising such a wondrous place as exists beyond the edgewoods.

Huxley capped his pen, leaned back and stretched, yawning fiercely. Outside, the late summer night was well advanced. He blotted the page of the journal, hesitated – tempted to turn back a few pages – then closed it.

Returning to the sitting room he found Jennifer reading. She looked up at him solemnly, then forced a smile.

'All finished?'

'I think so.'

She was thoughtful for a moment, then said gently, 'Don't make promises you don't intend to keep.'

'What promises?'

'A story for Steven.'

'I made him *no* promise . . .'

Jennifer sighed angrily. 'If you say so, George.'

'I do say so.'

But he softened his tone. Perhaps he had forgotten a promise to tell Steven a Roman story. Perhaps, in any event, he should have been gentler with the boy. Reaching into his pocket he drew out the wrist drum that Ash had left.

'Look at this. I found it at the Horse Shrine. I'll give it to Steve in the morning.'

Jennifer took the drum, smiled, shook it and made it beat its staccato rhythm. She shivered. 'It feels odd. It feels old.'

Huxley agreed. 'It *is* old.' And added with a laugh, 'A better trophy than that last one, eh?'

'Trophy?'

'Yes. You remember . . . that raw and bloody bone in my study. You kicked it and called it a trophy . . .'

'Raw and bloody bone?'

She looked quite blank, not understanding him.

Huxley stood facing her for a long while, his head reeling. Eventually she shrugged and returned to her book. He turned, left the room, walked stiffly back to his study and opened the journal at the page where Grey-green man had left his second message.

The message was there all right.

But with a moan of despair and confusion, Huxley placed his hand upon the page, upon the scrawled words, touched a finger-tip to the part of the paper where, just a few days ago, there had been a smear of blood, confusing and concealing part of Grey-green man's script.

And where now there was no blood. No blood at all.

He sat for a long time, staring out through the open windows, to the garden and the wood beyond. At length he picked up the pen, turned to the end of the journal and started to write.

> *It would seem that I am not quite home*
> *Confused about this.*
> *Maybe Wynne-Jones will have an answer*
> *Must return to Shrine again*
> *Everything feels right, but not right*
> *Not quite home*

Thorn

for John Murry

At sundown, when the masons and guild carpenters finished their work for the day and trudged wearily back to their village lodgings, Thomas Wyatt remained behind in the half-completed church and listened to the voice of the stone man, calling to him.

The whispered sound was urgent, insistent: 'Hurry! Hurry! I *must* be finished before the others. *Hurry!*'

Thomas, hiding in the darkness below the gallery, felt sure that the ghostly cry could be heard for miles around. But the Watchman, John Tagworthy, was almost completely deaf, now, and the priest was too involved with his own holy rituals to be aware of the way his church was being stolen.

Thomas could hear the priest. He was circling the new church twice, as he always did at sundown, a small, smoking censer in one hand, a book in the other. He walked from right to left. Demons, and the sprites of the old earth, flew before him, birds and bats in the darkening sky. The priest, like all the men who worked on the church – except for Thomas himself – was a stranger to the area. He had long hair and a dark, trimmed beard, an unusual look for a monk.

He talked always about the supreme holiness of the place where his church was being built. He kept a close eye on the work of the craftsmen. He prayed to the north and the south, and constantly was to be seen kneeling at the very apex of the mound, as if exorcising the ancient spirits buried below.

This was Dancing Hill. Before the stone church there had been a wooden church, and some said that Saint Peter himself had raised the first timbers. And hadn't Joseph, bearing the Grail of Christ, rested on this very spot, and driven out the demons of the earth mound?

But it was Dancing Hill. And sometimes it was referred to by its older name, *Ynys Calidryv*, isle of the old fires. There were other names, too, forgotten now.

'Hurry!' called the stone man from his hidden niche. Thomas felt the cold walls vibrate with the voice of the spectre. He shivered as he felt the power of the earth returning to the carved ragstone pillars, to the neatly positioned blocks. Always at night.

The Watchman's fire crackled and flared in the lee of the south wall. The priest walked away down the hill to the village, stopping just once to stare back at the half-constructed shell of the first stone church in the area. Then he was gone.

Thomas stepped from the darkness and stood, staring up through the empty roof to the clouds and the sky, and the gleaming light that was Jupiter. His heart was beating fast, but a great relief touched his limbs and his mind. And as always, he smiled, then closed his eyes for a moment. He thought of what he was doing. He thought of Beth, of what she would say if she knew his secret work; sweet Beth; with no children to comfort her she was now more alone than ever. But it would not be for much longer. The face was nearly finished . . .

'*Hurry!*'

A few more nights. A few more hours working in darkness, and all the Watchman's best efforts to guard the church would have been in vain.

The church would have been stolen. Thomas would have been the thief!

He moved through the gloom, now, to where a wooden ladder lay against the side wall. He placed the ladder against the high gallery – the leper's gallery – and climbed it. He drew the ladder up behind him and stepped across the debris of wood, stone and leather to the farthest, tightest corner of the place. Bare faces of the coarse ragstone watched the silent church. No mortar joined the stones. Their weight held them secure. They supported nothing but themselves.

At Thomas's muscular insistence, one of them moved, came away from the others.

With twilight gone, but night not yet fully descended, there was enough grey light for him to see the face that was carved there. He stared at the leafy beard, the narrowed, slanting eyes, the wide, flaring nostrils. He saw how the cheeks would look, how the hair would become spiky, how he would include the white and red berries of witch-thorn upon the twigs that clustered round the face . . .

Thomas stared at Thorn, and Thorn watched him by return, a cold smile on cold stone lips. Voices whispered in a sound realm that was neither in the church, nor in another world, but somewhere between the two, a shadowland of voice, movement and memory.

'I must be finished before the others,' the stone man whispered.

'You shall be,' said the mason, selecting chisel and hammer from his leather bag. 'Be patient.'

'I must be finished before the magic ones!' Thorn insisted, and Thomas sighed in irritation.

'You *shall* be finished before the magic ones. No-one has agreed upon the design of their faces, yet.'

The 'magic ones' were what Thomas called the Apostles. The twelve statues were temporarily in place above the altar, bodies completed but faces still smoothly blank.

'To control them I must be here first,' Thorn said.

'I've already opened your eyes. You can see how the other faces are incomplete.'

'Open them better,' said Thorn.

'Very well.'

Thomas reached out to the stone face. He touched the lips, the nose, the eyes. He knew every prominence, every rill, every chisel-mark. The grains of the stone were like pebbles beneath his touch. He could feel the hard-stone intrusion below the right eye, where the rag would not chisel well. There was a hardness, too, in the crown of Thorns, a blemish in the soft rock that would have to be shaped carefully to avoid cracking the whole design. As his fingers ran across the thorn man's lips, cold, old breath tickled him, the woodland man breathing from his time in the long past. As Thomas touched the eyes he felt the eyeballs move, impatient to see better.

I am in a wood grave, and a thousand years lie between us, Thorn had said. *Hurry, hurry. Bring me back.*

In the deepening darkness, working by touch alone, Thomas chiselled the face, bringing back the life of the lost god. The sound of his work was a sequence of shrill notes, stone music in the still church. John Tagworthy, the Watchman, outside by his fire, would be unaware of them. He might see a tallow candle by its glow upon the clouds, he might smell a fart from the distant castle on a still summer's night, but the noises of man and nature had long since ceased to bother his senses.

'Thomas! Thomas Wyatt! Where in God's Name *are* you?'

The voice, hailing him from below, so shocked Thomas that he dropped his chisel, and in desperately trying to catch the tool he cut himself. He stayed silent for a long moment, cursing Jupiter and the sudden band of bright stars for their light. The church was a place of shadows against darkness. As he peered at the north arch he thought he could see a man's shape, but it was only an unfinished timber. He reached for the heavy stone block that would cover the stone face, and as he did so the voice came again.

'God take your gizzard, Thomas Wyatt. It's Simon. Miller's son Simon!'

Thomas crept to the gallery's edge and peered over. The movement drew attention to him. Simon's pale features turned to look at him. 'I heard you working. What are you working on?'

'Nothing,' Thomas lied. 'Practising my craft on good stone with good tools.'

'Show me the face, Thomas,' said the younger man, and Thomas felt the blood drain from his head. *How had he known?* Simon was twenty years old, married for three years and still, like Thomas himself, childless. He was a freeman of course; he worked in his father's mill, but spent a lot of his time in the fields, both his family's strips and the land belonging to the Castle. His great ambition, though, was to be a Guildsman, and masonry was his aspiration.

'What face?'

'Send down the ladder,' Simon urged, and reluctantly Thomas let the wood scaffold down. The miller clambered up to the gallery, breathing hard. He smelled of garlic. He looked eagerly about in the gloom. 'Show me the green man.'

'Explain what you mean.'

'Come on, Thomas! Everybody knows you're shaping the Lord of Wood. I want to see him. I want to know how he looks.'

Thomas could hardly speak. His heart alternately stopped and raced. Simon's words were like stab wounds. *Everybody knew! How could everybody know?*

Thorn had spoken to him and to him alone. He had sworn the mason to silence and secrecy. For thirty days Thomas Wyatt had risked not just a flogging, but almost certain hanging for blasphemy, risked his life for the secret realm. Everybody *knew*?

'If everybody knows, why haven't I been stopped?'

'I don't mean *everybody*,' Simon said, as he felt blindly along the cold walls for a sign of Thomas's work. 'I mean the village. It's spoken in whispers. You're a hero, Thomas. We know what you're doing, and for whom. It's exciting; it's *right*. I've danced with them at the forest cross. I've carried the fire. I *know* how much power remains here. I may take God's name in oath — but that's safe to do. He has no power over me, or any of us. He doesn't belong on Dancing Hill. Don't *worry*, Thomas. We're your friends . . . Ah!'

Simon had found the loose stone. It was heavy and he grunted loudly as he took its weight, letting it down carefully to the floor. His breathing grew soft as he reached for the stone face. But Thomas could see how the young man drew back, fingers extended yet not touching the precious icon.

'There's magic in this, Thomas,' Simon said in awe.

'There's skill — working by night, working with fear — there's skill enough, I'll say that.'

'There's magic in the face,' Simon repeated. 'It's drawing power from the earth below. It's tapping the Dancing Well. There's water in the eyes, Thomas. The dampness of the old well. The face is brilliant.'

He struggled with the covering stone and replaced it. 'I wish it had been me. I wish the green man had chosen me. What an honour, Thomas. Truly.'

Thomas Wyatt watched his friend in astonishment. Was this *really* Simon the miller's son? Was this the young man who had carried the Cross every Resurrection Sunday for ten years? Simon Miller! *I've danced with them at the forest cross.*

'Who have you danced with at the crossroads, Simon?'

'*You* know,' Simon whispered. 'It's alive, Thomas. It's all alive. It's here, around us. It never went away. The Lord of Wood showed us . . .'

'Thorn? Is that who you mean?'

'*Him!*' Simon pointed towards the hidden niche. 'He's been here for years. He came the moment the monks decided to build the church. He came to save us, Thomas. And you're helping. I envy you . . .'

Simon climbed down the ladder. He was a furtive night shape, darting to the high arch where an oak door would soon be fitted, and out across the mud-churned hill, back round the forest, to where the village was a dark place, sleeping.

Thomas followed him down, placing the ladder back against the wall. But on the open hill, almost in sight of the Watchman's fire, he looked to the north, across the forest, to where the ridgeway was a high band of darkness against the pale grey glow of the clouds. Below the ridgeway a fire burned. He knew that he was looking at the forest cross, where the stone road of the Romans crossed the disused track between Woodhurst and Biddenden. He had played there as a child, despite being told never *ever* to follow the broken stone road.

There was a clearing at the deserted crossroads, and years ago he, and Simon Miller's elder brother Wat, had often found the cold remains of fire and feasts. Outlaws, of course, and the secret baggage trains of the Saxon Knights who journeyed the hidden forest trails. Any other reason for the use of the place would have been unthinkable. Why, there was even an old gibbet, where forest justice was seen to be done . . .

With a shiver he remembered the time when he had come to the clearing and seen the swollen, greyish corpse of a man swinging from that blackened wood. Dark birds had been perched upon its shoulders. The face had had no eyes, no nose, no flesh at all, and the sight of the dead villain had stopped him from ever going back again.

Now, a fire burned at the forest cross. A fire like the

fire of thirty nights ago, when Thorn had sent the girl for him . . .

He had woken to the sound of his name being called from outside. His wife, Beth, slept soundly on, turning slightly on the palliasse. It had been a warm night. He had tugged on his britches, and drawn a linen shirt over his shoulders. Stepping outside he had disturbed a hen, which clucked angrily and stalked to another nesting place.

The girl was dressed in dark garments. Her head was covered by a shawl. She was young, though, and the hand that reached for his was soft and pale.

'Who are you?' he said, drawing back. She had tugged at him. His reluctance to go with her was partly fear, partly concern that Beth would see him.

'Iagus goroth! Fiatha! *Fiatha!*' Her words were strange to Thomas. They were *like* the hidden language, but were not of the same tongue.

'Who *are* you?' he insisted, and the girl sighed, still holding his hand. At last she pointed to her bosom. Her eyes were bright beneath the covering of the shawl. Her hair was long and he sensed it to be red, like fire. 'Anuth!' she said. She pointed distantly. 'Thorn. You come with Thorn. With Anuth. Me. *Come*. Thomas. Thomas to Thorn. *Fiatha!*'

She dragged at his hand and he began to run. The grip on his fingers relaxed. She ran ahead of him, skirts swirling, body hunched. He tripped in the darkness, but she seemed able to see every low-hanging branch and proud beechwood root on the track. They entered the wood. He concentrated on her fleeing shape, calling, occasionally, for her to slow down. Each time he went sprawling she came back, making clicking sounds with her mouth, impatient, anxious. She helped him to his feet but immediately took off into the forest depths, heedless of risk to life and limb.

All at once he heard voices, a rhythmic beating, the

crackle of fire . . . and the gentle sound of running water. She had brought him to the river. It wound through the forest, and then across downland, towards the Avon.

Through the trees he saw the fire. Anuth took his hand and pulled him, not to the bright glade, but towards the stream. As he walked he stared at the flames. Dark, human shapes passed before the fire. They seemed to be dancing. The heavy rhythm was like the striking of one bone against another. The voices were singing. The language was familiar to him, but incomprehensible.

Anuth dragged him past the firelit glade. He came to the river, and she slipped away. Surprised, he turned, hissing her name; but she had vanished. He looked back at the water, where starlight, and the light of a quarter moon, made the surface seem alive. There was a thick-trunked thorn tree growing from the water's edge. The thorn tree trembled and shifted in the evening wind.

The thorn tree grew before the startled figure of Thomas Wyatt. It rose, it straightened, it stretched. Arms, legs, the gleam of moonlight on eyes and teeth.

'Welcome, Thomas,' said the thorn tree.

He took a step backwards, frightened by the apparition. 'Welcome where?'

In front of him, Thorn laughed. The man's voice rasped, like a child with consumption. 'Look around you, Thomas. Tell me what you see.'

'Darkness. Woodland. A river, stars. Night. Cold night.'

'Take a breath, Thomas. What do you smell?'

'That same night. The river. Leaves and dew. The fire, I can smell the fire. And autumn. All the smells of autumn.'

'When did you last see and smell these things?'

Thomas, confused by the strange midnight encounter, shivered in his clothing. 'Last night. I've always seen and smelled them.'

'Then welcome to a place you know well. Welcome to

the always place. Welcome to an autumn night, something that this land has always known, and will always enjoy.'

'But who are you?'

'I have been known by many names.' He came close to the trembling man. His hawthorn crown, with its strange horns, was like a broken tree against the clouds. His beard of leaves and long grass rustled as he spoke. His body quivered where the night breeze touched the clothing of nature that wound around his torso. 'Do you believe in God, Thomas?'

'He died for us. His son. On the Cross. He is the Almighty . . .'

Thorn raised his arms. He held them sideways. He was a great cross in the cold night, and his crown of thorns was a beast's antlers. Old fears, forgotten shudders, plagued the villager, Thomas Wyatt. Ancestral cries mocked him. Memories of fire whispered words in the hidden language, confused his mind.

'I am the Cross of God,' said Thorn. 'Touch the wood, touch the sharp thorns . . .'

Thomas reached out. His actions were not his own. His fingers touched the cold flesh of the man's stomach. He felt the ridged muscle in the crossbeam, the bloody points of the thorns that rose from the man's head. He nervously brushed the gnarled wood of the thighs, and the proud branch that rose between them, hot to his fingers, nature's passion, never dying.

'What do you want of me?' Thomas asked quietly.

The cross became a man again. 'To make my image in the new shrine. To make that shrine my own. To make it as mine forever, no matter what manner of worship is performed within its walls . . .'

Thomas stared at the Lord of Wood.

'Tell me what I must do . . .'

* * *

Everybody knew, Simon had said. Everybody in the village. It was spoken in whispers. Thomas was a hero. Everybody knew. Everybody but Thomas Wyatt.

'Why have they kept it from me?' he murmured to the night. He had huddled up inside his jacket, and folded his body into the tight shelter of a wall bastion. The encounter with Simon had shaken him badly.

From here he could see north to Biddenden across the gloomy shapelessness of the forest. The Castle, and the clustered villages of its demesne, were behind him. He saw only stars, pale clouds, and the flicker of fire, where strange worship occurred.

Why did the fire, in this midnight forest, call to him so much? Why was there such comfort in the thought of the warm glow from the piled branches, and the noisy prattle, and laughter, of those who clustered in its shadowy light? He had danced about a fire often enough: on May eve, at the passing of the day of All Hallows. But those fires were in the village bounds. His soul fluttered, a delighted bird, at the thought of the woodland fire. The smell of autumn, the touch of night's dew, the closeness to the souls of tree and plant; timeless eyes would watch the dancers. They were a shared life with the forest.

Why had he been kept in isolation? *Everybody knew*. The villagers who carried the bleeding, dying Christ through the streets on Resurrection Sunday . . . were they now carrying images of boar and stag and hare about the fire? He – Thomas – was a hero. They spoke of him in whispers. Everybody knew of his work. When had *they* been taken back to the beliefs of old? Had Thorn appeared to each of them as well?

Why didn't he *share* the new belief with them? It was the same belief. He used his craft; they danced for the gods.

As if he were of the same cold stone-stuff upon which he worked, the others kept him distant, watched him from afar. Did Beth know? Thomas shivered. The hours passed. He could feel the gibbet rope around his neck. Only one word out of place, one voice overheard – one whisper to the wrong man, and Thomas Wyatt would be a grey thing, slung by its neck, prey for dark birds. Eyes, nose, the flesh of the face. Every feature that he pecked for Thorn with hammer and chisel would be pecked from him by hard, wet beaks.

From the position of the moon, Thomas realised he had been sitting by the church for several hours. John the Watchman had not walked past. Now that he thought of it, Thomas could hear the man's snoring, coming as if from a far place.

Thomas eased himself to his feet. He lifted his bag gently to his shoulder, over-cautious about the ring and strike of iron tools within the leather. But as he walked towards the path he heard movement in the church. The Watchman snored distantly.

It must be Simon, the miller's son, Thomas thought, back for another look at the face of the woodland god.

Irritated, and still confused, Thomas stepped into the church again, and looked towards the gallery. The ladder was against the balcony. He could hear the stone being moved. There was a time of silence, then the stone was put back. A figure moved to the ladder and began to descend.

Thomas watched in astonishment. He stepped into greater darkness as the priest looked round, then hauled the ladder back to its storage place. All Thomas heard was the sound of the priest's laughter. The man passed through the gloom, long robe swirling through the dust and debris.

Even the priest knew! And that made no sense at all. Thomas slept restlessly, listening to the soft breathing of his wife. Several times the urge to wake her, to speak to her, made him whisper her name and shake her shoulders.

But she slumbered on. At sunrise they were up together, but he was so tired he could hardly speak. They ate hard bread, moistened with cold, thin gruel. Thomas tipped the last of their ale into a clay mug. The drink was more meaty than the gruel, but he swallowed the sour liquid and felt its warming tingle.

'The last of the ale,' he said ruefully, tapping the barrel.

'You've been too busy to brew,' Beth said from the table. 'And I'm not skilled.' She was wrapped in a heavy wool cloak. The fire was a dead place in the middle of the small room. Grey ash drifted in the light from the roof hole.

'But no *ale*!' He banged his cup on the barrel in frustration. Beth looked up at him, surprised by his anger.

'We can get ale from the miller. We've done it before and repaid him from our own brewing. It's not the end of the world.'

'I've had no time to brew,' Thomas said, watching Beth through hooded, rimmed eyes. 'I've been working on something of importance. I expect you know what.'

She shrugged. 'Why would I know? You never talk about it.' Her pale face was sweet. She was as pretty now as when he had married her; fuller in body, yes, and wider in the ways of life. That they were childless had not affected her spirit. She had allowed the wise women to dose her with herbs and bitter spices, to take her to strange stones, and stranger foreigners; she had been seen by apothecaries and doctors, and Thomas had worked in their fields to pay them. And of course, they had prayed. Now Thomas felt too old to care about children. Life was good with Beth, and their sadness had drawn them closer than most couples he knew.

'Everybody knows what I'm working on,' he said bitterly.

'Well, I don't,' she replied. 'But I'd like to . . .'

Perhaps he had been unfair to her. Perhaps she too was

kept apart from the village's shared knowledge. He lied to her. 'You must not say a word to anyone. But I'm working on the face of Jesus.'

Beth was delighted. 'Oh Thomas! That's wonderful. I'm so proud of you.' She came round to him and hugged him. Outside, Master mason Tobias Craven called out his name, among others, and he trudged up to the church on Dancing Hill.

His work was uneven and lazy that day. The chisel slipped, the stone splintered, the hammer caught his thumb twice. He was distracted and deeply concerned by what he had seen the night before. When the priest came to the church, to walk among the bustle of activity and inspect the day's progress, Thomas watched him carefully, hoping for some sign of recognition. But the man just smiled, and nodded, then carried the small light of Christ to the altar, and said silent prayers for an hour or more.

At sundown, Thomas felt his body shaking. When the priest called the craftsmen – Thomas included – into the vestry for wine, Thomas stood by the door, staring at the dark features of the Man of God. The priest, handing him his cup, merely said, 'God be with you, Thomas.' It was what he always said.

Tobias Craven came over to him. His face was grey with dust, his clothing heavy with dirt. His dialect was difficult for Thomas to understand, and Thomas was suspicious of the gesture anyway. Would he now discover that the foreigners, too, knew of the face of the woodland deity, half completed behind its door of stone?

'Your work is good, Thomas. Not today, perhaps, but usually. I've watched you.'

'Thank you.'

'At first I was reluctant to allow you to work as a mason among us. It was at the priest's insistence: one local man to work in every craft. It seemed a superstitious idea to me. But now I'm glad. I approve. It's an enlightened gesture, I realise, to allow local men, not of Guilds, to display their skills. And your skill is remarkable.'

Thomas swallowed hard. 'To be a Guildsman would be a great honour.'

Master Tobias looked crestfallen. 'Aye, but alas. I wish I had seen your work when you were twenty, not thirty. But I can write a note for you, to get you better work in the area.'

'Thank you,' Thomas said again.

'Have you travelled, Thomas?'

'Only to Glastonbury. I made a pilgrimage in the third year of my marriage.'

'Glastonbury,' Master Tobias repeated, smiling. 'Now that is a fine Abbey. I've seen it just once. Myself, I worked at York, and at Carlisle, on the Minsters. I was not a Master, of course. But that was cherished work. Now I'm a Guild Master, building tiny churches in remote places. But it gives fulfilment to the soul, and one day I shall die and be buried in the shadow of a place I have built myself. There is satisfaction in the thought.'

'May that not be for many years.'

'Thank you, Thomas.' Tobias drained his cup. 'And now, from God's work to nature's work – '

Thomas paled. Did he mean woodland worship? The Master mason winked at him.

'A good night's sleep!'

When the others had gone, Thomas slipped out of the sheltering woodland and made his way back to the church. The Watchman was fussing with his fire. There was less cloud this evening and the land, though murky, was quite visible for many miles around.

Inside the church, Thomas looked up at the gallery.

Uncertainty made him hesitate, then he shook his head. 'Until I understand better . . .' he murmured, and made to turn for home.

'Thomas!' Thorn called. 'Hurry, Thomas.'

Strange green light played off the stone of the church. It darted around him, like will-o'-the-wisp. Fingers prodded him forward, but when he turned there was nothing but shadow.

Again, Thorn called to him.

With a sigh, Thomas placed the ladder against the gallery and climbed up to the half-finished face. Thorn smiled at him. The narrow eyes sparkled with moisture. The leaves and twigs that formed his hair and beard seemed to rustle. The stone strained to move.

'Hurry, Thomas. Open my eyes better.'

'I'm frightened,' the man said. 'Too many people know what I'm doing.'

'Carve me. Shape my face. I must be here before the others. *Hurry!*'

The lips of the forest god twitched with the ghostly figure's anguish. Thomas reached out to the cold stone and felt its stillness. It was just a carving. It had no life. He imagined the voice. It was just a man who told him to make the carving, a man dressed in woodland disguise. Until he knew he was safe, he would not risk discovery. He climbed back down the ladder. Thorn called to him, but Thomas ignored the cry.

At his house a warm fire burned in the middle of the room, and an iron pot of thick vegetable broth steamed above it. There was fresh ale from the miller, and Beth was pleased to see him home so early. She stitched old clothes, seated on a low stool, close to the wood fire. Thomas ate, then drank ale, leaning on the table, his mason's tools spread out before him. The ale was strong and soon went to his head. He felt dizzy, sublimely detached from his body. The warmth, the sensation of drunkenness, his full stomach, all of these things made him drowsy, and slowly his head sank to his arms . . .

A cold blast of air on his neck half roused him. His name was being called. At first he thought it was Beth, but soon, as he surfaced from pleasant oblivion, he recognised the rasping voice of Thorn.

The fire burned high, fanned by the draught from the open door. Beth still sat on her stool, but was motionless and silent, staring at the flames. He spoke her name, but she didn't respond. Thorn called to him again and he looked out at the dark night. He felt a sudden chill of fear. He gathered his tools into his bag and stepped from the house.

Thorn stood in the dark street, a tall figure, his horns of wood black against the sky. There was a strong smell of earth about him. He moved towards Thomas, leaf-clothes rustling.

'The work is unfinished, Thomas.'

'I'm afraid for my life. Too many people know what I'm doing.'

'Only the finishing of the face matters. Your fear is of no consequence. You agreed to work for me. You must go to the church. Now.'

'But if I'm caught!'

'Then another will be found. Go back to the work, Thomas. Open my eyes properly. It *must* be done.'

He turned from Thorn and sighed. There was something wrong with Beth and it worried him, but the persuasive power of the night figure was too strong to counter, and he began to walk wearily towards the church. Soon the village was invisible behind him. Soon the church was a sharp relief against the night sky. The Watchman's fire burned high, and the autumn night was sweet with the smell of woodsmoke. The Watchman himself seemed to be dancing, or so Thomas thought at first. He strained to see better and soon realised that John had fallen asleep and set light to his clothing. He was brushing and beating at his leggings, his grunts of alarm like the evening call of a boar.

The moment's humour passed and a sudden anger took Thomas. Thorn's words were like sharp stab wounds to his pride: his fear was of no consequence. Only the work of carving mattered. He would be caught and it would be of no consequence. He would swing, slowly strangling, from the castle gallows and it would be of no consequence. Another would be found!

'No!' he said aloud. 'No. I will *not* work for Thorn tonight. Tonight is *my* night. Damn Thorn. Damn the face. Tomorrow I will open its eyes, but not now.'

And with a last glance at the Watchman, who had extinguished the fire and settled down again, he turned back to the village.

But as he approached his house, aware of the glow of the fire through the small window, his anger changed to a sudden dread. He began to feel sick. He wanted to cry out, to alert the village. A voice in his head urged him to turn and go back to the night wood. His house, once so welcoming, threatened him deeply. It seemed surrounded by an aura, detached from the real world.

He walked slowly to the small window. He could hear the crackle and spit of the flames. Wood smoke was sweet in the air. Somewhere, at the village bounds, two dogs barked.

The feeling of apprehension in him grew, a strangling weed that made him dizzy. But he looked through the window. And he did not faint, nor cry out, at what he saw within, though a part of his spirit, part of his life, flew away from him then, abandoning him, making him wither and age; making him die a little.

Thorn stood with his back to the fire. His mask of

autumn leaves and spiky wood was bright and eerie — dark hair curled from beneath the mask. His arms were wound around with creeper and twine, and twigs of oak, elm and lime were laced upon this binding. Save for these few fragments of nature's clothing he was naked. The black hair on his body gave him the appearance of a burned oak stump, gnarled and weathered by the years. His manhood was a smooth, dark branch, cut to the length of firewood.

Beth was on her knees before him, her weight taken on her elbows. Her skirts were on the floor beside her. The yellow flames cast a flickering glow upon her plump, pale flesh, and Thomas half closed his eyes in despair. He managed to stifle his scream of anguish, but he could not stop himself from watching.

And he uttered no sound, despite the pain, as Thorn dropped down upon the waiting woman.

As he ran to the church the Watchman woke, then stood up, picking up his heavy staff. Thomas Wyatt knocked him down, then drew a flaming wood brand from the brazier. Tool-bag on his shoulder he entered the church, and held the fire high. The ladder was against the balcony. Pale features peered down at him and the ladder began to move. But Simon, the miller's son, was not quite quick enough. Casting the burning wood aside, Thomas leapt for the scaffold and began to ascend.

'I was just looking, Thomas,' Simon cried, then tried to fling the ladder back. Thomas clutched at the balcony, then hauled himself to safety. He said no word to Simon, who backed against the wall where the loose stone was fitted.

'You mustn't touch him, Thomas!'

In the darkness, Simon's eyes were gleaming orbs of fear. Thomas took him by the shoulders and flung him to the balcony, then used a stone to strike him.

'No, Thomas! No!'

The younger man had toppled over the balcony. He held on for dear life, fingers straining to hold his weight.

'Tricked!' screamed Thomas. 'All a trick! Duped! Cuckolded! All of you knew. All of you *knew*!'

'No, Thomas. In the Name of God, it wasn't like that!'

His hammer was heavy. He swung it high. Simon's left hand vanished and the man's scream of pain was deafening. 'She had no other way!' he cried hysterically. 'No, Thomas! No! She chose it! She *chose* it! Thorn's gift to you both.'

The hammer swung. Crushed fingers left bloody marks upon the balcony. Simon crashed to the floor below and was still.

'All of you knew!' Thomas Wyatt cried. He wrenched the loose stone away. Thorn watched him from the blackness through his half-opened eyes. Thomas could see every feature, every line. The mouth stretched in a mocking grin. The eyes narrowed, the nostrils flared.

'Fool. Fool!' whispered the stone man. 'But you cannot stop me now.'

Thomas slapped his hand against the face. The blow stung his flesh. He reached for his chisel, placed the sharp tool against one of the narrow eyes.

'NO!' screeched Thorn. His face twisted and turned. The stone of the church shuddered and groaned. Thomas hesitated. A green glow came from the features of the deity. The eyes were wide with fear, the lips drawn back below the mask. Thomas raised his hammer.

'NO!' screamed the head again. Arms reached from the wall. The light expanded. Thomas backed off, terrified by the spectre which had appeared there, a ghastly green version of Thorn himself, a creature half ghost, half stone, tied to the wall of the church, but reaching out from the cold rock, reaching for Thomas Wyatt, reaching to kill him.

Thomas raised the chisel, raised the hammer. He ran back

to the face of Thorn and with a single, vicious blow, drove a gouging furrow through the right eye.

The church shuddered. A block of stone fell from the high wall, striking Thomas on the shoulder. The whole balcony vibrated with Thorn's pain and anger.

Again he struck. The left eye cracked, a great split in the stone. Dampness oozed from the wound. The scream from the wall was deafening. Below the balcony, yellow light glimmered. The Watchman, staring up to where Thomas performed his deed of vengeance.

Then a crack appeared down the whole side of the church. The entire gallery where Thomas had worked dropped by a man's height, and Thomas was flung to the balcony. He struggled to keep his balance, then went over the wall, scrabbling at the air. Thorn's stone-scream was a nightmare sound. Air was cool on the mason's skin. A stone pedestal broke his fall. Broke his back.

The village woke to the sound of the priest's terrible scream. He stumbled from the mason's house, hands clutching at his eyes, trying to staunch the flow of blood. He scrabbled at the wood mask, stripping away the thorn, the oak, the crisp brown leaves, exposing dark hair, a thin dark beard.

The priest — Thorn's priest — turned blind eyes to the church. Naked, he began to stagger and stumble towards the hill. Behind him, the villagers followed, torches burning in the night.

Thomas lay across the marble pillar, a few feet from the ground. There was no sensation in his body, though his lungs expanded to draw air into his chest. He lay like a sacrificial victim, arms above his head, legs limp. The Watchman circled him in silence. The church was still.

Soon the priest approached him, hands stretched out before him. The pierced orbs of his eyes glistened as he leaned close to Thomas Wyatt.

'Are you dying, then?'

'I died a few minutes ago,' Thomas whispered. The priest's hands on his face were gentle. Blood dripped from the savaged eyes.

'Another will come,' Thorn said. 'There are many of us. The work will be completed. No church will stand that is not a shrine to the true faith. The spirit of Christ will find few havens in England.'

'Beth . . .' Thomas whispered. He could feel the bird of life struggling to escape him. The Watchman's torch was already dimming.

Thorn raised Thomas's head, a finger across the dry lips. 'You should not have seen,' said the priest. 'It was a gift for a gift. Our skills, the way of ritual, of fertility, for your skill with stone. Another will come to replace me. Another will be found to finish your work. But there will be no child for you, now. No child for Beth.'

'What have I done?' Thomas whispered. 'By all that's holy, what have I done?'

From above him, from a thousand miles away, came the ring of chisel on stone.

'Hurry,' he heard Thorn call into the night. 'Hurry!'

The Shapechanger

ENGLAND, AD 731

(i)

The rain had eased off and the Wolfhead threw back the hood of his heavy cape. He turned to watch his young companion struggle through the wet and clinging mud of the track.

'You'll have to do better than that if you want to stay with me,' the shaman said.

The boy stopped and shrugged his heavy pack into a more comfortable position. 'We should have sheltered,' he complained.

'We *could* have sheltered,' the Wolfhead retorted. 'I chose not to.'

The young *Inkmarker* (the name by which he now knew himself) muttered vilely. He was burdened down beneath the pack in which they carried the skins for the tent and the various substances and flints that could make their fire. The Wolfhead carried the wood – for fire and shelter – and these sticks currently numbered five, and were not heavy at all; and his own pack was small, containing the tools, ten rolled-up masks, feathers . . .

Inkmarker was a small, fat youth, not yet ten years of age. He had been taught to write in the monastery at Cantabriagh, where he had been placed in his swaddling after his parents had been murdered (he had been told) by 'men from the northern regions'. He was not sure, now, that the oppressive regime within the monastery would not have been preferable to this life with the arcane stranger who had found him, starving, on his second attempt to escape the walls of his prison.

'If I break my fingers,' Inkmarker complained, 'it will be the worse for you.'

'If you break your fingers and cannot write, I'll leave you where you are. There isn't any magic in writing . . .'

'You can't write,' the boy said loudly, sloshing through the mire.

He was drawn up short by a thick, hard hand grabbing at his nose, twisting his face until his neck threatened to break. The Wolfhead breathed stale breath into his mouth. Grey eyes, wide grin, fixed stare. 'You have power over me then, do you?'

'No sir,' Inkmarker avowed. 'I'm just tired and hungry.'

The ferocious grip relaxed. Tall man, small boy, the tall regarded the short, and warmth flowed. 'Yes. I am too. But we're nearly there. That hill, ahead of us . . .'

'Is it Dancing Hill?'

'I'm certain of it.'

They stared ahead through the grey day. The hill was bordered by thick wood but itself was quite bare as if the chalk beneath had thrust too close to the air, denying the earth a chance to hold the trees. A small, strange building was in ruins there, ramshackle, ancient.

'No sign of the people,' Inkmarker said, his pale face showing the anxiety he suddenly felt. He stared all around, at the dark wood, the wet land.

'No-one has lived on Dancing Hill for a long time,' the shaman murmured. 'They're on the other side. To the south. That's why we approached from the north. I wanted time to get the sense of the place.'

'And the *Daemon*?' the boy asked shakily.

'If there *is* a daemon, then it will be in the village. Not here.'

There was a fallen tree. Its bark was wet, but it was a good seat. The Wolfhead led the way to it. 'Sit down and get a sheet ready. We'll make our recording from now.'

'I'll get my bum wet!'

The man watched the boy, who stood anxiously feeling the thin seat of his cloth britches. God knew, it was cold and miserable enough without asking for a chill in the bowels. The Wolfhead sighed and slipped off his heavy cape. He lay it over the tree, then helped the pack from the boy's back. 'His Lordship may now be seated.'

'Thank you.'

Without his cape, the Wolfhead was a strange sight, a man more skin and bone than flesh, clothed in sewn-together pelts: of rats, and hares, and lynx, and otter. He had encountered enough of the Christian world to have learned that he looked like the man called Jacob, who had worn a many-coloured coat. He was the many-coloured wolf. His colours were the colours of time, rich earth, grey stone, red blood, white bone, the grey of skies that watched the wandering of the first people. His magic, if magic it was, was tied to those colours, each strip of pelt warming both the body that wore them and the spirit that lurked within that walking corpse.

He was a gaunt man, teeth half gone, hands like the gnarled roots of a blackthorn. His hair was white, bound together in a long red sheath of linen, which he drew across his shoulder and pinned to his left chest, and stroked for luck as if it was a tail of Epona's horse.

The lice that crawled upon him were thin and starving, sucking at the hollow that was his body. They jumped and crawled to Inkmarker whenever they could, for a feast, for life, but the plump boy was meticulous in his preening, picked and squashed them, and complained that he was weak from loss of blood. When he wrote in the journal he smeared the creatures on the parchment. The words were the Wolfhead's, the blood was his own.

'Perhaps you would like to eat before we begin?' the seer said gently. Inkmarker smiled, eyes wide. 'Yes!'

The Wolfhead turned towards the trees, sniffed the air, then smiled. 'There is a boar in a thicket, four hundred of your pathetic paces to the west. It's a small creature, taller than you, but old. It has a spear-wound high on its chest. It is an easy kill. Go and kill it – you'll need only your bare hands – we'll cook it, eat it, and then we can work . . .'

Thinking, no doubt, of the tusks that could disembowel a man, the boy stayed just where he was, seated on the rotting trunk, eyes watching his master, hands white where they gripped the cape.

'I don't think I feel like boar today . . .' he said.

'Nor do I,' the Seer murmured. 'Yes. You're right. It's good to go without food. So we'll work, shall we?'

'Yes.'

And Inkmarker picked up his goosefeather quill, and the clay pot of ink, and leaned forward to the thick, yellow vellum that he had already strapped to his right leg, to hold it still. The Wolfhead began to speak.

They called for me. I have come to their village. The hill where the old fires once burned is to the south. There is a stream, and the daemon is beyond it. This place has colour and memory. The woods have been cut once, and there are places of burial. I feel no ghosts, but there is metal in the ground and it is not iron. I have watched the flight of three birds. Something is buried here, but perhaps this has no relevance. I placed my hand on the earth and a beetle crawled upon it, following the line of life. This will be a successful encounter with the daemon. I shall be more than kind to the boy Inkmarker. He will make a fine Wolfhead.

The Wolfhead reached round and grabbed the boy's wrist, lifting the quill away from the vellum. Inkmarker looked startled, then panicked. The man said, 'What are those last signs?'

'The last words?'

'What do they say?'

Gulping, the boy said, 'Written this day at Dancing Hill by the Inkmarker.'

'That's what I told you to say, but they don't say it. Show me how they say it.'

But when Inkmarker ran a finger along the line of symbols, the Wolfhead watched only the boy's eyes, and saw at once that he was lying. An ear was resoundingly clipped. The truth was quickly told. The line was deleted, obscured by the black fluid that flowed from the quill.

From the ruined shrine on top of Dancing Hill the Wolfhead stared down at the cluster of ragged tents and shelters that had been erected by the river, in the eastern lee of the woodland. He counted ten tents, four more permanent structures; roofs were of skins, walls were poles with turf or sacking fillings. The stockade that protected this makeshift habitation was fashioned from thorn and hazel, and was simple and insubstantial. A dog was barking loudly; the Wolfhead could see it, across the river, a scrawny creature, half wild, banished by the villagers. It darted in and among the thickets, prowling hungrily.

'Is this the haunted village?' Inkmarker asked.

'Just the villagers. The original settlement, the homestead they've abandoned, is further away . . .'

Two large fires burned, and the women, in their grey and green tunics, were gathered around them or at the riverside. There were clusters of men, all of them holding spears and small shields, Saxon farmers now nervously imitating their warrior forebears. The Wolfhead noticed how their cheeks and arms were patterned for war in the local fashion.

There was an aimlessness in the place. The fields, close by, were tall with wheat and weeds, untended, untouched.

'They must be starving,' the shaman mused.

'So am I,' said his Inkmarker.

The village-settlement which they had abandoned was just visible in the far distance, on a rise of land, which had been thrown up into steep earthen walls. It was a small place. The Wolfhead strained his ancient eyes to see it, and thought he could identify the remnants of the high wooden palisade. But even from here the man could see that there were structures and shapes within the compound that were wrong, that were strange. A haze hung over the deserted village, as if heat blasted the air. But it was a cold day, even if a spring one.

The shrine on the hill, long-since abandoned for different reasons to the village, was dedicated to a dark god. Ruined, the wooden walls decayed, the stone kneeling-places and altars weatherworn, their painted symbols faded ... nevertheless, there was a power here. The blind face that watched, from a corner where it had fallen, seemed almost to sneer at the Wolfhead.

Remember me? Does your ancient memory go back as far as MY first beginnings?

The grainy stone was worn and chipped. But the Wolfhead remembered him, remembered the god.

'I struck at you with an antler twice my height. Generations later I chased you across a land of wild horses. I cracked your skull in front of the first of the Warlords. Their bronze daggers were useless against my skills. I saw you torn down by the Legions; I stood by and watched. You don't frighten me.'

The sneer on the decaying head of the old deity seemed to fade a little.

'Is this place important?' Inkmarker asked.

'Probably not. We're up against a daemon. A shape-changer. Not a memory. Not a cracked stone god.'

'Which god was he?' the boy asked nervously.

'Which of his names would you like?'

'The Red Branch's.'

'Mabathagus. God of Hills. God of the Deep Earth.'
'Hecate . . .' the boy whispered.
'Hecate was his daughter. She killed him centuries ago.'
'Then we're safe from him?'
'I would think so. I can't promise so.'
The boy moved cautiously away.

Yes, this place is important. An event happened here. The place has magic in it. The people of the village have no knowledge of it. They have farmed the land. They have worshipped old gods and new. They have practised old ways and new. They have lost touch with the spirit of the land. Raiders from the North will have left their mark. The river could have helped them sail this far. I expect this is a forgotten place. Metal in the ground. A ruined shrine. A hill that cries with forgotten voices. A woodland that has grown back to cover the scars of another place. I feel only peace here. The shadows are still. Nothing has disturbed them. It is old. It stretches ahead. But the daemon is from outside. This will be a terrible encounter, I now realise.

He led the way through the crude thorn fencing, past the nervous guards, and into the circle of tents. The women took the children and huddled by the riverside. The men, looking angry and tired, formed a square about the strangers, their spears (few of them iron-tipped) and daggers held ready for attack.

'Is this the homestead of Gilla's people?'

A small man, the oldest of the group, stepped forward. His cloak was heavier than most, and he wore a dulled leather jacket over his stained linen shirt. 'I'm Gilla. These are my people. And this is our home while the daemon inhabits our settlement. You will be the Wolfhead, then. You came faster than I thought.'

'It was a good summoning,' the seer said. Inkmarker

shuffled uneasily behind him, not liking the enclosure of glowering, fair-haired men. The Wolfhead paced in a cross within the square of Gilla's people. He stopped at a certain point, smiled, then used his own knife to cut the greensward. After a few minutes he stabbed down into the ground and lifted out the decaying, wormy head of a wolf.

The men all relaxed. Gilla himself shook his head, amazed at the way the stranger had so easily located the sign of the summoning.

'The spell is an old one,' Gilla said.

'I know,' the Wolfhead agreed mildly. 'Who showed it to you?'

'My mother. She was a dreamer in that particular way that attracts magic. She had awarenesses of things beyond my simple senses. Now that I know the summoning spell works, I shall show my own sons.'

'Boil the head,' the Wolfhead stated flatly, tossing the revolting object to one of the men in the square. 'Give me the bones, then reduce the soup to a thick broth.' He turned and looked at Inkmarker, who suddenly turned more pale than ever.

'Make sure this apprentice of mine drinks a good bowlful.'

'Not me. I'm not that hungry.'

'Hunger has nothing to do with it. You want to be a Wolfhead. You want to work wolf magic. You had better know the taste of the spirit you'll be working with.'

Inkmarker looked green, now, staring frantically at the rotten object on the ground.

The Wolfhead and Gilla went beneath a canopy and sat on the bracken and rush floor. They ate a little food. The seer drank milk. Gilla drank the sour wine that was on offer.

'When did the daemon enter the village?'

'Twenty-five or so nights ago.'

'Where is it located?'

'That's hard to tell. But there is a deep well in the centre of the village, lined with stone. We were not the first people to settle in this place. We built partly out of the remains of an older town.'

'A well ... lined by stone ...' the seer murmured softly. His eyes narrowed and he nodded as if understanding something.

'It has been there for years,' Gilla said. 'More years than I can imagine.' He shrugged, then frowned, peering through age-worn eyes at the shaman. 'Why would the daemon come now?'

'Something was done to the stones,' the Wolfhead muttered. 'I have experienced such unwilling summoning many times.'

Gilla stared at him hard for a moment, then nodded. 'Yes. Two names were carved upon the top-stone. I'd hoped this wouldn't be the reason.'

'Two names?'

'Two young men. They had a minor triumph in a skirmish with raiders. There were only twelve of the Northmen, and two were killed, and the slayers boasted their names by scratching them on the well-stones.'

'And where are these two men now?'

Gilla looked pained. 'Still there. Still trapped. In the well-pit itself. The changes are occurring around them. They may even be dead, now. We haven't heard their cries, for help, of fear, of the *daemon-son* itself for some days.'

'The *daemon-son*?'

'That's what they screamed.'

'And the young men's names?'

'Ealgawan and Badda. My sons.'

It started to rain again and the gathered crowd dispersed to shelter. The Wolfhead watched the downpour, smelled the dank earth, and felt the presence of the daemon, an odd, smoky odour in the wet day.

'As I thought,' he said. 'The daemon is in the well. When it rains, the water bubbles, and the daemon reaches into the world, bringing a smell of fire with him. You say he is changing the village?'

'Nightmarish visions. One day a house as it was built, the next it looks as if it was stretched by a giant hand. Strange coloured stone appears,' Gilla went on, 'and slats of wood, dark and thinly cut. Then hard glass, as you see in churches. And when it cracks it splinters, like blades. Stone walls appear overnight, brilliantly white, and crumble before the dawn. And always, the silver ghosts: they move through the village like spectres, terrifying creatures. We fled while we could. The village *itself* is possessed, not just my two sons.'

In all the long generations of his wandering the Wolfhead had heard of nothing similar. He didn't tell this to Gilla. He rose and drew his hooded cape around his body. Inkmarker was crouched in one of the tents, watching the iron cauldron with the animal's skull as it boiled and gave off a rich, putrescent odour. 'Stay here,' the seer said to him.

He went, then, to find some objects that would resist the daemon's change. He picked a black, water-rolled stone from the river and quickly swallowed it. He smeared the unchanging soil onto his wrists. Then he moved among the women, searching their possessions, until he found a stone shell, petrified life, unchanging too. It was already made into a necklet and he slung it over his shoulders.

Thus protected, he walked through the tangled woodland to the deserted village. He stared up at the immense palisade on its steep bank of earth, higher by far than Gilla's people could or would have constructed. Trees grew from the bank, black-trunked and monstrous, warped into shapes as if twisted by winds from the four corners; their roots gripped and covered great blocks of stone, some carved with symbols and faces. These, too, were daemon-wrought.

The Wolfhead walked twice around the outer bank, then entered the village by the eastern gate. He gaped again in astonishment, this time at the twisted houses, their walls curved and angled, the stones coloured, their roofs a bizarre mixture of the thatching he would have expected and tiling as he had seen on Roman buildings. Everywhere, gruesome, ugly faces stared at him from statues, or from fragments of crumbled building.

A turret like a Roman tower, but round, grew from the village centre; a pennant flapped there, red and gold, the shape designed on it that of a dragon. The top of the tower was castellated. The whole structure gleamed a brilliant white.

In the air, the stink of the daemon was strong.

'Ealgawan! Badda!' the seer called, but there was just silence in reply. Somewhere in the confusion of impossible buildings lay the well, with its two trapped men. But the shaman could not see a way into this mess of stone and wood.

He called again, and as he did so, the earth shook. Walls crumbled further and the air *crackled*, as if the god Taran was sending his silent fire from the heavens. A sudden stifling wind sucked the rain away from the seer and the building in front of him twisted on its base, dry clay flaking and spilling from great cracks that appeared on it.

The Wolfhead stepped back quickly, drawing his cloak around his shoulders. He fought to keep confusion from his mind, but he was unnerved.

Through the rain came riders, a small band of them on enormous horses, each animal white and covered with coloured, heavy blankets. Their harnessing rattled like a

Legion on the march. Their riders were silver men, bright yet blurred, as if they rode from some icy hell.

They were as insubstantial as fog, and as quickly as the Wolfhead envisioned them, they seemed to fade, although the earth continued to shake to the sound of their riding. The seer had encountered nothing like them, but they were warriors, of that he was certain. He had seen their like from the dry forts of Babylon to the cold frontiers of the Roman Empire. He had followed in the wake of the Goths, and watched, from afar, as tall, dark-haired men in bright bronze armour had ridden in triumph around the great stones of this very land, the land of the Britons.

He had seen the ages, but the warriors he had just visioned were from an unknown region. Like the Wolfhead himself, they were ghosts.

He drew away from the haunted village, keeping low against the rain, frightened yet intrigued by this encounter.

(ii)

Head low in the rain, lean body glistening, the wild dog padded warily along the edge of the river, half an eye on the tents and the miserable farmers who inhabited them, half aware of the dense thickets that bordered the bank. Inkmarker rose from his forlorn crouch, close to the stinking stew of wolfskull, gathered his short cloak around his shoulders, glanced once at Gilla — who was preoccupied with thoughts of his own — and moved in the same direction as the hound.

The boy was hungry and angry at being so abused by his master. 'I need food. Doesn't he understand that?' His belly rumbled, the sound echoing in hollow bones. There was a scent of woodsmoke on the rain, and woodsmoke made him think of pork, charred and crispy from the fire. He kept pace with the hound, skidding on the slick turf close to the river, plunging through the briar and thorn of the thickets, listening to the dull patter of rain through trees in their full spring leaf.

The dog crossed the stream ahead of Inkmarker, close to the earthwork that surrounded the haunted village. For a moment or two the boy crouched below the bushes, peering through the hazel scrub at the ambling shape of his master as the man paced around the high wall.

The Wolfhead glanced his way just once, but seemed to have seen nothing. He vanished inside. A few moments later the earth shook and the trees on the earthworks twisted and groaned, seeming to reach towards the boy. Inkmarker's eyes widened with shock and fear, and he withdrew rapidly to the river.

The hound had caught a water rat, and was crunching through the limp, brown body, feral eyes on the boy, threatening: stay off.

Inkmarker sat below a tree, huddled and cold. The dog whined as it ate, then growled. In seconds it gulped down the small creature.

'Not even a *tail* for me? You miserable beast.' He threw a stick at the dog. The dog watched the weapon approach but didn't move and the wood struck its head. Now it rose and padded up to the boy below the tree. Inkmarker reached out a hand and the dog snapped at the wrist, closing its teeth over the exposed flesh, but not biting.

'Bite,' said Inkmarker. 'Draw blood. Show your independence. Don't be like me, too frightened to fight your master.'

But the wild dog had not been wild long enough; its memory of fire and companionship was too close. It watched Inkmarker through eyes that had suddenly gone soft.

It released the boy and ran through the wood to the earth wall, and the twisted-tree palisade. The rain drummed on the turf. Images, shapes, flickered in the air. Inkmarker could feel, rather than hear, movement in the wood. He dodged and ducked, felt the skin on his body crawl and tighten. His senses were heightened; his face bled water from the soft and gushing downpour.

There was a horseman in the woods. There was something prowling close by ... And out in the clear, the dog was behaving strangely. It was turning in circles, as if after its tail, but it seemed to be sniffing for something. Then it leapt into thin air, paws extended, and leapt again, as if battering against a closed door, or trying to ascend a steep bank.

The dog watched Inkmarker. Then it turned and ran around the village, yelping and barking, every bit the frantic animal, lost and frightened. Again it leapt into the air, dropped, seemed stunned, seemed to be watching something.

'What are you seeing?' the boy asked quietly.

The dog was motionless. It had raised its back and the fur stood on end. It snarled, walked in a strange, stiff way, backwards. Then it barked desperately, ran forward again, leapt and scrabbled in the air, falling to the wet earth.

A moment later there was a sudden, alarming noise behind Inkmarker, and the boy turned quickly; he stepped back into the open, and watched, terrified, as the cluttered, tangled thicket behind was parted. An immense face appeared there, a dog's face, a hound's maw, its teeth, daggerlike and gleaming, streaming wetness.

It came through the wood, walking like a horse, pushing against the trees. It passed out of the wood, brushing by the gasping, frozen boy. It stank of ferality and territory, a sharp, pissy odour that exuded from its towering flanks. The man who followed it was also gigantic, half-armoured,

THE SHAPECHANGER

kilted and helmeted in the fashion of the Northmen. He glanced at the cowering scribe, then tugged at the rope with which he held the great hound.

'Cunhaval,' Inkmarker breathed, and then sat down heavily as man and huge beast walked not through the gate into the village, but into hell, sliding into the rain, into nowhere, there one moment, and invisible the next.

The wild dog was apoplectic. It screeched and rolled, its legs in the air, its body flexing and twisting. It seemed to die. Inkmarker thought he heard the crack of bones. Was the wild dog being crushed by the feet of the gone-hound, the daemon dog?

'Cunhaval. Great Hound . . .' the boy again whispered. He remembered the tales of the beast, told to him when he had been younger and in the monastery. Cunhaval, hound of the underworld, running with its warrior master, its champion knight. And the Wolfhead too had told him about the creature, but for a different reason, a reason to do with *seeing* that underworld. The *mask* of Cunhaval, a way to watch the running of a hunting dog into the realm of spirits.

He approached the dying creature. All wildness had fled. Then the eyes faded as its spirit, perhaps, followed Cunhaval into the world within the world.

'What did you *see*?' Inkmarker whispered in the wet ear. 'What vision, I wonder.' The dog's breathing was soft; finally it stopped altogether. Inkmarker stroked its wet head for a moment, then dragged the corpse into the hollow of a thicket, drew out his knife and quickly skinned the fur from the face, cutting first around the neck, then splitting the tight flesh over the skull. Remembering what he had seen the Wolfhead do, he peeled away the face of the dog, and scraped the blood from the raw hide. He made a frame of twigs, tied with ivy strands, and secured the flesh mask to this crude base.

Nervously and cautiously he placed the mask across his own face. He went into the clearing, looked towards the village and peered at the world through the eyes of the wild dog, the spirit of Cunhaval, the Hunter of the Otherworld.

A moment of silence, then he was screaming and beating at the thin air in front of his face.

He was in a confined, almost airless place, leaping at a brightly painted door, paws striking the wood, body striking a soft fabric that covered the corridor along which he prowled and raged and whined . . . and leapt. He could hear a voice, plaintive at first, then hysterical: 'I want my dog. Let me have my dog. Please. Please. Let me have my dog . . .'

Almost instantly he was in a different space, still confined, and this too was airless. He could hear the sound of the dog, battering against the door. Pictures of warriors whirled before his eyes. Horses raced through dark woods. Hoofs thundered. The eerie ululations of war-trumpets sounded loud in this bizarre prison. Feathered plumes caught the wind. Light gleamed on strangely bright and silver armour.

And there was pain, and hunger, and the Inkmarker knew this hunger well . . .

The voice again, the child-daemon's voice, 'Merlin. Arthur. Sir Gawain. Sir Bedwyn. Sir Wulf. Come to me. Come now. Come now.'

More images: of tall turrets, high walls, a deep lake around a proud castle, and Inkmarker/wild dog scurried below the prancing legs of fine, high horses, while hounds ten times his height were sent on the hunt for stags that rose like trees above the forest, and roared and called, and thundered; and armour clashed. And music made meaningless sounds, while coloured flags streamed and high, wide tents gave birth to tall, silver men . . .

THE SHAPECHANGER

The fear became too much for Inkmarker and he was sick. He had eaten nothing for so long that he retched up only a pale, sour liquid. He ran from the cold, wet earthen wall, tearing the mask from his face, trying to block the screaming voice of the child-daemon and banish the frightening, incomprehensible pictures of silver men and white-walled castles from his mind. He found the cover of the edgewood, crawled below the thorns, wrapped the briar and the bramble around him, buried his face in the musty mould of bracken and leaf.

The daemon had touched him. It had touched him through the wild dog. It had trapped him, made him *become* the dog, and the dog-part of the daemon had caught his limbs and made him prance and twist and scrabble like the poor, mad beast.

But that voice. That poor voice: 'I want my dog . . .' Such sadness. Such fear. Such loneliness.

Someone moved swiftly, menacingly through the underbrush. Inkmarker whimpered and crawled deeper into the sylvan bosom. A hand reached for him, dragged him back by the damp seat of his pants. He was lifted bodily to his feet, and the Wolfhead shook him quiet. The old man reached down for the crumpled dog-mask, stared at it, then at the boy.

'You are just a simple Inkmarker. If you play with magic you will feel the bite of daemon teeth.'

The boy squirmed in the powerful grasp of his master. He said, 'I saw warriors in armour. They gleamed like moon on water. I saw white-walled castles. I touched the daemon, and the daemon's dog. He is very young.'

Slowly the grip relaxed. The Wolfhead lowered himself to a crouch. He was at first puzzled, then excited, at what his young scribe had told him.

'Indeed,' he whispered. 'Then you must have drunk that broth from the skull.'

'No! I didn't! And I won't. Although I am hungry . . .'

Ancient eyes tore apart the soul of the youth. But old magic bowed, in its wisdom, to the showing of youthful talent.

'You have done more than I could do,' the shaman murmured. 'If you can touch the daemon-son, then you can find the way to banish it back to the pits of the earth.' The man picked up the shattered mask, passed it back to his apprentice. He placed a hand on the boy's shoulder. 'Did you say you were hungry?'

'Hungry enough to eat a dog . . . no! Not a dog!'

The Wolfhead laughed, and his grip on the boy's neck tightened. 'Where *is* the body of that hound?' he asked softly, and Inkmarker's gorge rose again.

(iii)

When he had finished eating — a small bowl of thick broth and a hunk of oatcake — Inkmarker was instructed to write:

The nature of the daemon is strange. It is either youthful — a form perhaps of Mercurian or Mabdagda — or it has ingested the soul of a child, and it is this struggling soul whose nightmare is expressed in the ruins. The shape of the village is bent and twisted and given an appearance that is remote from my experience. These structures are from another world, from hell. Inkmarker is attuned to the child in the daemon. Through his eyes other pictures, other worlds, can be seen which are absent from my own vision. He, then, can see through the gate in the skull, into hell. I see only what the daemon sends through the gate in the world. To summon the daemon I shall use Inkmarker and the 'journeying' mask he has so cleverly made, to call upon the child's soul. The daemon may well follow, and I shall destroy it.

Hand resting lightly on the boy's shoulder, the Wolfhead returned along the rough track between the woods, to the rise of land that led to the earthworks. The day was still, now; the scent of rain was strong, bringing out the smells of the rich earth. In the trees, creatures shuffled restlessly, and Inkmarker glanced nervously about.

'What made you kill the dog and make the mask?' the Wolfhead asked.

Inkmarker clutched the wet hide tightly, glancing down at the crumpled features of the dog. 'Impulse,' he said. 'But you told me about the ten tracks into hell . . . I knew about Cunhaval . . . I didn't kill the dog . . .'

The Wolfhead smiled as he walked, his gaunt face tightening. 'Cunhaval: the running of a hound into the unknown region.' He nodded, slightly proud that his apprentice had absorbed so much of his own secret ways. 'The tracks are ancient. I myself carry *all* the "journey masks", but use only the ghost, Morndun. When I enter the otherworld, I pass in as a ghost. But today I shall try and draw the daemon into our world. It is you who will do the running.'

There had been more changes to the village. The stone walls that had so recently risen tall and turreted from the bank, now were crushed and decayed, overgrown with thorns and twisted oaks, small, gnarly trees that jutted from crevices and the tumbled brick. But a high pole, with a fluttering pennant, stood close to the ragged cluster of houses and ragged walls at the centre of the enclosure.

Everywhere was draped in a pale, heavy mist, which hung quite still despite the sound and sensation of a cold wind blowing through the ruins. As the Wolfhead led the way through the broken buildings, Inkmarker jumped and twitched at each odd sound: the whinnying of a horse, the sudden scampering of a dog, the creak of wood, the rattle of arms and armour.

Close to the well, the tattered rags of tents and pennants fluttered silently in that same impossible breeze. Broken lances of enormous length lay everywhere. Light gleamed suddenly on the face of a horse, carved out of steel. It was a mask of sorts, or perhaps protective metal for a war-beast, cast aside among the duller gleam of bones.

In his gentle grasp, Inkmarker began to shudder, and the shaman glanced down. The boy's face was ashen, his mouth moist and open. The Wolfhead reached down and lifted the crude mask of the dog, placing it against his apprentice's face, tying the wooden frame with the ivy thongs.

Inkmarker cried out, the words bubbled from him, causing a sudden flurry, birds perhaps, from the hidden recesses of the ruins.

'*Sir Gawain* came to the ruined castle, and there among the fallen stones found the remains of many knights! The battle standards fluttered in the chill wind, the last memory of the brave warriors! The King would be saddened to see so many places at the *table round* empty of his kin!'

The words fled into the misty stillness, but they seemed to set in motion a vibration in the earth. The Wolfhead crouched slightly, drawing the boy into the lee of a low wall. Out of the mist five riders galloped on black, blanketed warhorses. Their heads were bare, though they wore the same bright breastplates. Each carried a long lance, shaped of pale wood. They laughed as they rode, calling out at each other. They came from nowhere, they were swallowed by the air. Behind the shaman the wall corroded. He stepped away from it, eyes wildly alert as the shapechanger imposed a small, circular tower upon the decaying stone.

This was a dangerous place!

But the daemon was here, now. It was speaking through the boy. It was chanting through the boy. The word *sirgawain* meant nothing, but the rest of what Inkmarker had cried out sounded like . . . like a story, perhaps.

'What can you see? What can you hear?' the old man asked, his eyes gleaming as he watched the drooping features of the dog, and the terrified eyes of his apprentice through the widened orbits.

Suddenly, Inkmarker rubbed his legs, wincing and jerking as if being struck. His cries were of pain. His body seemed to be suffering from blows. He whimpered, then almost cooed: 'Don't hurt me. Please. Don't hurt me . . .'

Then he snarled; enraged, he turned on the Wolfhead and struck and scratched at the gaunt, stooped man. The shaman held the boy's hands, kept the bitten nails from tearing at his ancient flesh.

The apprentice shouted, 'Let me out! Let me out! Unlock the door! Don't hurt her! Don't hurt my mother! Let me out! Stop shouting! Stop screaming at her! *Drunken bastard!* I *will* use that language! Stop screaming at her!'

And then a third change, and he started to cry. He hunched down and the shaman let the body fall, but kept his own hands upon his young friend's tormented, possessed body. The tears flowed from the boy.

'Where *are* you?' he sobbed. 'Why don't you come? Gawain . . . Arthur . . . Where *are* you? I've called for you from the books. Why don't you come?'

Now the Wolfhead whispered to his Inkmarker, to the daemon which spoke through the unwilling scribe. 'Where do you exist? By what name are you known? Who is the child?'

Inkmarker was silent for a moment, then through his racking sobs he managed to say, 'My name's Stephen. My name's Stephen. Are you Gawain?'

'Where are you?' the seer persisted.

'I live in *Gillingham*. You should know. You should know. This is the place you fought to save. Now save me. Get me away from this house. Please! Get me away from my father . . .'

Before the Wolfhead could speak further, again Inkmarker was possessed. He struggled in his master's grasp, and cried out, as if reading loudly from a text: 'At the centre of the old town is a large well, which once reached a depth of a hundred *feet*. It is now reached through the basement of *Selfridges* and can be viewed by special request. Two of the stones, those with names scratched upon them, are in the local *museum*. Known as the *knights' stones*, the names, Ealgawan and Badda, are reputed by legend to be those of two of Arthur's knights (Gawain and Bedwyn, according to tradition) who tried to protect the town of *Gillingham* (then known as *Croucomagum* or stone mound) against the numerically superior forces of the Saxon warlord Gilla.'

The Wolfhead listened to this in astonishment. But slowly the words, the strangest words, made a certain sense to him.

Gillingham. The accent was odd, but that was clearly Gilla's homestead, this very village. Gilla's people had settled here. Arthur was a name. There were many warlords who were called such. The Wolfhead remembered the tall, Roman noble who had recruited from the horsemen in the townships around Camulodunum, on the east of this country. That had been centuries before. The man had been called Pwyl, but had carried the emblem of a bear locked in mortal combat with a dragon, and he had been nicknamed *Artorian of the Red Branch*. Artor. The shaman did not recognise the strange name *Sella Friggas*; it sounded something like a god, and perhaps the reference was to the temple of this unknown deity.

But it was the *form* of the chanting that intrigued the Wolfhead in particular. The reference to 'legend'.

From where was this daemon-son calling to the world of Gilla and his people? Why was it using the child? These thoughts, these anguished cries, were simply the child's *possession terror* . . . or were they?

The shaman's process of thought was abruptly ended. Inkmarker bayed and howled like a dog, dropped to a crouch, then began to leap and scrabble at the wall in front of him.

'My dog! My dog!' he cried in his own language. Then barked fitfully and terrifyingly.

The Wolfhead slapped him on the back. 'Yes! Seek and find. Go and find the daemon. Go!'

The boy/dog raced away, dropping his pouch of quills, parchment and ink, entering through gaps in the ruined wall, penetrating to the heart of the ruins, of the changing place. Finding the well. Finding the terrified farmers, whose brief skirmish, and triumphant killing, had led them to scrape their names on the well-stone.

The Wolfhead followed, entering the dank place, with its foetid water, its green-slimed walls, its powerful stink of evil.

For the shaman there was nothing to see but the crushed, petrified bodies of the two men, their grey, dead faces still showing the agony that had racked them as their limbs had somehow been *absorbed* by the stone of the well. They were half men, half rock, the shapes of hands and legs sculpted in the grey/green ragstone as if by the hands of those *greeks*, who had so beautifully wrought the shapes of the human body from the solid clay of the earth.

The Wolfhead noted all of this, and also that he had no power to free these men from their stony death.

Inkmarker was standing upright, looking up towards the slanting, greying light that shafted from the gaps in the wood and thatching of the roof.

His face was flexed with pain. The dog's mask was on the floor. His lips were moving, and slowly the words began to sound . . .

'High-walled *camelot* lay ahead of them . . . as *sirgawain* rode he could hear the sounds of the *joust* . . . he could smell the ox on the spit . . . a hundred flags blew in the wind from the tents of Arthur's gathered knights . . . from every country the champions of Kings had come to the white-walled castle . . . the Queen watched from the high tower . . . white silk favours fluttered down from the walls and the knights took them gladly . . .'

'*Stop!*'

The Wolfhead clapped a hand across the boy's face and suddenly the possession was gone. Inkmarker looked startled, then afraid. The more so as he felt the shifting of the earth, the cracking of stone . . .

Sudden whiteness, as if all colour drained from the walls and ledges . . .

Sudden summer breezes . . .

The sudden sound of horses . . .

Fragments of white gossamer seemed to drift in the air of the stifling well-space . . . A woman's voice sang gently, the words meaningless.

Inkmarker was shaking. He blurted out, 'It's all in a book. Pictures. Words. It's all he possesses in the place where he's trapped. He turns the pages. The ghosts are all there, the huge castles, the towers, the great horses, the silver men. He's reading from a book of story-spells. Oh! My head! It hurts so much! And he's so lonely!'

As the boy struggled with the daemon's pain, the Wolfhead was triumphant. A book of story-spells. Of course! As the daemon looked at the images in the spells, so the world was shaped. As he chanted the hellish tales of silver knights and battles, as he described the world of his own kind, so he changed the world of Gilla's village. In that otherworld the two men's names had been inscribed in the Book of Hell, made into story *themselves*. That was the link. As the daemon sought to escape from his prison, he was twisting the gateway — *this stone well!* — to try to find release into the world where farmers would live in terror of his power.

How clever to pretend to be a *child* reading from manuscript pages written as if *for* a child.

The Wolfhead must have spoken these thoughts aloud. Suddenly his Inkmarker, who had at first been watching him blankly, then with an expression of horror, shouted out, 'No! He's not a daemon! He's just a boy. Like me. A boy, trapped and punished. Somewhere very far from here, but tied to us through the well. The true daemons are the people who have trapped him. They are hurting him. They make him very lonely. This is his only escape from the pain. He's trying to reach to us for help. No! He *isn't* a daemon. You mustn't hurt him.'

'You are already possessed,' the seer murmured hoarsely, watching the contortions on his apprentice's face, the tears fill the eyes. 'I should have realised as much. The daemon is half way through to this place.'

Inkmarker backed away, fetched up hard against the wall, against one of the petrifying corpses. His fingers, reaching for support, brushed against one of the incised names, and he jerked his touch away, whimpering like the half-wild dog of earlier in the day.

The Wolfhead was reaching slowly into his bag of magic. He watched the boy as he did so, considering, planning, thinking how to treat this new possession.

'You don't understand,' Inkmarker breathed. 'If you put on the ghost mask, perhaps you'll see what I could see.'

The shaman had drawn out a bone knife, carved from the shoulder blade of a boar. It was polished, honed sharp. It caught the light from above.

Inkmarker sobbed. He was no match for this powerful man of magic. He darted round the strange well-room, skidding on the slick stones of the floor. The man moved after him. The boy snatched up his hound's mask, and held it to his face, frantically tying the ivy behind his head. He growled, wild and loud. He raised his hands in protection. His eyes glittered as they watched from Cunhaval's running track.

'I'm coming for you!' he shouted, and the other boy stopped turning pages. The dog leapt against the door. It grew larger. It grew fiercer. Its body hit against the door and the house shuddered. The boy ran from his bed to the battered door and listened.

'My dog! Let me have my dog!'

Inkmarker leapt again. His front legs were stretched out, his claws extended. He struck the Wolfhead, struck the door, and the door came down. There was a brief pain, then loving arms around his neck, ruffling the fur on his head and cheeks. Tears of delight. Cries of joy. There were shouts, hard, angry, drunken cries. A man's voice. A woman screamed.

But the boy and his hound were off and running, out through the landing window, over the roof of the garage, down towards the town, where the traffic growled and there was freedom to be had.

The Boy who Jumped the Rapids

The horn-helmeted man had come from the far west, following the ridgeways and woodland tracks, and crossing streams and rivers at the nearest point, not at their shallows. From the state of his clothes it was clear that he had journeyed through the dark forests where the Belgic peoples ruled; from the downwind smell of him, the hint of salt and sea, it was clear that he had travelled across the wide ocean that separated two lands. His hair hung lank and fire-red from beneath his strange helmet, a helmet with stubby horns and sparkling decorations. When the sun was bright the helmet flashed in the way of gold, and sometimes in the way of silver. And again, sometimes it gleamed in the way of bronze. But there was no iron there, not that the boy Caylen could see.

Word had already gone ahead to the forest community of Caswallon's people, and now only Caylen and two men discreetly trailed the stranger as he ran along the high ground, squinting at times into the distance, seeking smoke, perhaps, or the sea. Caylen moved stealthily through the undergrowth, pausing occasionally to watch the horned man as he ran and danced past in the open. The boy had never seen anything, or anyone, quite like this dark-cloaked foreigner; he didn't walk like a warrior; nor did he run, crouched and wary, like a hunter. He ran upright, his cloak streaming behind him, a narrow, skin-wrapped object held firmly in his right hand. At times he actually leapt into the air, twisting about and spinning as he touched the ground again so that his cloak swirled about him. His voice, at these times, was a loud cry, a triumphant cry, echoing away across the woodlands and the grassy downs, and frightening the dark carrion birds that nested in the spruce and ash trees.

At dusk the man came down from the ridgeway and followed the tracks, of hunters and animals both, through the forest until he came to the tall, wooden totem that stood where the river forked. This was the holy place at the apex of the streams.

Within minutes he had found the village, though the village had been expecting him since before noon.

He stood outside the heavy palisade, outside the open gate, and stared across the muddy compound at the low round-houses, the broken animal pens, the roped dogs, hysterical in their excitement and barking loudly, the huddle of women in their drab green robes, the children, excitedly gathered in a goat-house, peering at the stranger through the thin, wicker walls. He looked also at the line of dark-haired men who stood facing him, their spears and swords held across their chests. Chickens, ducks and grey puppies ran noisily between them, disturbed in their empty-headed ways by the tension in the air.

The man said one word, which might have been 'Food'. He said it loudly, and there was something in his voice that made the pain of his empty belly obvious. Then he said, 'Help', or a word that sounded similar. His eyes glazed a moment as he looked around at the people of the village, and then he flung back his cloak and held the long, thin package above his head. 'Help,' he repeated, and lowered the object to his lips, hugging it afterwards as he might hug a child. 'Rianna,' he said, but the name was strange to Caswallon and his kin, and they ignored it.

When at last the Chieftain, Caswallon — who was Caylen's father — stepped towards the horned man, it was to welcome him. The man removed his gleaming helmet and stepped inside the palisade. His scalp, below the helm, had been scarred savagely by a sword. Caylen grimaced at the sight of the hideous wound, and the thought of the agony this man must have borne.

It rained as it always rained in the forest: hard, for a while, driving man and beast into shelter; then gentle, almost like a sea spray. The rolling storm clouds passed away into the east, and the sky brightened. The children were driven out into the gleaming mud pond that had formed within the village walls, and set about the task of laying straw and wood walkways. When they had finished, they gathered the animals from the edge of the woodlands, chased them back into the compound, and then sneaked away among the trees.

Caylen followed the boys at a distance. The day before, he had suffered a beating from the two sons of his father's cousin, the warrior Eglin, blinded during a raid three years ago. These two boys were vicious and compassionless. They joked about their father in an open and openly derisory way, calling him 'blind stick', and bragging that they would have taken his head a long time before but it would not have been worth the effort. They spared no wrath from Caylen, stripping him and bruising him with malicious glee. They had carved something on his backside, but the scarring and scratching had obscured its nature from his friend, Fergus, who had helped Caylen to his special place, near the river, and bathed and patched the wound.

'Don't tell my father,' Caylen had said, and Fergus had laughed.

'What would *he* do? Nothing! He'd do nothing. Not even with the stranger here.'

Caylen had laughed angrily and said he knew that, but he always hoped that one day Caswallon would step in and defend his son from the other village children. It was a vain hope.

Now, with Fergus, he followed the pack, keeping low in

the undergrowth that lined a narrow boar-run. The other children walked boldly along the trampled bracken, snagging clothes on bramble and thorn and noisily knocking aside the wood and plant growth with sword sticks.

'That ol' pig'll hear them,' said Fergus. 'But it won't attack. Not until it thinks it's safe, and that will be us. So let's hurry.'

Caylen needed no second urging. He raced along the run and only dropped to a crouch when he saw the bobbing heads of the other boys in front of him, and of course on that heart-stopping occasion when he realised he was standing right by the thicket where the boar was calmly waiting for the noise to pass. He could smell it in there, musty, foetid; its breathing was rapid, almost hoarse. He thought he saw a shaft of sun glint off the cruel, curved tusks, and he realised this was a giant boar, a huge thing, that had probably come down from the deep forests inland.

Caswallon knew it was here, but it was taboo to kill boars for two seasons, because of the goring of the druid Glamach, in the season of Bel. It would make great eating, this one, and was a severe threat to the village while it was alive. But until the season of the fires, and the blessing of Lug, it would forage the nearwoods unhindered.

Caylen leapt past it and waited for Fergus. Fergus was a small lad, two years younger than the wiry Chieftain's son, and his face was red with effort, his tawny hair slick and plastered with animal grease which ran down his cheeks as the heat in his flesh melted it. He clutched a tiny wooden knife, and there was such an expression of childish excitement in his face that Caylen felt his own excitement surge again. They went on, breaking through the tangled, thorny undergrowth where the ground was marshy, and finding a clearer passage through the gnarled trunks of oak and elm, where bluebells covered the ground in a single, dazzling azure sheen. The other boys had gone through here too, and Fergus led the way after them, diving from tree to tree, listening to the rustling in the distance, and the sound of bird life disturbed by the intruders below.

When they were near the clearing known as Old Stone Hollow, Caylen led the way to the side. They wormed through nettles, hands behind their necks, and found an old trickle-stream, dried now that summer had been halfway exhausted. From this they peered, through dried bracken and the tangle of a rose bush, at the small, grassy clearing, with the great wind and rain-etched boulder poking up from deep in the ground. In front of this rock a small, wooden shelter had been built, and the red-haired man, stripped to the waist, was busy hammering iron nails into the sloping roof. No house, then, but a shrine of some sort. Smoke rose from his tiny fire, and a fish slowly grilled there. The wrapped object that was so precious to him stood against the boulder. Caylen could see that the man had painted things on that stone, strange shapes and symbols, and pictures of animals too. They were painted in blue and green, and he had painted similar symbols on his arms, and on his chest. Caylen knew of the tribes in the north and east who painted their bodies in this way, but this one was from the west, from the far west, or so his father had said in Caylen's hearing, from the land across a great sea, where a thousand kings ruled.

He didn't even speak their language, although he had learned enough words to indicate his needs. He was here because he was a fugitive, because he was protecting something from evil forces in his homelands.

After a while Caylen grew restless. He drew back from the glade, Fergus following, and began to walk towards the river. They were puzzled by the man, and intrigued, and they were aware, too, that Caswallon and the other villagers were uneasy with him, although he was in no way hostile.

Abruptly they were surrounded by boys, and Caylen felt a stinging blow on his face where a spiky, green nut had been thrown. There was laughter, and the screech of boyish anger that precedes a boyish punishment. But Caylen was in no mood for trouble and he found his temper at exactly the right moment, swinging a dead stick with a loud whack against the leader's head.

He was off then, the boys in pursuit. Where Fergus went he didn't know, and for the moment didn't care. His backside still hurt, and the head that he had struck had belonged to the boy whose knife had carved the pain. They chased him, shouting and yelling, but he was surefooted and swift, and knew the way to the river better than they. He ducked through dense stands of oak, and plunged into bramble thickets, not caring about the scratches to his legs and arms, preferring that pain to the pain of the senseless beatings.

The boys closed on him where the forest thinned, but now he could hear the water, the rushing waters of the great river, and he sensed he was safe, even though a part of his mind still questioned the strangeness of the fact.

He ran down the bank, waded in and felt the river's coldness sting all the way to his waist. The flow was gentle, the mud below soft and sucking. It was a long way across, a good minute's wade, and then he scrambled out, just as Domnorix led the gang of panting youths out of the woods and to the water's edge. Fergus appeared, farther away, and shook his head, smiling but smiling uncertainly. He crouched, exactly as Caylen was crouching, and stared at the gentle water.

The boys threw stones for a while, which Caylen dodged with arrogant ease, even lobbing a few back. Domnorix taunted him. 'Only a demon could get across those rapids.

Only someone possessed by evil magic could float across those waters. You're an evil thing, Caylen, your father knows it, your mother knows it. Evil. Evil.' And others cried, 'Possessed, possessed!' And still others taunted him with, 'Unbirthed, unbirthed!' or, 'Crow's spawn, crow's spawn!'

All of this Caylen had heard a hundred times before, and so he sat on the river bank and grinned, watching the boys across the calm waters until they went away.

Fergus walked down to stand across from him. 'How *do* you get across, Caylen?' he called, and smiled almost nervously, as if he didn't want to hear the answer.

'I've told you,' said Caylen, not angrily, but with a patience that he was determined to preserve for this one friend of his. 'I waded across. The water is *calm*. Why don't you try it? It's easy.'

Fergus shook his head. He looked at the river, then at Caylen, and he seemed lost; he was more of a child than his nine years made him; and he needed Caylen very much. He seemed stick thin in his baggy cotton trousers and ragged shirt, his limbs scratched by bramble and thorn. Across the water the two boys watched each other, each longing for closer company, each aware that they were united in friendship through the vagaries of life in such a small community.

'No one could wade through that, Caylen,' Fergus said. 'You have a trick, don't you? There's a way across that we can't see, but which you found. Tell me where it is . . . go on, tell me!'

'It's right in front of you,' urged Caylen, and now a sudden edge of desperation entered his voice, and his manner. He stood up, tossed a pebble into the river. It splashed and the water was so calm that the ripple was able to spread slowly outwards before it was carried away. Above the placid surface, Caylen could glimpse the ghostly image of the tumbling rapids; faintly, he could hear their rush. 'Please, Fergus . . . Please! Wade across. Honestly, there's nothing dangerous here, nothing at all.'

Fergus shivered, wrapped his arms about his shoulders and again shook his head. His eyes were kindly, his smile telling Caylen that it was all right, that though he didn't dare wade across, it wasn't going to change their friendship.

Oh Fergus, thought Caylen desperately. If you would just find the courage not to believe your eyes, to come across to me. That would show the other boys that I'm not some evil spirit. It would convince my father that the things I see are not abnormal, not unnatural. One friend, bearing out my word, and it could be so different, and the chief of the village would not have to stay hidden in the forests for the shame of his son.

But Fergus had heard movement in the woods and waved a brief farewell to Caylen before slipping into the gloom of the undergrowth. Caylen saw a figure passing along the river, hidden by darkness and the bramble thickets. For a second he saw the gleam of sun on metal, and made out the stubby horns of the stranger's helmet. But then that glimpse had been lost in the great confusion of movement as a brisk wind disturbed everything, including the river. Caylen sat for a long while watching for the horned man, but he had gone.

The wind dropped, and with its passing Caylen realised what an unnatural wind it had been, neither a summer breeze, nor a storm wind blowing in advance of a fall of torrential rain. It had been wind like a breath, blowing in a wide circle so that the branches of trees moved one way, and across the river blew oppositely; it was a warm wind, like the passing of some spirit, and Caylen felt the hair on his neck prick up with apprehension. He looked up the river, and down, but saw nothing apart from the wide, gentle waters as they curved from north to south.

Behind him the forest was eerily still. Small animal trackways led through it to the rising hills deeper inland, and the overgrown valleys of a country into which none of the people of Caswallon had ever ventured. From the tree tops on the village side of the river those hills could be seen, cloud-shadowed, green, and the marks of a ridgeway were obvious. But it was a ridgeway that no man had ever travelled, or could remember anyone having ever travelled. There were those who had sought it; it would have made easier passage of the journey north to the edge of the truly deep and dense forests where no tribes lived and the hunting was good. But however the voyager approached that ridge he came upon some impossible barrier – the rapids, or cliffs, or impenetrable, marshy woodlands. The land beyond the rapids was a mystery, even to the boy who could see beyond the illusion of danger.

Caylen had ventured through the silent tangle-woods only once, and that was recently. He had stood in a clearing by a wood-choked stream, and looked up the slopes of a hill. He had thought he could hear the sound of a village on the other side. But as he had tried to cross the blocked stream he had become suddenly overwhelmed with fear, and had turned and run frantically back to the river.

Strangely, he had known that the fear was mere foolishness, more of the illusion that guarded this piece of land from the rest of his village.

Still, he felt something of that apprehension now as he stood and faced the gloomy woodland. He took a deep breath, lobbed a stone among the trees, then took a few paces towards them, kicking through the fern and bracken until he was fully shaded by the foliage.

As his eyes grew accustomed to the gloom he could see the metal totem standing there. Tall, spindly legged, its arms reaching outwards, its eyes wide and dead ... He caught just a glimpse of it as sun broke through the foliage, and he could see that it was silvery, metallic, like some iron god erected at the edge of a tribal land. There was a sound, a wailing like some banshee, but it was distant and it merely made him glance about, frightened.

He walked a little deeper into the forest, picking his way carefully. The place was unnaturally silent, no birds, no rustling of wind-blown foliage. He felt he was being watched.

At the wood-clogged stream, again the heart-stopping fear snagged at him, but he fought it down, stepped over the rotting carcases of tree and branch, and came, within a few paces, to a thistle-choked clearing.

What he saw here astonished him. It was the ruin of a building made all of stone. It rose nearly as high as an oak, and its windows were straight sided, perfectly regular. Creepers, ivy, weeds of all sorts had grown up through the strange structure, adding to its aura of desertion.

Caylen had heard of stone buildings – in the north of his own lands, it was said, houses were made of white stones piled one on another; and across the ocean, in lands where the sun shone all year round, there was a race of warlike men who built stone houses as high as the clouds.

A thin strip of iron surrounded the ruined building. It hummed softly and when Caylen reached to touch it he felt an unpleasant tingling on his skin that made him draw back.

The next moment a bat shrieked down close to him, its audible screech so loud in his ear that he himself screamed, and turned and ran, watching as the huge night-beast circled twice through the trees, its wings outstretched, its mouth still emitting that supernatural cry. It was gone, then, into the woods, back to its daytime resting place.

Caylen caught his breath, tried to stop his hands trembling, then walked shakily back to the river and quickly crossed it.

He stood on the far bank for a moment, and stared at the water. He could see the great swirling rapids. Jagged rocks poked up and broke that awesome flow of water, as they would break a man who slipped and was carried onto them. He watched the raging foam-covered river, and the drowning eddies, and he looked through them at the placid river as it truly was. He would never understand why only he could see beyond this illusion, and he would never understand who created the dream, and why.

But for the moment he was cold, and wet. His heart was still racing, and his body was still tied in knots of fear, the sort of fear that not even a rampaging wild boar would normally induce in him.

Every day the horned man came to the village for food and drink, and every day he sat and for a while tried to communicate with Caswallon and the others. The sense of unease was almost tangible. Not a man crouched without his sword, even the stranger, who detected the tension and was wary of a sudden fury. To thank the village for their help he spent a whole day rebuilding a ruined outhouse, a thatched building, more than a man's height from the ground to point, roomy enough inside for the sheep to huddle when the winter snows covered the forest and made the ground hard as rock.

The job was finished swiftly; the stranger was skilled at his job, and of course, once he had tokened his gratitude by working alone for an hour, the others helped. He placed his helmet on his head, then, and towards dusk ran back into the forest, his black cloak flowing behind him. When Caylen ventured near to his glade, even though it was night, he could hear the sound of building, the expansion of the ceremonial place that the stranger was constructing for his own ends.

After a week the sounds of hammering could no longer be heard, and the stranger had vanished. None ventured to the glade itself, for Caswallon had warned that until the horned man communicated otherwise the glade was his, since he had requested it.

That which he built there was a temple, a shrine, a tomb ... that which he buried there was more precious to him than life itself. Not a man, nor a woman, nor child from the village was allowed to interfere with this burial, until the stranger departed and took his memories with him, leaving only the monument in Old Stone Hollow, which would pass under the care of the village.

After a week of nights made restless by rain and Caswallon's continuing despair with his son, Caylen, word came of warriors approaching along the ridgeway from the west. Red-haired, black-cloaked, they came fast, and with weapons. They sought the horn-helmeted man, and they were coming to kill him.

Caylen was crouched in the corner of his father's house as this news was brought. He had a fever, and his throat was sore. He was miserable because the druid had recommended that he be starved for a week, to help the illness, and to give a chance for those who had sent his evil to take him away. 'The body, unresisting, can be taken by the dark world,' he had told Caylen's father, and then had come and smeared foul-smelling substances on his lips and eyes and ears, and cut off a lock of his greased hair. This he had tied to a rabbit bone and slowly burned on the fire. Caswallon had watched all this, crouched close to the warmth, his strong features sad in the firelight, his eyes filled with anger, and remorse, and not even a hint of pity for his son.

'Is there no way to shake the possession? To make him like us, a man among men?'

The druid, squatting and eating his father's food as he burned the hair, shook his head. He was not an old man, but his lank grey hair, and untrimmed beard, gave him a wild look, and an aged appearance. His woollen tunic was dyed blue and cut short to the knees. He wore animal-bone beads and sparkling torques of bronze on each upper arm and round his neck. He was painted with mud, of course, the grey mud from the far-off rivers close to the sea. The mud on his body was to protect him from the evil presence in Caylen, that which made the boy able to jump over water and walk through the sheer cliff wall known as Wolfback.

'It's just a hill,' Caylen had said (two years before). 'A gentle hill, with boulders. There's no cliff!' He had walked among the stumpy trees and jutting stones, making his way up the rise of the slope. The men of the village had hung back, horrified. When Caylen walked further, there was a sudden panic. The druid, Glamach, had screamed a torrent of abuse at him, and made passes with his hands that effectively condemned Caylen to the dark fires.

Afterwards, when the shock had gone, and only the resentment remained, Caylen had sought out his friend Fergus. Fergus was terrified, then puzzled, and finally cried against his friend and confessed his confusion.

'But what did it *look* like I did?' Caylen asked.

'Can't you see them?' Fergus begged, pointing to the hill. There was a sheer cliff there, Fergus explained, and at the base of the cliff were sharpened spikes of wood on which were impaled the bloody corpses of men and women, and below the corpses, the bones of others. The air was strong with the stink of decaying flesh. Whoever lived beyond the cliff was dangerous. But Caylen had walked through the spikes and the corpses, and then right on up to the cliff itself, passing through the rock as if it had not been there.

Caylen looked hard, narrowing his eyes. When cloud

shadowed the sun he imagined he could glimpse the spikes; but it was like a dream, a ghostly image that didn't last.

'He must be killed,' the druid was saying, in Caswallon's lodge. Hostile eyes, high-lit by the red fire, watched Caylen from across the room. 'But killed in the correct way. As yet I have not decided how best to use the spilling of his blood for the good of the village, and the cleansing of the stain of possession that is on it.'

And as if the words had induced in Caswallon a warlike anger, the man came across the lodge and stared down at his son, then raised his hand and dealt him such a blow that Caylen cried out. The cry fuelled the fires of hatred and frustration and Caswallon struck him again and again, dizzying him with the constant blows to the head. When the fury was passed, Caylen slumped back in his corner and sobbed. The druid came across to him and bathed his face in a pungent liquid, murmuring the secret words as he went, and calming the boy.

The pain passed away, but not the hurt. Caylen decided that he must leave the village and flee to his own special land, the land across the water where none of the village dared go. He rose after dusk, when the sky was twilight, and the forest quiet and dark. He ran lightly through the compound and entered the woods. But he had been seen and the slight, fleet-footed shape of Fergus came after him. 'I heard the beating,' he said. 'What are you going to do?'

'Go across the water and live there. It's the only safe place. The druid says I must be killed in a special way.'

Fergus grimaced. 'Horrible, horrible. I've seen a special killing. It's horrible.'

'I don't need you to tell me that,' said Caylen grimly. But he was glad of Fergus's company. It made his life bearable, if not attractive.

'I'll come with you across the rapids,' said Fergus, and in the twilight Caylen saw that his friend was crying.

'I'm glad,' he said. 'You'll be quite safe. And when we're old enough we'll raid the village and take all the women. That'll teach them.'

'Good idea,' said Fergus, wiping a hand across his eyes. Caylen could see that he was genuinely frightened; having made the declaration to cross the river he could not now back down. He was sad for his friend, so brutally treated by the village, and now he was frightened by his own rashness.

Someone stirred in the lodge, and it would not be long before Caswallon noticed that his demon son had slipped away. Before tonight this would not have bothered Caswallon; but Caylen suspected that from now until they killed him they would not allow him to leave the village. It was now or never, his last chance for freedom and peace.

They ran along the boar track, passing the thicket with hardly a glance, though they could hear the animal in there, snuffling sleepily. Without thinking they burst into Old Stone Hollow, where the small wooden temple had been built. Caylen stopped, catching his breath in surprise. His intention had been to go to the river, and unthinkingly he had come here. Fergus had just followed blindly, not really wanting to leave his friend, not wanting to think too hard about what was happening.

It was quite dark, but the moon, a fairly full crescent shining through the thin, wind-blown clouds, gave light enough to show what the stranger had made of his shrine. He had built it high, and wide, and he had built it all about the stone in the centre of the glade. A wide open doorway led to the interior. Inside, on the floor, Caylen could see a small tallow candle burning, its yellow flame hardly enough to show him anything of the interior. The wood of the shrine was fresh hewn, and expertly chopped into thick and lasting planks; it was bright, not yet dulled either by pitch or rain. Nor, yet, was it carved, though it would surely be represented with the symbols of the gods before the stranger was finished.

Caylen, feeling now that he had little to lose by any action, boldly stepped up to the shrine, and with Fergus following nervously behind, ducked and stepped inside.

The stone rose from the ground; the floor was still rough grass and the remnants of thorn and nettle. It smelled rich and earthy inside, though near to the door there was the pleasant tang of fresh cut wood, and near to the stone the musty smell of a tomb, the rock and all the grey dust that clung to it exuding an odour that was unmistakable.

On the stone rested a spear, and Caylen picked up the candle so he could see it better. This, he was quite sure, was what had been in the protective hides. A spear, a precious weapon, which the horn-helmeted man had carried from his land of kings, hiding it from his pursuers, rescuing it, no doubt, from those who would abuse whatever power it contained.

Unhesitatingly, Caylen picked it up and hefted it; nearly a man's height in length, it was carved from some dark wood, but lightweight, and the shaft was inscribed with rings and patterns from the very tip of it, to where the wide, leaf-shaped blade was fastened to the wood. The blade was iron, grooved and serrated, and on each side of the central rib there had been scratched an eye. It was the spear not of a warrior, for no warrior's spear could be so small, but of a child, a child's weapon, as deadly as any flung on the field of battle; the spear of a prince.

A hand reached past Caylen and took the weapon from him. He started with shock, gasped and turned to find himself looking up at the heavy features of the stranger, who stood with Fergus gripped firmly in his other hand, the palm stifling any sound his friend would have made.

Caylen tried to run, but the man used the spear to block his path. Then he let go of Fergus and smiled at them both, raised finger to lip and gently placed the spear back on the stone. He dropped to a crouch, now looking up at Caylen, who was a tall lad. His wild eyes were bright in the candle flame, his teeth gleaming white, his breath sweet as if he had been eating berries. His hands on their arms were strong, gentle. He looked from one to the other, but mostly he looked at Caylen. 'Come,' he said. 'Tell. Come, tell,' and as he spoke he rose, picked up the spear, and led the way from the shrine. Caylen hesitated only a second before following, and Fergus (with one compulsive grip of Caylen's hand, the squeeze of reassurance from one who is mortally afraid) also went after the stranger, out into the moonlit night, and into the forest.

They walked at first, Caylen keeping pace well along the overgrown animal trackways and through the bramble thickets. Fergus straggled a little, but every time they passed through a clearing in the forest he raced after Caylen and caught up, tugging once on Caylen's shirt to let him know that he was there again. The horned man, his helmet gleaming in the moonlight, paced on, and Caylen sensed he walked faster and faster, his cloak billowing behind him, catching on branches and rose thorns, but always tearing free. Suddenly the man made a sound, like a bird cry, but deep and long. He raised his arms, still walking, and then said a single word, 'Follow,' before he began to run.

Caylen ran too, and Fergus after, and they both watched as the horned man leapt high, then crouched low, twisting and turning as he ran until he became a source of crashing, stumbling, shrieking darkness, his helmet, the metal of his belt and necklet, flashing and glinting in the stray silvery light. His cloak swirled about his body, at times a wing, at other times a flowing robe of darkness, and always he ran, the forest loud with the sound of his noisy progress, and with the laughing and shrieking of the boys who followed.

Caylen joined the spirit of the wild dance, leaping and twisting himself, and staggering as he landed, struggling to keep his balance. He struck branches and tree trunks, and waved his hands through bracken and fern, and through the tight clumps of flower-covered moss; he felt everything in the forest, letting its night dew soak his clothes and his skin. The horned man jumped higher, touching branches more than twice his height above the ground, and at times, as he ran, Caylen thought he was actually walking through the air. He seemed to leap into the forest sky, and run through the very foliage, before gently landing and spinning round, his arms outstretched, his body whirling in the gloom.

At length, breathless, they came to the river, and Caylen realised that this was the illusory river that guarded his private haven. The man had led their merry dance in a wide and perfect circle. They were nearly back to the glade, but here he stopped, and reached to brush water across his perspiring face.

Caylen could almost hear the rushing of the waters, but the sound was on the edge of a waking dream, a distant sound, unreal, unrealised. He looked at Fergus and Fergus smiled brightly, not speaking the words but almost saying that he would still wade across with Caylen the next time Caylen went.

The stranger had torn a strip of bark from a tree and now he pushed his dagger twice through the wood and made two holes for eyes. This woody mask he held against his face, peering at the boys through the slits. He spoke to them, then, in their own tongue, in perfect language, his voice thrilling them with its texture of sound, soft yet deep, a woodland sound, a wild sound. While he was speaking he kept the mask of bark to obscure his lips from them.

'Like you, she was young, full of the wonder of life. A girl of looks so fair that she caught every heart, was sought by every king in our king-ridden lands. Her name was Rianna. She was not the daughter of a king, but she was a princess, and it was a king who guarded her when his own soldiers razed her village and killed her kinfolk. A compassionate king, who looked at her, the tender child, and never again raised his army against the land. He built a great stone fort, a great city, and shaped a great people. Rianna was the queen of that people, not in rank, but in heart. No man or woman could tear their gaze away from young Rianna. She was a child born to be a queen, a queen born to be a goddess.

'But the great land, and the great king, fell to a dark host from the north, men without feeling, men of war. They swept through the hills and took the stone fort, putting to the sword all who were noble born. They chased families into the hills and marshes, subjugated every town that had known this time of peace. This is the way in our land, and it was the king who was wrong, to be unprepared and unwilling for battle. And yet, none of his people condemned him, even though he had betrayed them. One thing kept hope alive. Rianna. Rianna had escaped the butchery, and the conquest, for on the eve of the invasion a man had come out of the night, out of the earth itself, and taken this girl from the fort. He fled with her to safety. She took only her clothes and her childish spear, the weapon fashioned to mark her adoption to the royal line.

'This is how it ended for her: in a valley, mist-obscured and deep, where not even animals ventured for fear of the emptiness of the place, there went Rianna, carried by the man of earth, that clay man who had come from the grave to take her beyond the savagery of the northern host. But another went there, one of that dark host who knew too well the danger of the girl should she return a queen and draw the people to her. He found her, and before her guardian could act he turned her own spear against her, twisted the blade in her heart to ensure the deed was properly done. But the earth one, before she died, had magicked her spirit to the very blade of the spear. Here she lives, and while she lives so the people of her land live in hope. Here is that spear. Here is Rianna. I have brought her to these lands, for safety, to erect a shrine to her, to protect her for the years while the storm passes in our country.'

The horn-helmeted man ceased to speak, and he moved the mask from his face. Caylen saw the tears there, and watched in silence as he raised the blade of the spear to his lips and kissed it, kissed the iron that had once tasted so bitter with the blood of his young queen. He looked towards the river, then raised the mask again. 'This place I saw in a dream. There are other places like it, concealed, guarded. Powerful places. But this is the one that was shown to me.'

Caylen watched him, curiously disturbed. In the same way that when he stared at the rapids he saw only the calm waters that were the truth of the river, so, as the man had spoken, the flowery, sad words of the story had fallen away. Caylen had been aware of the flowing, rather pleasant tongue that was the stranger's natural language; he had been aware, too, of starker, less romantic images: a cold, bleak stone fort, a desolate, windswept land, a bloody battle, a complacent warlord, gruesome slaughter, an escape into the night for a screaming, terrified girl, a mercenary sent to kill her, and achieving that end swiftly and brutally.

Time had passed more swiftly than the reason could accommodate, and Caylen was startled as he heard the first chorus of forest birds, marking their awareness of the dawn. Turning, where he sat, he saw the glow of light in the east, above the trees, above the water. Fergus was sleeping, and Caylen grinned as he saw this. The horned man seemed to smile as well, and Caylen turned to him.

'Then you claim to be a magician, a man with dark powers, who uses them for good purpose...'

The stranger inclined his head. From behind the mask he said, 'Dark powers? Not I. None save the power to run without stopping.'

'But why did you come to save her, why ride from the earth? Who were you that you felt the need to save her, to bring her to safety?'

The horn-helmeted man laughed, but the laugh was bitter, not amused. 'You have misunderstood me, young Caylen. I was the man who followed them. I was the man who killed her.'

Five men came, like braying hounds, down from the ridgeway and through the glades of the forest until they found the village, following the spoor of the man they pursued. They talked for an hour with Caswallon, but the village was weak in arm when compared to such seasoned soldiers as these. Caswallon spoke firmly with one of the strangers who had a smattering of the village tongue; at no time did he bend to any whim of theirs, but from the outset it was clear that he would not hinder them in their quest. Each of these men was sturdily built, and heavily bearded; long hair, bound back with green linen, was ungreased and fair; they carried round shields on their backs, made of alder and beaten leather, rimmed and studded with iron; they carried fighting spears and throwing darts, and each wore a sword so richly decked and turned with gold and silver on the pommel that there could be no question of their nobility, and their warrior status.

Caylen saw them as he walked, unsuspecting, from the woods. Even as he turned to run back to the Old Stone Hollow, and the shrine of Rianna, so Caswallon was pointing the way to the glade, and the chase was on.

The guardian of the shrine heard Caylen coming towards

him, through the thickets, along the old boar trail. The boar had gone two nights previous, foraging in some other part of the forest, perhaps tired of the activity in its vicinity. When Caylen burst from the trees, breathless, screaming, the man already had the spear, and was fleeing towards the river.

The horned man stumbled, and Caylen caught up with him. As he helped the man to his feet the sound of the pursuers was loud, close; they seemed to know every twist, every turn that their prey had taken. They had followed him across two lands and an ocean, and they had not put a step wrong.

The man staggered to his feet, but his leg was twisted. Wild-eyed, fearful for more than his own life, he thrust the spear at Caylen, pressed it on him, and said to him to run swiftly and cross the illusory river. 'It will be safe there, safe with you. Guard her, Caylen. Guard little Rianna, as I have guarded her since I took her life.'

Caylen turned and fled, the man staggering after him, but slow, now, and crying with the pain.

Caylen found the river. Clutching the spear he ran through the shallows, emerging cold and wet on the other side. He could hear the sound of children, approaching along the far bank, but all he could see for the moment was his friend Fergus, racing towards him, tears in his eyes.

Then the horned man came through the trees, cried loud and fell to his knees, his face racked with pain, yet smiling. For a moment he stared at Caylen, met the boy's gaze and raised his arm towards him. 'Rianna,' he cried, and again, and again, until a fair-haired man stepped up behind him and dealt him a blow with his sword that cut through the bone and sinew of his neck. The sound of Rianna's name died on his lips, spilled to the wind as his dark blood spilled to the earth.

Caylen ran away from the river, towards the woods, and

felt the prickle of fear, fear of the unknown, fear of the magic force that worked here to keep this place of hill and woodland guarded from mortal man. He squatted then, the spear held across his lap, his hand resting lightly on the vibrant, cold metal blade. The hunters prowled up and down the water's edge, but none ventured to try and cross; all were taken by that vital fear, induced not just by the violent waters, but by the wall of magic that was dazzling their senses.

They called to him in their strange, flowing tongue, and sometimes they were begging him, and sometimes they were threatening him. Domnorix and four of the village boys were crouched some yards away, afraid to come closer to the strangers. Only Fergus stood with them, watching Caylen through wide, fear-filled eyes.

Caylen clutched the spear tighter. He was safe here, and so was the memory of Rianna, and he would never go home, never in all his life. He would stay here and hide her, and he knew that when the time was right some man of earth would come for her, to take her home.

But how could he have forgotten Fergus? Fergus, who had been his friend through the weeks of hatred and the months of pain; the young boy who had counted his friendship with Caylen so high that he had determined to break through his fear of magic, and follow Caylen across the river. 'Wait for me!' he cried, and Caylen came to his feet in shock, and with a great cry of, 'No, go back! No, Fergus, not now, not now!' he raced to the water's edge, the spear gripped tightly in his right hand.

'I'm coming with you,' shouted Fergus, confusion painting panic on his face. He was ankle deep in water. 'I said I would come with you, and I shall. I'm not afraid, Caylen, I'm truly not. I shall cross the river and we'll run together, just like we always said.'

He came deeper, and the river rose against him. There

were tears in his eyes, and the fear on his face grew visibly as he went towards the rapids. Behind him the men who had killed the stranger watched in silence, fearful for the boy's life, yet puzzled as to the courage of the lad, a courage that made him risk his life in the foulest waters they had ever seen.

'Oh Fergus, no ... you *must* listen to me. Go back, *please*! Don't follow me, don't give me away ... go *back*!'

But the boy came on, fear overwhelming reason, courage and the pursuit of honour blinding him to Caylen's panic, deafening him to the terrible words of his lifelong friend.

And Caylen saw that soon every man on the bank would know the illusion for what it was, and then there would be no haven for the boy, no place of refuge for the ghost of a girl that might one day spirit the life back into a people as distant and as alien from Caylen as were his own people.

And yet to stop him, to stop him ... such a decision, such a tearing of heart and mind, to sacrifice his friend for the sake of freedom. And even then it was not resolved. For how could Caylen save himself except by using that same spear which was a symbol of peace, of compassion, everything that might make a nation great in greater times than these?

Even as he thought this, the stark images of the stranger's story became vivid again — the killing, the running, the cold-blooded murder of an hysterical girl by a man paid to do the deed, a man whom remorse, some awareness of the beauty he had killed, had changed from mercenary to guardian. He had run with the spear, creating in his own mind the legend of a supernatural presence in the blade. But there had been no magic, Caylen realised. The spear, a cold, dead weapon, was all that remained of her. It was the horn-helmeted man himself who threatened those who pursued him, a man with a memory that needed obliteration. He was dead now, and the weapon was just a weapon. Whether it was destroyed or not, whatever memory of Rianna remained in that far-off land would be the same. This spear, or another, what mattered were the words that spoke the legend.

Old enough to grasp this simple truth, Caylen was too young to realise that the illusion of hope was best served by less complex symbols. He flung the spear back to the far shore and watched as the strangers destroyed it. By the time Fergus had waded to the nearer shore, face aglow with triumph, the strangers were gone.

Caylen turned from his friend and walked quickly away from the river.

Time of the Tree

Tundra

All the signs are that the long winter is coming to an end. The great expanse of tundra, with its strange bluish hue, still shimmers and shivers in the biting winds of early morning. Yet to the south, below the swollen hill with its deep lake, Omphalos, there are signs of green. I am certain that a fresh and vibrant grassland is beginning to spread across the land. From my fixed point of observation it is hard to see so far to the south, but sometimes the cold and stinking winter wind, the stench of the foetid tundra, is replaced by the scent of new meadow and flowers.

I no longer feel so cold.

As the day advances, the tundra dries slightly. Its slick shine fades and I imagine that the air is filled with the buzz and hum of insects. The lake, though, remains full. I have abandoned my game of emptying the pool. The water is rich and ripe. If I could see clearly enough I imagine it would be scum-laden, dense green growth feeding on the stagnancy and the dead life that falls into its murky depths. But as further evidence of the coming of the spring, there are rushes at its borders. Again, seeing in any detail is hard, but the tiny growth is evident, and the wind from the caves in the north takes the tall rush-heads and blows them wildly.

I suspect that a migrating bird-life has already settled at the shores of the lake. To see this would be too much to ask. One thing, though: I have sensed a darker movement on the swathes of tundra, in the shallow valley between the Pectoralis hills. Since this is closer to my point of observation, and my lens is more effective, I can say with certainty that the shadow is *separate* from the land. It may be nothing more than that: the shadow of cloud. But I think I may have witnessed the first migrating herds of some cervine species, perhaps reindeer. My dreams are often filled with the eerie cries of the wild.

The Birch Accession

The first forests are beginning to appear, and with their growth they bring with them a strange sense of pain, and a new sense of time. I realise how much I have been living by the time of the empty plains; those centuries of silence, save for wind and water. How slow that time has been, following the retreat of the ice from the north of the land. Time has been as stagnant as the standing water on the peat. Time has been in suspension. Sunrise to moonrise, the land has whispered and shivered, and dried and become wet, but there has been no change. The bursting life of the forests had remained asleep below the skin of the land, the cells as quiescent as the marshes.

Suddenly that life has begun to erupt, and now at last I begin to live by the time of the tree. Now there is *vibrancy*. There is a *swaying* feel to time, a wind-whipped and vital sense to time, as if time is being *stretched*. It hurts. It brings a strange discomfort to the land, and to the perception of the land. The forests strain to grow. The trunks thicken and reach out and up. They spread, they expand, they quiver at their tips, and in their roots. They suck the memory of the forest from the cells below the land, draining the genetic code, feeding hungrily upon the mass of silent chromosomes.

Silent? Silent no longer. *The tree in the man*, that forgotten part of history, that unacknowledged presence of the primordial plant, has taken root upon the man himself, and the swathes of birch begin to spread. They are in the Pelvic Valleys; they cover the slanting length of the Man-Hill. They reach across the Thigh-Ridge Mountains, down almost as far as the sharp Bone-Ridge of the Calf-Plain. They reach across the Pelvic Plain as far as the lake in the navel itself. Omphalos.

The water gleams with a new and enticing light. It is silver, now. The smell has gone. When I dip my finger into its depths, the taste on my tongue is sweet. All foulness flees before the surging spread of birch and spruce.

I am living by the time of the tree, yet I have no conception of how that time compares with the time of the world outside the land. For me — observing from the north — a day in the passage of the world seems to be . . . how *many* years, I wonder, in the time of the forest? Two hundred? Three?

Each day the winter woodland stretches north, surrounding the lake, covering the hollow of the Solar Plexan Plain, spreading up the Sternal Valley and over the Pectoral Hills, even surmounting the flattened mounds (like the barrows of some forgotten civilisation) which top the knolls. Hard to see, these winter trees, yet their roots are like spikes into the flesh. They are like thorns. It is a thin forest, this, struggling for life in the cold air, consuming and taming the acid land that for so many centuries has covered the skin.

It is a long time since the ice retreated. Sharing time between that of the tree and that of the land, I begin to forget the accident that precipitated the glacial movement. The Ice Age is fading from memory, just as is the event that started all of this. I struggle sometimes to hold these unreal images in my mind: the 'cold room' at my University; the high-tech lab where I worked on Primordial-DNA, those sequences of genes that retain memories of the primaeval environment, codons that contain bizarre echoes of a world long since lost; the sudden alarm in the cold room; my own surprise, then slip; the slamming of the door across my body; the sensation of ice building up across my face and shoulders.

I know I was dragged from the freezer room, but I have no memory of that rescue. I know that ice had coated me from head to chest, a millimetre of ice, which slowly melted, a glacial advance that was thwarted but which somehow activated the hidden memory in the land below . . .

This is how the forest came into being. It is unbelievable to contemplate. Now, though, all that matters is how it will develop!

The Coming of the Wildwood

A milder climate envelops the microcosm of the land. Outside my room it is cool and raining, a typical early summer's day. Inside, a dry, pleasant heat occupies that volume of space that has become the woodland microenvironment. The birch forest still occupies the high land to the north, but there is much pine, now, and its scent is *wonderful*.

The bristles cover me completely. They itch where they enter the softer skin below my chin. When the hairs of the human land dropped away they left me sensitive. I wonder, sometimes, if the trees have grown from the follicles of the hairs themselves. The tree-line ceases below my lips, but spreads slightly to cover my cheeks. My crown is quite bald, and is cold to touch, as if winter still holds sway there. When I brush my cheeks I wonder what damage I might be doing, but through the lens and in the mirror I can see the proud stands of pine, still extant after the brutalising touch of the Giant, on whose corpse this world is starting to evolve.

The tallest tree rises from the skin by no more than a fraction of a millimetre. In profusion, though, they make my body shimmer green; the canopy is dense. But around the lake of Omphalos, and below, across the Pelvic Valleys and the stump of the Man-Hill, down across the ridges of the thigh, the forest has become softer; it gleams like velvet, and is gentle on the fingers. The wildwood, the deciduous forests, have replaced the scrawny evergreens. Now the trees crowd and fight for light. The elms and the oaks can be clearly seen. Round the Omphalos great stands of alder crush together. Over the flank of the land a stand of hazel has a touch like emery paper. The Scar of the Appendix is covered by a coarse thornwood, painful to the touch despite the minuteness of its size. Where the land grows colder, above the Line of the Eleventh Rib, a battle for supremacy occurs between the pine and the gleaming ranks of hornbeam and ash. But the wildwood is spreading north, and in the lower valleys it is dense and rich, the trees tall, some of them giants, rising higher than the canopy, the great standard oaks and elms that grow where destruction has occurred around them.

Sometimes I pass my hands above the land, letting darkness fall. I pour water over my skin; great floods. I moisten myself for comfort: showers of rain, sometimes storms. I wonder how the forest perceives these actions. I have ceased to sweat. My skin exudes the scent of sap, of undergrowth. I am in no discomfort. The creases in my body flow with water, small streams, rivulets, supplying the root needs of the body forest. I eat from cans. It is sometimes painful to walk. There is no growth upon my back, which remains a pristine, unconquered realm. When I lie, I lie supine, legs apart, arms to the sides, and in this position, like some slumbering god, there is a wonderful sense of peace.

Below my chin, below the relaxed face of the world, a

terrible struggle for the light ensues. The sounds of the wildwood occupy my mind, the cries, the screams, the creaking, twisting growth of trees. These are the first sounds of the world. Among them I can hear the shrieks of birds, the howls of wolves, furtive movement in the dense, dank undergrowth.

At dawn all is silent; from Glottal Mound to the Phalangeal Rocks in the far south, the land is a rich and vibrant green, catching the light. The land rises and falls with peaceful steadiness, a gentle wind blowing across the virgin swathes of forest, catching the branches of the giant elms that reach so high above the canopy; watchtowers; guardians of the hidden world below.

The Elm Decline

There is a smell of woodsmoke in the air, just a hint, penetrating the pungency of the rotting food and unwashed bedding of my room. I am used to the smells of my own decay, and so this new odour is sharp to my nostrils. In the slanting sunlight from the world outside I can see the tiny drifting coils of smoke.

Pain! Sharp pain, that takes me by surprise. It comes from the area around the lake. Through the lens I can see that it is from here that smoke is unfurling. The pain is a tiny focus, like a pinprick, a prick of fire.

There can be only one explanation . . . *The forest is being cleared!*

It is hard to make out detail. The clearing is being made on the shores of the lake, which is brim full and brilliant in the dawn sun. Now I have a decision to make: do I extinguish the fires? But that might risk destroying whatever or whoever is burning the forest. If I leave them, however, they may bring barrenness to the land.

There are other fires. As the day in the real world advances, so coils of smoke drift up from my right groin, from an area in the dense mass of wildwood over my belly, and from two locations on my right leg. The pricks of pain are tolerable. I wonder if the communities are related?

They have begun to fell the great elms. Through the lens I see one of them topple, a tiny shard, no bigger than a trimmed whisker, yet majestic for all of that. I suppose that whoever is clearing the wildwood is also building the first settlement lodges.

The First Totems

In my dreams I can hear the ululations and strange chanting of the forest clearers. At night, they sing and dance around the smouldering fires of the day's clearing. They are dressed in the raw, red hides and heads of beasts. The people by the lake are the Clan of the Spiny Boar. Their youngest and fittest male wears the carcase of an immense wild pig; his body is impaled with sharpened tusks, and he dances and screams his invocation to this ancestral creature. They are called *Kalokki*. In my dreams I feel the presence of forty or more individuals. They shelter in lodges made of bone and wood, whose roofs are branches sealed with lake mud. They hunt at dawn. They are building crude boats and I sense that the mist-covered lake is a place of worship to them. They drift across the lake and throw huge wooden carvings into the water. It is here, when they are on the surface of Omphalos itself, that the sound of their voices is loudest.

All sensation of hunger seems to have gone from me. The forest itself sustains me, drawing nutrients from the air, from the light. A fine mist fills my room. The sounds of the outside world have faded. There is no light, no heat, save that which streams through the window.

Creatures move on the floor of the room, among the debris. Sometimes I hear thunder, but it passes: people at the door, friends perhaps, or colleagues, but I cannot move to answer them. Time is too precious. The body forest is too fragile.

The dwellers by the lake fight for survival. A Wolf Clan has attacked them. I dreamt the pain. They burned a lodge, then were driven away. But the Wolf Clan is hungry and restless and hovers in the wildwood, watching the clearing on the lake shore, biding its time.

All of this is in the form of glimpses, half seen, half felt scenes in my restless sleep. During the night the land heaves. No doubt it disturbs the Kalokki.

If only I could communicate with them. If only their words could be heard ...

I pass my hand over the lake. I hold the lens toward them, peering through its rounded glass. Perhaps they see my face. What manner of heavens do they witness, I wonder.

The Temple Builders

Over the weeks, dust and dirt, the grime of my room, has settled on the cleared land, and fallen in and among the dense wildwood.

I have been sensing the deliberate movement of these great stones for some time now. The Clans are organised. They drag the monolithic particles of dust from the forest edges and shape them, working by day, by night, chanting to the instruction of the priests. They are erecting the massive sarsens into a great circle, on the very edge of the lake itself. A mightier stone circle has never been created. By fire they dance within its ring. Travellers have come south, from the cold woods of the Sternal Valley, to witness this great construction. They have journeyed north, from the now-desert land below the Plain of the Patella. Even in those dark communities, where the forest flanks the edge of the world itself, even there they have heard of the Great Stone Ring of Omphalos. And in my dreams I hear the crying and the singing of votive dedication. They are singing up the gods. They are dancing up the powers of the forest, and the lake. And they are planning a sacrifice . . .

Ritual Sacrifice

Her scream of fear alerts me. In a half dreaming, half waking state, I feel the pounding of her heart. It is dawn in their world, and a heavy, cold mist hangs above the clearing and the lake. Bone horns are being sounded, and bone rattles, and skin drums, beaten with a ferocity that makes the whole lakeside shiver with anticipation of the murder to come.

She is very young. They bind her with willow wood, arms behind her back, legs crooked behind her, tied to staffs of wood. Her neck is bent back. Creeper and ivy entwine her body. She is trussed and helpless, laid in a boat on a bed of leaves. They strike out into the water. A young male voice calls for her. The drums thunder, the bone horns blast eerily through the dawn fog. Water laps at rushes against the shores of Omphalos.

Soon I sense the stillness in the centre of the waters. Something is whirled around a head, and it creates a strange humming sound. Voices drone. The girl struggles, but is held so tightly that she cannot even flex a finger. A thong is tied around her neck. It tightens and her heart screams for help. The blood thunders in her head. A blow by oakwood to her skull and the water is reddened and enriched. She is placed, face down in the lake, and sinks by weight of stone to its bottom.

I feel her enter me. She is sublime in her dying. She trails her life vertically in a coil of warmth to the surface of the lake where the small boats bob and the priests watch for signs of acceptance of their sacrifice. When she settles in the debris of the navel, her eyes are closed. Something slips into my mind.

She seems to have risen from the corpse and is running...

Journey to the Underworld

Where is she running?

She seems to be in a moondream wood. The trees gleam white. They grow from the roof and sides of a great winding passage. Where is she?

The moonforest is all around her. She expands to drift among the moonbright branches. Moonlakes glimmer. She floats above them. She travels through the caverns of the underworld, round the spiral tracks, into and out of dark caves, where the land heaves and shifts, like the pulsing body of some great creature.

And in this way she spreads to the north, to the place where the ice had once lain so heavily upon the rock, scouring the soil, feeding upon the seeds below. Here is a place where the trees hum and fire burns, great streaks and flashes of fire, running through the roots and branches. Here is a fire-forest where the voices of the ancestors sing loudly, where faces peer, bodies shift, and a whole world of image echoes through the crowded wood.

She is in the fire. She spreads herself to sink into the fire-trees. She spreads through the forest, stretched thin, touching the coils of the seeds, where the forest co-exists with the creatures of the past, where the codes snap and fold, twist and replicate.

Our Lady of the Chromosomes

The Boar is threatened by the Wolf.

She means that war between the Clans is killing her people. She drifts there, in the seed-codes of the forest, enveloped by nucleotides, fed by ribosomes, arrows of RNA winging from her spectral presence. What do I say to her?

MAKE A FIRE THAT IS HOTTER THAN YOU KNOW. MELT ROCK. SOME ROCKS FLOW. WHEN THE ROCK FLOWS IT WILL HARDEN INTO BRIGHTNESS AND CAN BE SHAPED INTO A BETTER KNIFE THAN BONE OR FLINT.

I must return to the lodges of the Boar. I must return from the wasteland. I must take this vision back to them.

How do I help her? She is a ghost in the man-forest-machine that lies upon its bed in a rancid, rotting room. The forest above has disposed of her, thinking her dead. The forest within is a place of spectres and she is a ghost.

FLOW INTO THE RIVERS OF THE WORLD. FLOW INTO THE SAP. I WILL GUIDE YOU BACK THROUGH THE CAVERNS. I WILL GUIDE YOU THROUGH THE CAVERN IN THE MAN-HILL. YOU WILL RETURN TO YOUR PEOPLE IN A GREAT FLOOD FROM THE OTHERWORLD.

She dissolves from the roots of the fire-forest, flows into the blood, and drifts into the channels that drain sap from the tissues and the organs of the land. I feel the building of the flood, and the rising of the Man-Hill. By the lake, the Kalokki watch the skies in awe. An immense shadow is across the land. The cave that opens at the head of the mountain gushes. The lake is filled. The Kalokki escape the flood by climbing the giant trees. The naked goddess returns to them, ghostly white, floating above the waves, bringing her vision from the dark and fiery wastes of Hell.

Anger of the Gods

I have slept for too long. Much time has passed, and I wake to great pangs of hunger. And yet hunger had been banished from me, and thirst too. The forest had sustained me, as all forests sustain the land. Why, then, hunger now?

The Kalokki have gone. They ceased to be in my dreams. With their passing came a time of resting and sleep. I have let the world on my body grow and flourish in its own, inexorable way.

Now, though, there is a great itching. I am swathed with the cracking, crusty signs of eczema. My skin seeps a thick and stinking exudate. What has happened? Great swathes of the Pectoralis Valley, and the Belly Plain, are barren. The wildwood exists in patches only, small, amoebic spreads of green in the orange and yellow wasteland. And even through that greenness I can see great lines and tracks of red, roadways, perhaps, although what travels along them is too small to see.

A heavy smog hangs above the groin. It is an impenetrable smoke, oily to the nostrils, and sulphurous ... The air of the room is filled with a distant buzzing, like machines. Even as I watch I see the edge of the forest shrink a little. The itching increases. There is pain in my bowels.

Someone is drilling deeply into the world. Seeking for what, I wonder?

I have slept too long. I have let too much time pass. I cannot stand the itching. Whilst the pain of the Kalokki's forest clearing had been a pin prick, suffered to allow them to establish their presence upon the world, this eczema is too much.

I smear and squeeze, scratch and smudge. I blow away

the smoke from above my groin. I scratch at the soreness
and the hard scabs of the cities. A black and tarry residue
fills my finger-nails and I scrape it out between my teeth.

Soon there is stillness on the land. And peace.

I will have to find food for a while, but the grasslands will
soon be re-established upon the world. Then, the first seeds
of the forest will germinate and the wildwood will return.

And once more I will dream by an ancient light.

Magic Man

Crouched in the mouth of the shrine-cave, One Eye, the painter, shivered as black storm clouds skated overhead and the wind whipped down from the northern ice-wastes to plague the grasslands with its bitter touch.

The tribe should be gathered together before the darkening skies could loose their volleys of rain and lightning; then they would huddle into the cliff wall and wail and moan their misery. When the rains passed the women would come, invading the shrine-cave and screeching at One Eye because he had not stopped their soaking.

He squatted, looking out across the grasslands to the man-high rushes that waved and danced in the biting winds. Stupid women, he thought. Stupid, stupid women. They should understand that his drawings were for the spirit of the hunt, not for their own comfort. They should be pleased when their men brought home bison, deer and, increasingly, the reindeer that strayed from the snows of the northern valleys.

'One Eye!' hailed a child's voice. One Eye looked down to where a small boy scrambled up the slopes of the cliff towards the cave.

'Go away, child. Go away!' shouted the old man angrily. But he knew it would be no use. The boy, brown and dusty, crawled into the mouth of the cave and squatted there, breathing heavily. The sight of One Eye's empty eye socket staring at him no longer perturbed the would-be painter as once it had.

'I want to draw.'

One Eye let his grey hair fall over his one good eye, clenched his mouth tight in an obstinate gesture of annoyance and shook his head. 'Go away, child. Wait for the hunters.' Outside, the wind howled against the cliff and the dark sky grew perceptibly darker.

'I want to *draw*.' Big eyes stared at the old man, childish features, open, honest. The boy was filthy; his hair was lank and filled with grass from his earlier romping. 'I'm tired of making *these*!' He threw the inaccurately made axe from his hand and it clattered down the slopes to land heavily among the women below. One of them looked up and shouted angrily. She was cleaning a skin and had blood up to her elbows. The fire around which the group squatted burned low, and charred bones and wood poked blackly from the pile of ashes. An adolescent girl, underdeveloped and sulky, prodded the dying embers with a spear. The boy, in the shrine-cave above, was angry. 'I want to draw a bear. One Eye, please! Let me draw a bear, please?'

'Look,' snapped One Eye, pointing. Black shapes against the grey sky, the hunters returned. They walked slowly, spears clutched tightly, animals slung over their shoulders. Leading them came He Who Carries a Red Spear, his scarred face angry, bleeding from gashes on his cheeks. He waved his red-ochred spear at the group and the women stood, shouting their greeting. Red Spear, thought One Eye. How I wish a bison would get *you*. The tall hunter strode into the camp. He had a deer slung over his shoulders. His fur and leather tunic had been torn away and he walked naked, black hair coating his body from neck to toe, acting as a fur in itself. He was unaware of the death-thoughts of the old man above his head. Today he had not killed a bison. Today the hunt, for him, had failed. He was angry.

The men dropped their kills close in to the cliff wall and then dragged the skins and axe baskets from where they had been distributed about the fire. The women crouched against the sloping wall of the overhang and giggled as the hunters covered them with taut skins, making rough and ready tents against the cliff face. They hammered special narrow points through the skins to hold them down, propping them up in the middle with spears. The skies darkened, distant thunder rolled and the grass whispered and sang as it bowed to the groaning winds.

'Go down,' snapped One Eye. 'Into the tents with you. Leave me in peace, brat. Leave me.'

The boy darted back into the cave and laughed as One Eye screeched with surprise. He waited for the painter to come after him, but One Eye had fallen suddenly quiet, watching the slope below him. There was the sound of someone climbing up to the cave. The boy crawled to the entrance and began to shake as he saw his father coming up towards them.

He Who Carries a Red Spear crouched beside One Eye and snarled. 'What happened to your magic today, old man? Why didn't I kill a bison, uh?' Mouth stretched back into a hideous grin, eyes narrowed, Red Spear struck fear into the heart of One Eye. One Eye cowered back, but a hairy and powerful hand reached out and grabbed him by the neck. The hunter snarled, increased the grip until the bone nearly snapped, then released the painter, looking back into the cave.

'Drawings! Paintings!' Hard eyes turned on One Eye. 'Only *spears* kill animals, you old fool. Spears, stones . . . and *these*.' He held up his bare hands, the fingers curved with the power they possessed. 'I have killed bison with my bare hands, old man. I have twisted their heads, their necks twice the thickness of my body. I have twisted them until the bones snapped and splintered, the muscle tore and the blood spurted over my body. Drawings! Pah!' He smashed One Eye across the face. 'If it weren't that *they*, stupid fools, believed this nonsense, I should kill you. I should break your neck between my thumb and forefinger. I should snap you in two and throw your useless body to the scavengers. I should give you to the Grunts to devour.'

'My paintings,' mumbled One Eye, 'show the hunt. They protect you. They give you power over beasts.'

Red Spear laughed. Behind him a hunter climbed into the cave and touched the bitter man on his arm. 'Your wife is singing for you, Red Spear. She is eager.'

He Who Carries a Red Spear grunted. 'Hear that, old man? My wife sings for me. All the women in this tribe I could have if I so desired. Because I am the best hunter!' He pounded his naked chest and inched towards the painter, the stench of his body strong and sickening. 'I hunt with weapons, not with paintings . . .' And as he said it he clutched dirt in his hand and threw it over the ochred walls. He took his son by the arm and threw him down the slope before him, sliding down and disappearing into the tent.

The other hunter looked sympathetically at the old man. 'He killed no bison today. You must forgive his anger.'

One Eye shook his head. 'He is the half-kin of a Grunt — that explains much to me.' Thunder crashed nearby and the black skies flared with the streaking lightning to the north. 'He sneers at the magic of my paintings,' One Eye murmured. 'The paintings bring luck, they bring kills.' He looked at the blood-smeared hunter. 'They don't say *who* shall make the kills. They bring kills to the tribe. He *must* understand that . . .' He looked away. 'But I fear he never shall — he cannot understand, just as none of his father's spore can understand, that beasts and men have spirit.'

The hunter nodded. 'He only understands *kill*. And soon, One Eye, he will kill *you*. Be careful.' The hunter turned to go. One Eye reached out a hand and stopped him. 'How many kills today? How many?'

'Ten,' said the hunter. 'More than enough. But we shall go into the herds again tomorrow.' His eyes flickered beyond One Eye to the cave walls. 'Paint us luck, old man.'

Then he was gone and the storm broke, rain sheeting

down and drumming off the taut animal hide tents below. The women moaned and cried and the men laughed and loved. One Eye sat in the darkness at the back of the cave and thought over and over of the ten dead animals he had drawn the day before.

Always it was the same. The number he drew was the number killed. And yet, he felt he had no real power. But one day *true* power over the paintings would come to one of the tribe, and then, from here to the seas in the south, beasts would be at the mercy of men — and men, perhaps, would no longer be at the mercy of the moving ice wastes to the north. The tribe must never die, One Eye realised, not with the inherent power it contained, hidden somewhere in the bodies of its hunters.

With the breaking of the sun above the eastern horizon the boy came scrambling up to the shrine-cave. He found One Eye hard at work, drawing the shapes of hunters with a charred-wood stick.

'Why don't you draw them full?' asked the boy as he sat, absorbed by the growing picture of a hunt. 'Why so thin? And black?'

'Men are black,' said One Eye mysteriously. Then, pausing to glance at the boy, he lifted his eyes to the cave entrance. 'Inside . . . we are thin and shallow.' His eyes dropped to the boy. 'Beasts kill other beasts in a *natural* way. Man kills beasts with more than his hands. He uses spears and slings, and traps and nets. Man is more than a beast, but he has lost his goodness.' The old man looked at the coloured portraits of his animals. 'They have goodness and they are full and whole. But man is shallow.' He turned to the boy. 'That is why I draw the hunters thin.'

The boy did not understand the old man's talk. But he knew he was right. And when he, too, was a great painter, magicking animals into the traps, on to the spears, of his brothers, he would follow the tradition of One Eye.

'Let me draw. Please. Let me draw.'

One Eye muttered with annoyance but he passed the yellow and red pastes he had made that dawn. The boy dipped his fingers in and smudged the wall with yellow. With his left hand he used a charred stick to draw an outline around the smear. He remembered how the ribs of the bison stood out and he marked them in. He drew the legs and the way the muscles rippled with the power of the beast. One Eye concentrated on his own drawing, but again and again he glanced at the bison taking form at the hands of the boy. Finally he stopped and watched as his small apprentice drew a spear, thrust deep into the neck of the animal.

'It is good,' said One Eye. 'You have skill.' He smiled.

The boy beamed. 'May I draw a bear? Please?'

One Eye shook his head with finality. 'The bear is a hunter of man and he must never be drawn in the shrine-cave — he is beyond our magic.'

'A bear is just a beast,' argued the boy.

'The bear is *more* than a beast. We must only draw animals that *run* from man. Never those that attack him. Do you understand?'

The boy nodded, bitterly disappointed.

'Old man!' He Who Carries a Red Spear crawled into the cave. 'How many kills today, old man?' he sneered. 'You, down!' He looked angrily at his son and the boy left the cave. Red Spear raised a fist at One Eye. 'If I find him here too many more times I shall begin to think you are stopping him from being a great hunter, like me. I shall be forced to kill you . . . hear me?'

He was gone before One Eye could answer. The hunters gathered together their spears and furs and walked from the cliff towards the plains where they would find bison and deer, and smaller animals to eat on the way home.

The boy, grinning, scampered back into the cave. One Eye ignored him, staying in the mouth of the cave, watching the distant figures and wishing he was going with them. Behind him he heard charred wood scrape on the wall. He ignored it. The scraping ended and there was silence. Eventually One Eye looked round. 'What do you draw, child?'

The boy said nothing but continued working. One Eye crawled over to him.

What he saw made him gasp with horror. He slapped the boy away from the wall and reached out to try to erase the fully drawn man from the painting of the hunt.

'No!' cried the boy, but he fell silent. The ochre was too dry; only the arm was erased. One Eye sat and looked at the man with one arm. Then he looked at the bison with the spear in its neck. Then he looked at the boy and his face was white beneath its dusty covering.

When the hunt returned, one of the hunters was dead. They carried him in, stretched on a fur and laid across two poles. His left arm had been severed above the elbow and he had bled to death. One Eye heard the word 'bear' and he knew what had happened. Then his eye wandered to the kills of the day, to the bison still with a spear-head buried deep in its neck.

The women mourned that night. The hunter lay in a shallow pit at the edge of the camp and his wife rubbed ochre into his ice-cold body, groaning and keening with every pass of her hand across her dead husband's strong chest. The fire burned high in the still night and the faces of the children and women who squatted around its warmth were solemn and drawn. Red Spear sat apart from the tribe and time and again his eyes flicked up to the dark cave mouth, where he could see One Eye squatting, watching the gathering.

Suddenly he jumped towards the fire and kicked the burning wood. 'What happened to your magic today, old man?' he screamed up at the figure in the cave. 'Why didn't you save him?' He turned to look at the dead hunter, and there were tears in his eyes, but tears of frustrated anger rather than sorrow. 'He was a *good* hunter. He killed many beasts for the tribe. Nearly as many as me!' Swinging round he raised one clenched fist. 'If you can work magic, old man, why couldn't you have saved him?'

A hunter jumped up from the ring and caught Red Spear by the shoulders. 'One Eye cannot know the unknowable! He merely spirits the animals into our traps!'

He Who Carries a Red Spear flung the man aside. 'He does *nothing*!' he cried angrily. 'We no longer need One Eye and his stupid paintings.'

As he ran through the circle of seated hunters and their women, a hand reached out and tripped him. Furious, he twisted on the ground and reached for the woman who had insulted him. He stared into the calm face of his wife, brown eyes insolently watching him. 'Leave the old man,' she said softly. 'He does no harm and many here believe him possessed of magical power. Why waste energy and respect on killing the useless?' Her smile was the last straw in the cooling of angry fires in the hunter. He leered up at One Eye and shook his fist. But he spared him.

A wood torch burned in the shrine-cave. A wolf pack howled somewhere on the tundra, and as the night progressed so the sound of their baying moved farther away to the south. One Eye was oblivious of their cries, he was oblivious of the howling wind and the sound of rocks falling outside the cave mouth. He worked on his picture. The boy knelt beside him, watching. He had begged to be allowed to draw, but One Eye had said no, not yet. The anticipation kept the boy silent and now he watched as animals took shape upon the cave wall, overlapping animals that had been drawn in the past, but that did not matter because those animals had been killed and now they were just ochre smears, without meaning, without consequence.

As he worked, One Eye repeatedly glanced at the attentive boy. There was a strange look in the old man's eye, an expression of awe.

Well into the night, when the boy was beginning to yawn, One Eye sat back and handed the charred wood to his apprentice. Wrapped tightly in animals' skins, still One Eye shivered as he began to guide the boy's hand in the drawing of men on the wall scheme. The boy, with small furs round his shoulders, hardly noticed his chill. He was enthralled.

'Draw . . . your father, here. That's right,' breathed One Eye as the boy's hand traced the pin shape. 'Arch the back, that's right. Throw the arms up . . . no, don't stop . . .'

'I don't understand . . .' murmured the boy.

'See,' explained the painter, 'see how he scares the bison into the traps – see, they run before him and he has no weapon. Red Spear *needs* no weapon.'

The boy nodded, satisfied, and continued the picture.

'Tomorrow,' said One Eye, 'I shall accompany the hunters. That surprises you?' His whiskered face broke into a smile at the expression on the boy's face. 'I used to be a hunter, long years ago. This hunt . . . see how it spreads across the wall. Tomorrow will be a *great* day for the tribe. There will be *many* kills . . .' His voice trailed off. 'Many kills. And I wish to join in on such an occasion. Now.' He guided the tiny hand to the wall. 'Draw me, here. See, standing *behind* your father. Draw me a spear. See how I throw it at the bison your father scares . . .'

Pin shapes took form upon the grey wall. The boy, excited, creating, drew as the old man instructed him. When it was finished he was beaming. One Eye was satisfied. The boy settled against the cave wall and One

Eye looked at the picture of the hunt and dreamt of the kill that would be least expected tomorrow. And by the boy's magic hand it had been depicted so! He closed his eyes and slept.

When he was sure One Eye was asleep, the boy crawled to the wall and picked up the charred wood. Carefully he drew more hunters. But he was tired and they didn't form as they should – they were too small, too stooped ... like Grunts. Uncomfortable at what he had done, the boy smudged them away. They remained, shadows on the wall.

A fine mist hung over the grasslands as the hunters, followed by One Eye, moved off towards the grazing herds. There was the feel of snow in the air and the women had wrapped up tightly and insisted that their men put thicker skins around their shoulders, binding them into place with extra thongs. Silently, feet trudging across the cold, dewy grass, the band moved off, away from the cliff, and was swallowed by the mist.

The boy watched them go, and when they were out of sight he scrambled up to the shrine-cave and disappeared inside.

The hunters had moved silently across the mist-covered land for several hours when the first feelings of unease came to them. The fog was dense and they could see only a few paces around them. They grouped together and Red Spear motioned them to silence. One Eye watched him, breath steamy with the cold, as he pricked his ears to the low winds and listened.

There was movement all around them, shuffling, the sound of invisible feet padding across the frozen grass.

A stir went through the hunters. Was it Grunts, was it the squat and ugly men who lived in the shadow of the moving snow walls? Clutching his red-ochred spear, Red

Spear motioned for the band to move on. One Eye, his own spear held ready to stab, followed, but now his eye was wide and watchful, his heart thundering. Grunts were unpredictable. They might pass by or they might attack. There was no way of telling.

The hunters spread out as they neared where they could hear the bison grazing. Still the wall of white separated them from anything that lay ahead or behind. Each hunter was a vague grey shape as he moved through the mist, spear held ready, head turning from side to side. Behind them the sound of creatures grew louder.

'Look!' breathed a hunter close to One Eye. His voice caused them all to stop and turn. What they saw made them howl with fear . . .

White shapes, running through the mist. Ghosts, shimmering and flickering in and out of vision. Ghostly spears held high, mouths open in a silent war cry. Grunts, spirits, the spirits of the ugly creatures that had died at the hands of the hunters over the years gone by.

One Eye ran. He ran hard and he ran fast and he was aware of the other hunters running beside him, breathing fast and hard, eyes wide and constantly turning to regard the apparitions that pursued them.

All at once they were among the bison. Their approach, not the most silent, had been muffled by the heavy air, and the animals were taken by surprise. The huge black head of a male bison looked upon One Eye, and the creature stood, for a moment, stunned. Then it snorted and turned, lumbering heavily away and out of sight.

From his left there came a scream and the sound of flesh torn. One Eye moved over and saw the shape of a hunter spreadeagled on the ground, being gored by the huge leader of the herd. And beyond the sight of the man threshing against the veil of death, the white ghosts of dead men came running through the fog.

One Eye staggered backwards, his head turning frantically from right to left as he searched for a way out. The silent shapes were all around and now he could see their tiny eyes, black orbs in the white of their spectral faces. Their bodies were naked, squat and heavy, their brows huge and jutting, giving them a peculiarly blind look.

They ran through the fog, and ghostly spears flew from ghostly hands, sailing silently past the hunters and vanishing as they flew from sight. The bison snorted and raged and ran amok among the terrified hunters. One Eye came up to the steaming flank of a small animal, and when it saw him it turned on him. He stabbed at it with his spear and felt the point sink into flesh. The bison roared and thundered away. One Eye stood alone, surrounded by the shifting wall of white. He could see the ghosts moving closer, their bodies swaying as they neared him, mouths open, screaming their silent screams of anger.

Behind him he heard the thunderous approach of a large bison and ran to avoid its maddened gallop. Distantly, a hunter screamed, and the scream was cut off as his life ended at the razor tip of a bison's horn. One Eye ran towards the scream, and as he ran he passed bewildered and terrified hunters who stood still, now, almost ready for the death that was overtaking so many of the tribe.

A bison snorted close by and lumbered out of the mist, its flank catching One Eye and sending him sprawling. As he staggered to his feet a new sound reached his ears. He paused, on his knees, breath coming short and painfully. There was blood on his tightly wrapped fur breeches, but he felt no pain.

A throaty growl, like no sound he had ever heard in his life. And it was near, very near. A hunter screamed, and it was a scream of terror, not of death. One Eye jumped to his feet and crouched with his spear-point centred unwaveringly on where he could hear something big and cumbersome moving in his direction. The hunter who had screamed so loudly came running out of the mist, face smeared with blood and sweat, eyes open, mouth open. He carried no spear and ran past One Eye as if he hadn't seen him. He disappeared into the mist and a moment later One Eye heard a grunt and a gasp. The hunter reappeared, staggering, a red-ochred spear thrust deep into his belly.

The roar of the animal that approached came again, nearer. One Eye backed away carefully and his eye searched the fog for any sign of what it could be. The ghosts appeared again, dancing towards the lost hunters, and now they seemed almost . . . taunting.

Behind One Eye there was the snort of a bison. He swung round but could see nothing. As he walked forward, ears keened for the sound of the beast behind him, he came to He Who Carries a Red Spear, standing with his back to One Eye, crouched and waiting for the bison to charge. One Eye could hear its snorting in the mist and realised that any moment it would tear into sight and Red Spear would either kill or be killed. But that could not be! Remembering how he had drawn the hunt, how he had spirited Red Spear's life into his own hands, One Eye edged forward.

He raised his spear high and threw it with all his strength at the centre of the leader's naked back. Red Spear screamed and arched over backwards, and One Eye saw two feet of spear protruding beyond the other man's chest. Naked, blood pumping down his glistening limbs, Red Spear lay dead at One Eye's feet.

A shadow fell across One Eye and, as he was about to defile the body with his hand axe, he froze. Straightening up, he became aware of the heavy breathing close behind, of the rumbling roar of a wild beast . . .

'NO!' he screamed, flinging his body round and staring up at the black creature which towered over him. 'NO!' His hands flew to his face and he staggered backwards, tripping over the body of Red Spear. The monster lumbered forward, rising on to its hind legs and reaching down with its front paws. Claws as long as a man's forearm glinted and slashed down at the painter, caught him just below his throat and ripped downwards, disembowelling him and throwing him twenty feet across the grass with a last jerk of a bloodstained paw. One Eye had a brief second to assess his killer. It was like a bear, yet so unlike a bear – the muzzle was long and twisted, the teeth too long, too white. The eyes, huge, staring, were the eyes of a dead man, not a living beast. And the fur . . . the fur was unlike the fur of any bear that One Eye had ever seen. It was black and red! Black and red!

Then there was only pain for One Eye, intense pain and the sight of his own blood and entrails seeping on to the grass. Followed by the blackness of death.

Crouched in the mouth of the shrine-cave, the boy shivered as black storm clouds skated overhead and icy winds whipped down from the northern ice-wastes, driving the mist before them, clearing the grasslands to the eyes of the desperate women.

The hunters were late, very late. The women were frightened and they wailed. The fire burned high as a beacon for their men, and soon, tired and bloody, spearless and without a single kill between them, the few hunters that survived returned to the camp.

The boy crawled into the deep of the cave where a small fire burned and illuminated the drawings and paintings on the wall. He reached out a hand and traced the figure of his father, moving his finger to the outline of One Eye poised, ready to throw his spear. Then the boy's fingers traced the great bear that reared up on its hind legs, body finished with red ochre and black charred wood, teeth pearly white with root gum . . . It had taken him a long time to draw and he was proud of it. That it was not a realistic likeness of one of the bears which roamed the tundra he was not to know, for he had never seen a bear.

He settled back and regarded the towering shape as it seemed to swoop on the little figure of One Eye, dancing among the smudges of the hunters the boy had drawn earlier.

The boy laughed as he reached out and smudged away the black drawing of his teacher. One Eye would not be coming back. The tribe had a new painter, now.

Scarrowfell

1

In the darkness, in the world of nightmares, she sang a little song. In her small room, behind the drawn curtains, her voice was tiny, frightened, murmuring in her sleep:

> Oh dear mother what a fool I've been . . .
> Three young fellows . . . came courting me . . .
> Two were blind . . . the other couldn't see . . .
> Oh dear mother what a fool I've been . . .

Tuneless, timeless, endlessly repeated through the night, soon the nightmare grew worse and she tossed below the bedclothes, and called out for her mother, louder and louder, *Mother! Mother!* until she sat up, gasping for breath and screaming.

'Hush, child. I'm here. I'm beside you. Quiet now. Go back to sleep.'

'I'm frightened, I'm frightened. I had a terrible dream . . .'

Her mother hugged her, sitting on the bed, rocking back and forward, wiping the sweat and the fear from her face. 'Hush . . . hush, now. It was just a dream . . .'

'The blind man,' she whispered, and shook as she thought of it so that her mother's grip grew firmer, more reassuring. 'The blind man. He's coming again . . .'

'Just a dream, child. There's nothing to be frightened of. Close your eyes and go back to sleep, now. Sleep, child . . . sleep. There. That's better.'

Still she sang, her voice very small, very faint as she drifted into sleep again. '*Three young fellows . . . came courting me . . . one was blind . . . one was grim . . . one had creatures following him . . .*'

'Hush, child . . .'

Waking with a scream: 'Don't let him take me!'

2

None of the children in the village really knew one festival day from another. They were *told* what to wear, and *told* what to do, and *told* what to eat, and when the formalities were over they would rush away to their secret camp, in the shadow of the old church.

Lord's Eve was different, however. Lord's Eve was the best of the festivals. Even if you didn't know that a particular day would be Lord's Eve day, the signs of it were in the village.

Ginny knew the signs by heart. Mr Box, at the Red Hart, would spend a day cursing as he tried to erect a tarpaulin in the beer garden of his public house. Here, the ox would be slaughtered and roasted, and the dancers would rest. At the other end of the village Mr Ellis, who ran the Bush and Briar, would put empty firkins outside his premises for use as seats. The village always filled with strangers during the dancing festivals, and those strangers drank a lot of beer.

The church was made ready too. Mr and Mrs Morton, usually never to be seen out of their Sunday best, would dress in overalls and invade the cold church with brooms, brushes and buckets. Mr Ashcroft, the priest, would garner late summer flowers, and mow and trim the graveyard. This was a dangerous time for the children, since he would come perilously close to their camp, which lay just beyond the iron gate that led from the churchyard. Here, between the church and the earth walls of the old Saxon fort — in whose ring the village had been built — was a tree-filled ditch, and the children's camp had been made there. The small clearing was close to the path which led from the church, through the earth wall and out onto the farmland beyond.

There were other signs of the coming festival day, however, signs from outside the small community. First, the village always seemed to be in shadow. Yet distantly, beyond the cloud cover, the land seemed to glow with eerie light. Ginny would stand on the high wall by the church, looking through the crowded trees that covered the ring of earthworks, staring to where the late summer sun was setting its fire on Whitley Nook and Middleburn. Movement on the high valley walls above these villages was just the movement of clouds, and the fields seemed to flow with brightness.

The wind always blew from Whitley Nook towards Ginny's own village, Scarrowfell. And on that wind, the day before the festival of Lord's Eve, you could always hear the music of the dancers as they wended their way along the riverside, through and round the underwood, stopping at each village to collect more dancers, more musicians (more hangovers) ready for the final triumph at Scarrowfell itself.

The music drifted in and out of hearing, a hint of a violin, the distant clatter of sticks, the faint jingle of the small bells with which the dancers decked out their clothes. When the wind gusted, whole phrases of the jaunty music could be heard, a rhythmic sound, with the voices of the dancers clearly audible as they sang the words of the folk songs.

Ginny, precariously balanced on the top of the wall, would jig with those brief rhythms, hair blowing in the wind, one hand holding on to the dry bark of an ash branch.

The dancers were coming; all the Oozers and the Pikers and the Thackers, coming to join the village's Scarrowmen;

and it was therefore the day of Lord's Eve: the birds would flock and wheel in the skies, and flee along the valley too. And sure enough, as she looked up into the dark sky over Scarrowfell, the birds were there, thousands of them, making streaming, spiral patterns in the gloom. Their calling was inaudible. But after a while they streaked north, away from the bells, away from the sticks, away from the calling of the Oozers.

Kevin Symonds came racing round the grey-walled church, glanced up and saw Ginny and made frantic beckoning motions. 'Gargoyle!' he hissed, and Ginny almost shouted as she lost her balance before jumping down from the wall. 'Gargoyle' was their name for Mr Ashcroft, the priest. A second after they had squeezed beyond the iron gate and into the cover of the scrub the old man appeared. But he was busy placing rillygills – knots of flowers and wheat stalks – on each gravestone and didn't notice the panting children just beyond the cleared ground, where the thorn and ash thicket was so dense.

Ginny led the way into the clear space among the trees in the ditch. She stepped up the shallow earth slope to peer away into the field beyond, and the circle of tall elms that grew at its centre. A scruffy brown mare – probably one of Mr Box's drays – was kicking and stamping across the field, a white foal stumbling behind it. She was so intent on watching the foal that she didn't notice Mr Box himself, emerging from the ring of trees. He was dressed in his filthy blue apron but walked briskly across the field towards the church, his gaze fixed on the ground. Every few paces he stopped and fiddled with something on the grass. He never looked up, walked through the gap in the earthworks – the old gateway – and passed, by doing so, within arm's reach of where Ginny and Kevin breathlessly crouched. He walked straight ahead, stopped at the iron gate, inspected it, then moved off around the perimeter of the church, out of sight and out of mind.

'They've got the ox on the spit already,' Kevin said, his eyes bright, his lips wet with anticipation. 'It's the biggest ever. There's going to be at least two slices each.'

'Yuck!' said Ginny, feeling sick at the thought of the grey, greasy meat.

'And they've started the bonfire. You've got to come and see it. It's going to be huge! My mother said it's going to be the biggest yet.'

'I usually scrub potatoes for fire-baking,' Ginny said. 'But I haven't been asked this year.'

'Sounds as if you've been lucky,' Kevin said. 'It's going to be a really big day. The biggest ever. It's *very* special.'

Ginny whispered, 'My mother's been behaving strangely. And I've had a nightmare . . .'

Kevin watched her, but when no further information or explanation seemed to be forthcoming he said, '*My* mother says this is the most special Lord's Eve of them all. An old man's coming back to the village.'

'What old man?'

'His name's Cyric, or something. He left a long time ago, but he's coming back and everybody's very excited. They've been trying to get him to come back for ages, but he's only just agreed. That's what Mum says, anyway.'

'What's so special about him?'

Kevin wasn't sure. 'She said he's a war hero, or something.'

'Ugh!' Ginny wrinkled her nose in distaste. 'He's probably going to be all scarred.'

'Or blind!' Kevin agreed, and Ginny's face turned white.

A third child wriggled through the iron gate and skidded into the depression between the earth walls, dabbing at his face where he had scratched himself on a thorn.

'The tower!' Mick Ferguson whispered excitedly, ignoring his graze. 'While old Gargoyle is busy placing the rillygills.'

They moved cautiously back to the churchyard, then crawled towards the porch on their bellies, screened from the priest by the high earth mounds over each grave. Ducking behind the memorial stones — but not touching them — they at last found sanctuary in the freshly polished, gloomy interior. Despite the cloud-cover, light was bright from the stained-glass windows. The altar, with its flowers, looked somehow different from normal. The Mortons were cleaning the font, over in the side chapel; a bucket of well-water stood by ready to fill the bowl. They were talking as they worked and didn't hear the furtive movement of the three children.

Kevin led the way up the spiralling, footworn steps and out onto the cone-shaped roof of the church's tower. They averted their eyes from the grotesque stone figure that guarded the doorway, although Kevin reached out and touched its muzzle as he always did.

'For luck,' he said. 'My mother says the stone likes affection as much as the rest of us. If it doesn't get attention it'll prowl the village at night and choose someone to kill.'

'Shut *up*,' Ginny said emphatically, watching the monster from the corner of her eye.

Michael laughed. 'Don't be such a scaredy-hare,' he said and reached out to jingle the small bell that hung around her neck. Her ghost bell.

'It's a small bell and that's a big stone demon,' Ginny pointed out nervously. Why was she so apprehensive this time, she wondered? She had often been up here and had never doubted that the stone creature, like all demons, could not attack the faithful, and that bells, books and candles were protection enough from the devil's minions.

The nightmare had upset her. She remembered Mary

Whitelock's nightmare a few years before – almost the same dream, confided in the gang as they had feasted on stolen pie in their camp. She had not really liked Mary. All the same, when she had suddenly disappeared, after the festival, Ginny had felt very confused . . .

No! Put the thought from your mind, she told herself sternly. And brazenly she turned and stared at the medieval monstrosity that sat watching the door to the church below. And she laughed, because it was only frightening when you *imagined* how awful it was. In fact, it looked faintly ludicrous, with its gaping V-shaped mouth and lolling tongue, and its pointed ears, and skull cheeks, and its one great staring eye . . . and one gouged socket . . .

Below them, the village was a bustle of activity. In the small square in front of the church the bonfire was rising to truly monumental heights. Other children were helping to heap the faggots and broken furniture onto the pile. A large stake in its centre was being used to hold the bulk of wood in place.

Away from where this fire would blaze, a large area was being roped off for the dancing. The gate from the church had already been decked with wild roses and lilies. The Gargoyle himself always led the congregation from the Lord's Eve service out to the festivities in the village. Ginny giggled at the remembered sight of him, dark cassock held up to his knees, white bony legs kicking and hopping along with the Oozers and the local Scarrowmen, a single bell on each ankle making him look as silly as she always thought he was.

At the far end of the village, the road from Whitley Nook cut through the south wall of the old earth fort and snaked between the cluster of tiled cottages where Ginny herself lived. Here, two small fires had been set alight, one on each side of the old track. The smoke was shattered by the wind from the valley. On the church tower the three children enjoyed the smell of the burning wood.

And as they listened they heard the music of the dancers, even now winding their way between Middleburn and Whitley Nook.

They would be here tomorrow. Sunlight picked out the white of their costumes, miles distant; and the flash of swords flung high in the air.

The Oozers were coming. The Thackers were coming. The wild dance was coming.

3

She awoke with a shock, screaming out, then becoming instantly silent as she stared at the empty room and the bright daylight creeping in above the heavy curtains of her room.

What time was it? Her head was full of music, the jangle of bells, the beating of the skin drums, the clash and thud of the wooden hobby poles. But now, outside, all was silent.

She swung her legs from the bed, then began to shiver as unpleasant echoes of that haunting song, the nightmare song, came back to her.

She found that she could not resist muttering the words that stalked her sleeping hours. It was as if she had to repeat the sinister refrain before her body would allow her to move again, to become a child again . . .

'Oh dear mother . . . three young men . . . two were blind . . . the third couldn't see . . . oh mother, oh mother . . . grim-eyed courtiers . . . blind men dancing . . . creatures followed him, creatures dancing . . .'

The church bell rang out, a low repeated toll, five strikes and then a sixth strike, a moment delayed from the rest.

Five strikes for the Lord, and one for the fire! It couldn't *be that time. It couldn't!* Why hadn't mother come in to wake her?

Ginny ran to the curtains and pulled them back, staring out into the deserted street, crawling up onto the window ledge so that she could lean through the top window and stare up towards the square.

It was full of motionless figures. And distantly she could hear the chanting of the congregation. The Lord's Eve service had already started. Started! The procession had already passed the house, and she had been aware of it only in her half sleep!

She screeched with indignation, fleeing from her bedroom into the small sitting room. By the clock on the mantelpiece she learned that it was after midday. She had slept... she had slept fifteen hours!

She grabbed her clothes, pulled them on, not bothering with her hair but making a token effort to polish her shoes. It was Lord's Eve. She *had* to be smart today. She couldn't find her bell necklace. She had on a flowered dress and red shoes. She pulled a pink woollen cardigan over her shoulders, grabbed at her frilly hat, stared at it, then tossed it behind the hat rack... and fled from the house.

She ran up the road to the church square, following the path that, earlier, the column of dancers must have taken. She felt tears in her eyes, tears of dismay, and anger, and irritation. Every year she watched the procession from her garden. *Every year!* Why hadn't mother *woken* her?

She loved the procession, the ranks of dancers in their white coats and black hats, the ribbons, the flowers, the bells tied to ankle, knee and elbow, the men on the hobby horses, the fools with their pigs' bladders on sticks, the women in their swirling skirts, the Thackers, the Pikermen, the Oozers, the black-faced Scarrowmen... all of them came through the smouldering fires at the south gate, each turning and making the sign of peace before jigging and hopping on along the road, keeping time to the beat of the drum, the melancholy whine of the violin, the sad chords of the accordion, the trill of the whistles.

And she had missed it! She had slept! She had remained in the world of nightmares, where the shadowy blind pursued her...

As she ran she *screamed* her frustration!

She stopped at the edge of the square, catching her breath, looking for Kevin, or Mick, or any others of the small gang that had their camp in the earthen walls of the old fort. She couldn't see them. She cast her gaze over the ranks of silent dancers. They were spread out across the square, lines of men and women facing the lych-gate and the open door of the church. They stood in absolute silence. They hardly seemed to breathe. Sometimes, as she brushed past one of them, working her way towards the church where Gargoyle's voice was an irritating drone in the distance, sometimes a tambourine would rattle, or an accordion would sigh a weary note. The man holding it would glance and smile at her, but she knew better than to disturb the Scarrowmen when the voice was speaking from the church.

She passed under the rose and lily gate, ducked her head and made the sign of peace, then scampered into the porch and edged towards the gloomy, crowded interior.

The priest was at the end of his sermon, the usual boring sermon for the feast day.

'We have made a pledge,' Mr Ashcroft was intoning. 'A pledge of belief in a life after death, a pledge of belief in a God which is greater than humankind itself...'

She could see Kevin, standing and fidgeting between his parents, four pews forward in the church. Of Michael there was no sign. And where was mother? At the front, almost certainly...

'We believe in the resurrection of the Dead, and in a time

of atonement. We have made a pledge with those who have died before us, a pledge that we will be reunited with them in the greater Glory of our Lord.'

'*Kevin!*' Ginny hissed. Kevin fidgeted. The priest droned on.

'We have pledged all of this, and we believe all of this. Our time in the physical realm is a time of trial, a time of testing, a testing of our honour and our belief, a belief that those who have gone are not gone at all, but merely waiting to be rejoined with us . . .'

'*Kevin!*' she called again. '*Kevin!*'

Her voice carried too loudly. Kevin glanced round and went white. His mother glanced round too, then jerked his attention back to the service, using a lock of his curly hair as her means. His cry was audible to the Gargoyle himself, who hesitated before concluding,

'This is the brightness behind the feast of the Lord's Eve. Think not of the Death, but of the Life our Lord will bring us.'

Where was her mother?

Before she could think further someone's hand tugged at her shoulder, pulling her back towards the porch of the church. She protested and glanced up, and the solemn face of Mr Box stared down at her. 'Go outside, Ginny,' he said. 'Go outside, now.'

Inside, the congregation had begun to recite the Lord's Prayer.

He pushed her towards the rose gate, beyond which the Oozers and Scarrowmen waited for the service to end. She walked forlornly towards them, and as she passed the man who stood closest to her she struck at his tambourine. The tambours jangled loudly in the still, summer square.

The man didn't move. She stood and stared defiantly at him, then struck his tambourine again.

'Why don't you *dance*?' she shrieked at him. When he

ignored her, she shouted again. 'Why don't you make *music*? Make *music*! Dance in the square! Dance!' Her voice was a shrill cry.

4

There was no twilight. Late afternoon became dark night in a few minutes and a torch was put to the fire, which flared dramatically and silenced all activity. Glowing embers streamed into a starless sky and the village square became choking with the sweet smell of burning wood. The last smells of the roasted ox were banished and in the grounds of the Red Lion the skeleton of the beast was hacked apart. A few pence each for the bones with their meaty fragments. In front of the Bush and Briar Mr Ellis swept up a hundredweight of broken glass. Mick Ferguson led a gang of children, chasing an empty barrel down the street, towards the south gate where the fires still smouldered.

For a while the dancing had ceased. People thronged about the fire. Voices were raised in the public houses as dancers and tourists alike struggled to get in fresh orders for ale. A sort of controlled chaos ruled the day, and in the centre of it: the fire, its light picking out stark details on the grey church and the muddy green in the square. Beyond the sheer rise of the church tower, all was darkness, although men in white shirts and black hats walked through the lych-gate and rounded the church, talking quietly, dispersing as they re-emerged into the square. Here, they again picked up sticks, or tambourines, or other instruments of music and mock war.

Ginny wandered among them.

She could not find her mother.

And she knew that something was wrong, very wrong indeed.

It came as scant reassurance when a bearded youth called to the Morrismen again, and twelve sturdy men, all of them strangers to Scarrowfell, jangled their way from the Bush and Briar to the dancing square. There was laughter, tomfoolery with the cudgels they carried, and the whining practice notes of the accordion. Then they filed into a formation, jiggled and rang their legs, laughed once more and began to hop to the rhythm of a dance called the *Cuckoo's Nest*. A man in a baggy, flowery dress and with a big frilly bonnet on his head sang the rude words. The singer was a source of great amusement since he sported a bushy, ginger beard. He wore an apron over the frock and every so often lifted the pinny to expose a long red balloon strapped between his legs. It had eyes and eyelashes painted on its tip. The audience roared each time he did this.

As Ginny moved through the fair towards the new focus of activity, Mick Ferguson approached her, grinned, and went into his Hunchback of Notre Dame routine, stooping forward, limping in an exaggerated fashion and crying, 'The bells. The bells. The jingling bells . . .'

'Mick . . .' Ginny began, but he had already flashed her a nervous grin and bolted off into the confusing movement of the crowds, running towards the fire and finally disappearing into the gloom beyond.

Ginny watched him go. Mick, she thought . . . Mick . . . why?

What was going on?

She walked towards the dancers and the bearded singer and Kevin turned round nervously and nodded to her. The man sang:

'Some like a girl who is pretty in the face
And some like a girl who is slender in the waist . . .'

'I missed the procession,' Ginny said. 'I wasn't woken up.'

Kevin stared at her, looking unhappy. He said, 'My mother told me not to talk to you ...'

She waited, but Kevin had decided that discretion was the better part of cowardice.

'Why not?' she asked, disturbed by the statement.

'You're being denied,' the boy murmured.

Ginny was shocked. 'Why am I being denied? Why me?'

Kevin shrugged. Then a strange look came into his eyes, a horrible look, a man's look, arrogant, sneering.

The man in the hideous dress sang:

'But give me a girl who will wriggle and will twist
Each time I slap my hand upon her cuckoo's nest ...'

Kevin backed away from Ginny, making 'cuckoo' sounds.

'It's a *rude* song,' Ginny said.

Kevin taunted, '*You're* a cuckoo. *You're* a cuckoo ...'

'I don't know what it means,' Ginny said, bewildered.

'Cuckoo, cuckoo, cuckoo,' Kevin mocked, then jabbed her in the groin. He cackled horribly then raced away towards the blazing bonfire. Ginny had tears in her eyes, but her anger was so intense that the tears dried. She glared at the singer, still not completely aware of what was going on except that she knew the song was rude because of the guffaws of the adult men in the watching circle. After a moment she slipped away towards the church.

She stood within the lych-gate watching the flickering of the fire, the highlit faces of the crowds, the restless movement, the jigging and hopping ... hearing the laughter, and the music, and the distant wind that was fanning the fire and making the flames bend violently and dangerously towards the south. And she wondered where, in all this chaos, her mother might have been.

Mother had been so supportive to her, so gentle, so kind. During the nights when the nightmare had been a terrible presence in the house by the old road, where Ginny had lived since her real parents had died in the fire, during those terrible nights the Mother had been so comforting. Ginny had come to think of her as her own mother, and all grief, all sadness had faded fast.

Where *was* the Mother? Where *was* she?

She saw Mr Box, walking slowly through the crowds, a baked potato in one hand and a glass of beer in the other. She ran to him and tugged at his jacket. He nearly choked on his potato and glanced round urgently, but soon her voice reached him and, although he frowned, he stooped down towards her. He threw the remnants of his potato away and placed his glass upon the ground.

'Hello Ginny . . .' He sounded anxious.

'Mr Box. Have you seen mother?'

Again he looked uncomfortable. His kindly face was a mask of worry. His moustache twitched. 'You see . . . she's getting the reception ready.'

'What reception?' Ginny asked.

'Why, for Cyric, of course. The war hero. The man who's coming back to us. He's finally agreed to return to the village. He was supposed to have come three years ago, but he couldn't make it.'

'I don't care about him,' she said. 'Where's mother?'

Mr Box placed a comforting hand on her shoulder and shook his head. 'Can't you just play, child? It's what you're supposed to do. I'm just a pub landlord. I'm not part of the Organisers. You shouldn't even . . . you shouldn't even be *talking* to me.'

'I'm being denied,' she whispered.

'Yes,' he said sadly.

'Where's mother?' Ginny demanded.

'An important man is coming back to the village,' Mr Box said. 'A great hero. It's a great honour for us . . . and . . .' He hesitated before adding, in a quiet voice, 'And what he's bringing with him is going to make this village more secure . . .'

'What *is* he bringing?' Ginny asked.

'A certain knowledge,' Mr Box said, then shrugged. 'It's all I know. Like all the villages around here, we've had to fight to keep out the invader, and it's a hard fight. We've all been waiting a long time for this night, Ginny. A very long time. We made a pledge to this man. A long time ago, when he fought to save the village. Tonight we're honouring that pledge. All of us have a part to play . . .'

Ginny frowned. 'Me too?' she asked, and was astonished to see large tears roll down each of Mr Box's cheeks.

'Of course you too, Ginny,' he whispered, and seemed to choke on the words. 'I'm surprised that you don't know. I always thought the children knew. But the way these things work . . . the rules . . .' He shook his head again. 'I'm not privileged to know.'

'But why is everybody being so horrible to me?' Ginny said.

'Who's everybody?'

'Mick,' she said. 'And Kevin. He called me a cuckoo . . .'

Mr Box smiled. 'They're just teasing you. They've been told something of what will happen this evening and they're jealous.'

He straightened up and took a deep breath. Ginny watched him, his words sinking in slowly. She said, 'Do you mean what will happen to *me* this evening?'

He nodded. 'You've been *chosen*,' he whispered to her. 'When your parents were killed, the Mother was sent to you to prepare you. Your role tonight is a very special one. Ginny, that's all I know. Now go and play, child. Please . . .'

He looked suddenly away from her, towards the dancers. Ginny followed his gaze. Five men, two of whom she recognised, were watching them. One of them shook his head slightly and Mr Box's touch on Ginny's shoulder went away. A woman walked towards them, her dress covered with real flowers, her face like stone. Mr Box pushed Ginny away roughly. As she scampered for safety she could hear the sound of the woman's blows to Mr Box's cheek.

5

The fire burned. Long after it should have been a glowing pile of embers, it was still burning. Long after they should have been exhausted, the Scarrowmen danced. The night air was chill, heavy with smoke, bright with drifting sparks. It echoed to the jingle of bells and the clatter of cudgels. Voices drifted on the wind; there was laughter; and round and round the Morrismen danced.

Soon they had formed into a great circle, stretched around the fire and jigging fast and furious to the strident, endless rhythm of drums and violin. All the village danced, and the strangers too, men and women in anoraks and sweaters, and children in woolly hats, and teenagers in jeans and leather jackets, all of them mixed up with the white-and-black clothed Oozers, Pikers, Thackers and the rest.

Round the burning fire, stumbling and tottering, shrieking with mirth as a whole segment of the ring tumbled in the mud. Round and round.

The bells, the hammering of sticks, the whine of the violin, the Jack Tar sound of the accordion.

And at ten o'clock the whole wild dance stopped.

Silence.

The men reached down and took the bells from their legs, cast them into the fire. The cudgels, too, were thrown onto the flames. The violins were shattered on the ground, the fragments tossed into the conflagration.

The accordions wept music as they were slung onto the pyre.

Flowers out of hair. Bonnets from heads. Rose and lily were stripped off the lych-gate. The air filled suddenly with a sharp, aromatic scent . . . of herbs, woodland herbs.

In the silence Ginny walked towards the church, darted through the gate into the darkness of the graveyard . . . Round between the long mounds to the iron gate . . .

Kevin was there. He ran towards her, his eyes wide, wild. 'He's coming!' he hissed, breathlessly.

'What's going on?' she whispered.

'Where are you going?' he said.

'To the camp. I'm frightened. They've stopped dancing. They're burning their instruments. This happened three years ago when Mary . . . when . . . you know . . .'

'Why are you so frightened?' Kevin asked. His eyes were bright from the distant glow of the bonfire. 'What are you running from, Ginny? Tell me. Tell me. We're friends . . .'

'Something is wrong,' she sobbed. She found herself clutching at the boy's arms. 'Everybody is being so horrible to me. *You* were horrible to me. What have I done? What have I done?'

He shook his head. The flames made his dark eyes gleam. She had her back to the square. Suddenly he looked beyond her. Then he smiled. He looked at her.

'Goodbye, Ginny,' he whispered.

She turned. Kevin darted past her and into the great mob of masked men who stood around her. They had come upon her so quietly that she had not heard a thing. Their faces were like black pigs. Eyes gleamed, mouths grinned. They wore white and black . . . the Scarrows.

Unexpectedly, Kevin began to whine. Ginny thought he was being punished for being out of bounds. She listened, and then for one second . . . just one second . . . all was stillness, all was silence, anticipation. Then she reacted as any sensible child would react in the situation.

She opened her mouth and screamed. The sound had barely echoed in the night air when a hand clamped firmly across her face, a great hand, strong, stifling her cry. She struggled and pulled away, turned and kicked until she realised it was the Mother that she fought against. She was no longer wearing her rowan beads, or her iron charm. She seemed naked without them. Her dress was green and she held Ginny firmly still. 'Hold quiet, child. Your time is soon.'

The iron gate was open. Ginny peered through it, into the darkness, through the grassy walls of the old fort and towards the circle of great elms.

There was a light there, and the light was coming closer. And ahead of that light there was a wind, a breeze, ice cold, tinged with a smell that was part sweat, part rot, and unpleasant in the extreme. She grimaced and tried to back away, but the Mother's hands held her fast. She glanced over her shoulder, towards the square, and felt her body tremble as the Scarrows stared beyond her, into the void of night.

Two of the Scarrows held tall, hazel poles, each wrapped round with strands of ivy and mistletoe. They stepped forward and held the poles to form a gateway between them. Ginny watched all of this and shivered. And she felt sick when she saw Kevin held by others of the Scarrows. The boy was terrified. He seemed to be pleading with Ginny, but what could she do? His own mother stood close to him, weeping silently.

The wind gusted suddenly and the first of the shadows passed over so quickly that she was hardly aware of its transit. It appeared out of nowhere, part darkness, part chill, a tall shape that didn't so much walk as *flow* through the iron gate. Looking at that shadow was like looking into a depthless world of dark; it shimmered, it hazed, it flickered, it moved, an uncertain balance between that world and the real world. Only as it passed between the hazel poles held by the Scarrows, and then into the world beyond, did it take on a form that could be called ... ghostly.

Distantly the priest's voice intoned a greeting. Ginny heard him say, 'Welcome back to *Scarugfell*. Our pledge is fulfilled. Your life begins again.'

A second shadow followed the first, this one smaller, and with its darkness and its chill came the sound of keening, like a child's crying. It was distant, though, and uncertain. As Ginny watched, it took its shadowy form beyond the Scarrows and into the village.

As each of them had passed over, so the Scarrowmen closed ranks again, but distantly, close to the fire in the square, an unearthly howling, a nightmare wind, seemed to greet each new arrival. What happened to the spirits then, Ginny couldn't tell, or care.

Her mother's hand touched her face, then her shoulder, forced her round again to watch the iron gate. The Mother whispered, 'Those two were his kin. They too died for our village a long time ago. But Cyric is coming now ...'

The shadow that moved beyond the gate was like nothing Ginny could ever have imagined. She couldn't tell whether it was animal or man. It was immense. It swayed as it moved, and it seemed to approach through the darkness in a ponderous, dragging way. Its outlines were blurred, shadow against darkness, void against the glimmering light among the trees. It seemed to have branches and tendrils reaching from its head. It made a sound that was like the rumble of water in a hidden well.

It seemed to fill her vision. It occupied all of space. Its breath stank. Its single eye gleamed with firelight.

One was blind ... one was grim ...

It seemed to be laughing at her as it peered down from beyond the trees and the earth walls that surrounded the church.

It pushed something forward, a shadow, a man, nudged it through the iron gate. Ginny wanted to scream as she caught glimpses, within that shadow, of the dislocated jaw, the empty sockets, the crawling flesh. The ragged thing limped toward her, hands raised, bony fingers stretched out, skull face open and inviting ... inviting the kiss that Ginny knew, now, would end her life.

'No!' she shouted, and struggled frantically in the Mother's grip. The Mother seemed angry. 'Even now it mocks us!' she said, then shouted, 'Give the Life for the Death. Give it now!'

Behind Ginny, Kevin suddenly screamed. Then he was running towards the iron gate, sobbing and shouting, drawn by invisible hands.

'Don't let him take me! Don't let him take me!' he cried.

He passed the hideous figure and entered the world beyond the gate. He was snatched into the air, blown into darkness like a leaf whipped by a storm wind. He had vanished in an instant.

The great shadow turned away into the night and began to seep back towards the circle of elms. The Mother's hands on Ginny's shoulders pushed her forwards, towards the ghastly embrace.

The shadow corpse stopped moving. Its arms dropped. The gaping eyes watched nothing and nowhere. A sound issued from its bones. 'Is she the one? Is she my kin?'

Mother's voice answered loudly that she was indeed the one. She was indeed Cyric's kin.

The shadow seemed to turn its head to watch Ginny. It looked down at her, then reached up and pulled the tatters of a hood about its head. The hood hid the features. The whole creature seemed to melt, to descend, to shrink. Ginny heard the Mother say, 'Fifteen hundred years in the dark. Your life saved our village. Our pledge to bring you back is honoured. Welcome, Cyric.'

Something wriggled below the tatters of the hood. The Mother said, 'Go forward, child. Take the hare. *Take him!*'

Ginny hesitated. She glanced round. The Scarrows seemed to be smiling behind their masks. Two other children, both girls, stood there. Each was holding a struggling hare. Her Mother made frantic motions to her. 'Come on, Ginny. The fear is ended, now. The day of denial is over. Only you can touch the hare. You're the kin. Cyric has chosen you. Take it quickly. Bring him over. Bring him back.'

Ginny stumbled forward, reached below the stinking rags and found the terrified animal. As she raised the brown hare to her breast she felt the flow of the past, the voice, the wisdom, the spirit of the man who had passed back over, the promise to him kept, fifteen hundred years after he had lain down his life for the safety of *Scarugfell*, also known as the *Place of the Mother*.

Cyric was home. The great hunter was home. Ginny had him, now, and *he* had her, and she would become great and wise, and Cyric would speak the wisdom of the Dark through her lips. The hare would die in time, but Cyric and Ginny would share a human life until the human body itself passed away.

And Ginny felt a great glow of joy as the images of that ancient land, its forts, its hills, its tracks, its forest shrines, flooded into her mind. She heard the hounds, the horses, the larks, she felt the cold wind, smelled the great woods.

Yes. Yes. She had been born for this. Her parents had been sacrificed to free her and the Mother had kept her ready for the moment. The nightmare had been Cyric making contact as the Father had brought him to the edge of the dark world.

The Father! The Father had watched over her, as all in the village had often said he would. It had been the Father she had seen, a rare glimpse of the Lord who always brought the returning Dead to the place of the Lord's Eve.

Cyric had come a long, long way home. It had taken time to make the Lord release him and allow Cyric's knowledge of the dark world back to the village, to help Scarrowfell, and the villages like it keep the eyes and minds of the invader muddled and confused. And then Cyric, too, had waited ... until Ginny was of age. His kin. His chosen vehicle.

Ginny, his new protector, cradled the animal. The hare twitched in her grasp. Its eyes were full of rejoicing.

She felt a moment's sadness, then, for poor, betrayed Kevin, but it passed. And as she left the place of the gate she joined willingly in reciting the Lord's prayer, her voice high, enthusiastic among the rumble of the crowd.

> *Our Father, who art in the Forest*
> *Horned One is Thy name.*
> *Thy Kingdom is the Wood, Thy Will is the Blood*
> *In the Glade, as it is in the Village.*
> *Give us this day our Kiss of Earth*
> *And forgive us our Malefactions.*
> *Destroy those who Malefact against us*
> *And lead us to the Otherworld.*
> *For Thine is the Kingdom of the Shadow, Thine is the Power and the Glory. Thou art the Stag which ruts with us, and We are the Earth beneath thy feet.*
> *Drocha Nemeton*

The Time Beyond Age

The day before the experiment was scheduled to commence, Martin and Yvonne, our two MAA-grown subjects, were allowed into the observation laboratory for the last time.

As usual they caused chaos, thundering around the small room, arms flying, bodies taking unexpected turns until every technician in the place was clinging to his or her equipment for dear life. As Martin, a small figure clad all in white, raced past me I made a grab for him and sat him firmly upon the desk by my keyboard. Yvonne squealed (brake-like) and stopped behind me before deciding which way she would jump on to my lap. She chose to arrive from the left; I had been expecting her from the right and her arrival was painful!

Through her visor she watched me typing. Martin, sitting remarkably still, studied the posters and pictures all around the walls, twisting his protective helmet so that he could see further to each side. I told him not to do that, since the seal would loosen if the helmet were twisted through more than one hundred and eighty degrees.

I was typing a pre-experimental report for *Nature*, and was trying to get a decent title. Yvonne watched my fingers at work, every so often adding a letter of her own. Thus I typed:

NEWZ STU DTITES ON THE AC£CELERAT¹/₃ION OFXLIFE BY CHEMBIC AL MEANS%

'What does that say?' she asked, pointing to the line.
'A little more than I intended,' I replied. *Chembical* I quite liked. I read the proper title to her and Martin launched

himself from the bench, made a motorcycle-like noise, with appropriate hand gestures, and accelerated around the laboratory again. He was stopped by a middle-aged nurse (whose eyes popped open with hilarious effect when the human motorcycle collided with her) who picked him up and carried him, complaining, into the small decontamination cubicle. Coming outside she waited for the air inside to sterilise then snapped instructions to him to disrobe. He complained again, but stripped off his protective suit and the nurse placed her arms into the arm-gloves that reached into the chamber and reduced Martin to hysterics as she tried to administer the various prophylactics with which our two subjects were pumped every day.

The following morning the experiment began.

The first stages, of course, were the familiarisation procedures, and our two subjects were introduced to the closed environment that was to be their home for the rest of their natural and unnatural lives. There was something almost depressing in watching the children, conceived, grown and matured to the age of six in a Morris Artificial Amnion, now facing an incarceration in a second womb, this time for good.

The environment itself was an enclosed area nearly a quarter of a mile wide and exactly a quarter of a mile deep. In the middle, directly outside our laboratory, was a park ground, equipped with trees, benches and bushes. This was the environmental focus and the area within which Martin and Yvonne would be conditioned to spend most of their time. Outside the park was a mock city, houses and offices, detailed on the exterior but empty within. Only ten buildings were complete – the parental homes of our two subjects, their subsequent married homes (two, one far larger than the other) and the offices where they would work during their lives.

Into this environment they were led and left alone, under

THE TIME BEYOND AGE

a light hypnosis necessary to guard their awareness from the falsity of the city.

Martin, to our surprise, reacted against the environment in a difficult and worrying way. He lost his sense of security in the open space of the park — it didn't frighten him, but it made him unhappy and this was something we had not expected to happen.

I watched him carefully during this acquaintance phase. At first he walked among the trees very slowly, seeming very dubious that anything so irregular could be at all efficient. His examination of the town was almost perfunctory, an acknowledgement of its existence. He returned to the park and I watched him chip bark from the bigger of the two oaks we had grown in the environment. He spent a long time scrutinising the carefully selected microfauna that seethed beneath the fragment. He had no conception, of course, of the essential artificiality of the ecology, although it was plain to him — and we did not hide the fact, save as regarded the town itself — that the environment was contrived. The extent of our contrivance it was not necessary for him to know for the familiarisation to have its effect.

Yvonne, by contrast with her chosen mate, warmed immediately to the environment and it was all we could do to get her to return to the laboratory. It became a game — three or four sterile-suited technicians chasing one sterile-suited girl in and out of the shells that comprised the town. In conversation with her later in the evening, as I implanted one more of the interminable number of monitoring devices she would carry to her death, she told me how wonderfully free she had felt sitting on actual grass, picking flowers that were actually growing. It was an unpleasant thought to me that the young girl, knowing only sterility and starkness in the complex prior to this time, was now finding in an equivalent piece of unreality all the reality she would ever need. She had yearned to see the outside world, longed for nature and pined, perhaps, for the instinctively realised sensation of wind and rain on her face. Now she was content with a park that encapsulated all her dreams. And she sat in the middle of a construct, half knowing the fact, but finding it completely adequate.

Yvonne was a very chubby child, round faced and pretty. She had dark brown eyes and she chose to wear her hair in an elaborate display of curls, but had been complaining, as she matured these last months, that her hair was getting greasy. By the time we closed her off in the artificial world beyond our laboratory, she had begun to wear her hair straight, in a style that didn't suit her. She was growing quite fat, nothing that wouldn't soon vanish as she grew to adulthood, and it didn't seem to bother her, whereas Martin was naturally, and almost pathologically, ashamed of his protruding ribs.

It was May of '94, a feverish summer forcing itself upon us. The environment looked inviting and in the final weeks when children and technical staff both were in frantic final preparation for Closing Off Day, it was regarded as almost criminal that the cool parklands should be a prohibited area. After all, the disease-free status of the ecology was secured every day, now that Martin and Yvonne were spending time inside without their protective suiting.

In time, towards August, the atmosphere in the laboratory became almost unbearable as our two subjects underwent full acclimatisation. We watched as they played and explored their new territory, Martin gradually coming to terms with the area, but obviously still unhappy; and as we watched we sweltered and wondered who the true masters of the situation might have been.

It was at this time that the last member of our team joined us. She was a young woman, Josephine Greystone, only two years out of her basic training, and she brought to the laboratory not only reasonable looks, but a great enthusiasm for biology in general, and it was she who precipitated what were to become almost routine late-night sessions evaluating the utility of biological research as a whole.

She soon became very interested in Raymond McCreedy, a man in his mid-thirties, unmarried, unforthcoming about himself, a scientist totally involved in his work, to the great benefit of the scientific community, but to the detriment of any personal relationships between the members of the various teams. McCreedy was the head of our team, and had supplied the initial impetus for this particular experiment; it was also his own applied pressure that had secured the necessary funding from the Rockefeller Foundation.

Josephine worked hard trying to draw the man out of his test-tube shell, and indeed, before the full programme had begun, he was amenable enough to conversational foreplay; but any emotional involvement was destined to be just a dream on Josephine's part. The full programme began and McCreedy's interests became centrally directed upon the two human subjects behind the observation wall.

In September the programme of deep hypnosis began: hours and hours of factual adjustment and psychological disguise. Martin's prevailing disquiet with the environment was buried very deeply. In tests in the next few days there were signs that he would accept the environment long enough for it to become so familiar to him that he would be able to control the insecurity as it crept back to his awareness.

Three weeks before the first of the rapid growth treatments was administered, the two subjects received their Life Education. The Life Plan team, led by Doctor Martin Rich, had spent six months devising and recording nearly four hundred years of everyday experiences. A complete catalogue of friends, acquaintances and enemies, of events and non-events, of tragedy and success. One for Martin and one for Yvonne, the two systems knitting together gradually as they grew together themselves according to blueprint. The events they would live through were implanted first, followed by the complex series of visual and sonic codes with which the Life Operator in charge could direct events beyond the wall.

Finally, the enormous bank of experiences that they would never actually participate in – the twenty-nine 'false' days that would pass as they slept each night, giving them the illusion of a full and active life.

On the first day of November there was a promise of snow, but the skies, overcast and depressing, vanished into night without releasing their burden in any form. This was the day the full programme began.

I was lucky to draw my Christmas leave over the Christmas period itself. I returned to the Institute on the twenty-seventh of December to find Josephine, two nurses and two of the technicians in attendance. The Life Plan team had left an auto-programme in operation for seven days, and McCreedy himself had succumbed to the need for rest and was spending time in London.

'You could have taken your leave with McCreedy,' I remarked to Josephine, tactless as ever. 'Any of the technicians who were here over Christmas would have been glad to swop.'

'Why should I have wanted to swop?' she asked as we prepared for the day's observation.

'To be with McCreedy?' Oh hell, I thought. I've put a foot in somewhere.

Her look at me was pure contempt. 'Why should I have wanted to be with Doctor McCreedy?'

I had received all the warning signals, but momentum carried me to desperate conclusion. 'I'm sorry, I just thought . . .'

'I very much doubt, Doctor Lipman,' she said stonily, 'if you thought anything at all. What you laughingly call thinking rarely transcends a naïve and superficial curiosity.'

'Look, I'm sorry, let's drop the subject, shall we?'

Her look changed from contempt to distress. 'Yes, why not. Let's drop the subject of McCreedy, let's forget him for three days and have ourselves a real ball. For your information, and to ensure that you don't open your mouth again, Doctor Lipman, I have nothing going with McCreedy, and have no desire to try and change that state of affairs.'

I couldn't think of any suitably witty remark with which to extricate myself from my wretched corner, so I fell silent and monitored the two subjects, aware that Josephine was sitting staring at nothing in particular.

In the five months of Yvonne's life that I had missed — by taking a five-day break — she had altered remarkably. Her hair was very short, now, cut in the style of her currently favourite singer, and she was beginning to discover the versatility of cosmetics. She was still living in a separate building from Martin, ostensibly with her parents, but, as dictated by the programme within her, she was finding Martin's pre-adolescent form an attraction. He, according to script, was not too keen on his playmate. She was still plump, but the lipid-metabolism figures were indicating that soon this would fall away.

She was approaching adolescence at the late age of fifteen.

Although it is difficult to admit to such predictable behaviour, it was about now that I realised that my affection for the increasingly beautiful girl went far beyond fatherly emotion. On that first night back from my break

I followed Josephine and the nurse into the environment and approached the sleeping form of Yvonne with a strange sensation of anticipation. The nurse seemed oblivious of my feelings and in the matter-of-fact mannerism of a woman who regards the human body as an organism to be stripped, scrubbed, powdered, plugged and buried, she exposed the maturing body of the girl and proceeded to inject the ageing chemical known familiarly as *Chronon*. The hiss of the parcutaneous inoculation snapped me from my lingering contemplation of Yvonne and I performed the ritual of recording with an almost blank mind: I took whole body temperature scan, a tiny skin biopsy that would not be noticed the following day; I took smears and scrapes, tested reflexes and conductivity, obtained a ten-second recording of the girl's heart (probably the most vital organ she possessed, and the part of her body likely to give us the most trouble in later years), and finally stood back, flushed, shaking, aroused.

Perhaps the nurse was not as insensitive as I had thought for she was suddenly very quiet, watching me curiously. My embarrassment became acute and I glanced at Josephine who was standing silently beside me, looking at Yvonne. Quickly I said, 'I can't decide if she's losing weight or not . . .'

The nurse nodded slowly, then covered Yvonne's body, blowing the sound signal to bring her back into normal sleep.

As we walked to Martin's 'house' I considered my feelings. I was not really surprised that now, in December of '94, I should be feeling love for a young woman, since my marriage, never a satisfactory affair from the beginning, was awaiting legal dissolution and had been doing so for six months. What perturbed me was that I should have responded to the experimental subject and not to one of the technicians or nurses, or even Josephine.

Josephine. Had she noticed my momentary lapse of self-discipline? As we examined Martin so I studied the girl and I decided that she was too preoccupied with her own troubles to have read anything into my actions.

She suddenly said, softly, perhaps afraid of rousing Martin although she knew that he was in deep sleep: 'What do you make of people who are so one tracked they can't think of anything but work?'

'McCreedy?'

She looked at me. She seemed sad, and after a moment, 'He's an example, yes.'

'Annoying,' I said. 'Pointless.'

'You don't believe in dedication?'

I concluded the examination and we walked from the environment, sealed it and sterilised it again.

'I don't believe in isolation,' I said. 'And McCreedy is becoming isolated because of what you mistakenly label as dedication. His reactions, his behaviour, his approach to all of us working for him is becoming unreal. He begins to think we're machines, and should never turn off.'

Josephine said nothing. After a moment I asked, 'How do *you* see him?'

'With increasing difficulty,' she said after a while. 'It's something I can't explain.'

Perhaps these days, or if you prefer, these months, were the worst. By the end of February '95 Yvonne was a fully grown woman of twenty, and Martin, though the same age, was an immediately post-adolescent young man, still self-conscious, still unsure of himself, still given to the sort of tantrum directed at the ghosts who surrounded him that one expects in a normal male in his late teens.

The two months of my subjective time had done nothing to drown my desire for Yvonne, but more worrying to me, as a supposedly impartial observer, was the feeling of resentment I began to nurture, resentment directed at the young man I now watched and monitored as he devised some scheme to avoid parental retribution for his being out so late.

Josephine watched over my shoulder as Martin walked across the environment, oblivious of his watchers, concerned only with the non-existent forms awaiting him in his house. Yvonne, whom he had just left, was already in bed and — as our monitors showed us — peacefully asleep, about to age a month in the passing of her dreaming hours.

Tonight they had approached each other as adults, that much was apparent. I had watched them kiss in the shelter of the first oak that Martin had ever interested himself in, fourteen of his years ago. He had held her and explored her, and I could feel what he was feeling as his fingers had invaded her body.

Josephine turned away and sat staring into space. I was glad because my face was burning and I could feel my hands shaking as I directed the remote sensors to record all heartbeat and temperature changes, and instruct me if there was anything abnormal in their physical and physiological response to love-play. There was no satisfaction in the green panel that flashed 'normal' in a repetitive insult to my stricken ego.

That night, as the nurse and I monitored and examined each of them, it was with Martin that I lingered, noting his emerging masculinity and the involuntary ejaculation that occurred as my fingers brushed him during perfunctory examination. I hated his youth, and I hated his good looks; I hated his smugness as he lay in sleep, I hated the fact that he was fully entitled to everything that was Yvonne. I hated his dreams. What he dreamed I shall never know for certain, but in my uncertainty lies an impression that choked me at the time. And I hated him for that too.

Three days of my night shift passed in the Institute,

and I received promising news from my lawyer — that the separation would be made legal within days — and received a substantial cutback of my monthly stipend which would make even my bachelor life very difficult. Josephine had finished her spell on nights and it was the intense and disinterested McCreedy who sat with me at the beginning of March. I wondered if he knew of Josephine's feelings, I wondered if he had detected her waning enthusiasm . . . Almost certainly he had. Perhaps he had even told her of it. He was becoming more abstract with every passing day.

Since there was nothing to talk about with the intense young man who gave orders, I watched Yvonne with greater concentration than was usual or than I would have liked.

Now she was long-haired and slim, her breasts small and perfect and seeming fuller behind the attractive blouses she wore. She worked in an imaginary office and took every opportunity to meet Martin in the park, and on the third night of March, my last day on nights . . .

I shall record it for the sake of completeness.

In each other's arms beneath that tree they passed a few minutes, petting and kissing, then undressed and he made love to her, and the recording instruments said, heart beat 137 per minute, deep body temperature 0.5 degrees high, slight blood loss, loss of lachrymal fluid . . .

And so on, and so forth, as Yvonne cried and a significant moment in the life plan was reached and passed.

The loss of her virginity was five years in Yvonne's past before the pain of that incident faded from me. It was the beginning of May, and the first really hot day of the year. Long-range weather predictions were for a summer as hot and stifling as the last, and the thought of it was not welcomed by the Institute staff.

I looked at Yvonne, and at Martin, and saw mature people, Yvonne a full and lovely woman, delighting in life and love, almost passionately hungry for her husband. Martin was a strong, lean man, full bearded and fierce tempered. It was hard to remember that just a year ago they had been infants.

The years between twenty-five and thirty passed normally and uneventfully, and our first report, on the fifth of August, was summarised by the words: 'In all aspects of their lives the two subjects are normal thirty-year-olds. The effect of the chemical *Chronon* is seen only in the acceleration of their developmental rates, and the false experience implants seem fully capable of compensating for their accelerated lives. There is no evidence at all that mentally the subjects are anything but reasonably secure, reasonably stable thirty-year-olds. There is no evidence that either subject suspects their true situation. The experiment is continuing.'

It was heartening news to our sponsors, and a mood of exhilaration enveloped our laboratory. We began to feel that we had a breakthrough in our grasp.

A breakthrough into *what* was difficult to say. The kudos for the original discovery of *Chronon* was not ours. The chemical of age, the simple protein that accumulates in body cells at a steady rate and dictates the phenomenon of ageing, was the discovery of a Swedish biochemist seven years before. The acceleration of development, and of ageing, under the influence of artificially high concentrations of synthetic *Chronon*, was the contribution of a Scottish behaviourist at the University of Edinburgh, four years later.

The fact that synthetic *Chronon* worked as well on human beings as on rats would make a name for us, but hardly a reputation.

McCreedy was well aware of this, and we had both been aware of this when we had met nearly two years before to discuss the phenomenon of ageing, and the newly discovered facts about its chemical dependence.

THE TIME BEYOND AGE

With old age, McCreedy had said, comes a lowering of resistance not just to disease but to the environment and to life itself. We think of age as a barrier that none of us will pass. But is it? If we remove those agents of death that find they can operate better as a person gets older, will age *itself* be a barrier? Might not something, some form, some existence that we are unaware of lie beyond our four score and ten?

In rats there was nothing. They lived twice as long as normal and became twice as old. But rats were without souls, McCreedy had declared, and we should not be disheartened.

This was the first time that McCreedy had referred to a metaphysical concept, and it rather surprised me. He made no great play of his religious beliefs, and directed his actions under no religious dogma. I came to believe that he equated self-awareness with the concept of *soul*, and that he extended his favour towards the metaphysical only to the unscientific degree of regarding self-awareness as having an effect upon the physical form. He believed in mind over matter! But detailed consideration of such things was beyond his scope. At the time this narrowness did not seem significant to me, and it was not until well after the experiment had begun that I remembered his words, and his idle reflections.

Not until late November did any serious psychological stress symptoms begin to develop in the subjects. They were now into their thirty-eighth year and the monitoring consoles were still reporting their physical and physiological condition as completely normal. Certainly there was a slight increase in the incidence of embryonic cell formation, but – with our help – they were maintaining completely adequate control of their body systems. Martin was an enviable sight, advancing into middle age with muscles that were as firm and hard as a twenty-five-year-old's. And Yvonne, whilst showing signs of age in the lines that were tracing themselves around her eyes and on her legs, was still a beautiful woman. But now I felt only sadness when I looked at her, for more and more I was remembering her childhood, her innocence and her fixed gaze from which it was impossible to escape.

There was no trace of that innocence now, and the beautiful eyes were narrower and more canny. When she made love to Martin she was physically demanding but seemed no longer to need the concomitant affection.

Martin, whilst undoubtedly in love with his wife, was tending more and more towards solitariness, and in this I saw a reflection of his first acquaintance with the enormous environment. He was unhappy with his situation, seemed restless and morose, and returned again and again to the realistic-looking oak tree that he had first scrutinised so long, by his terms, in the past.

Here he sat for hours, during the day and often into the night, brooding, staring, perhaps trying to identify some feature, some element of his universe that would give him a clue as to why he felt so wrong.

Perhaps – again – such speculation by those of us who monitored and watched was just a sublimation on our parts of the fact that the experiment, stuck as it was in the 'normal' years, had become unbearably boring. We were looking for trouble, or so it seemed to some of us.

With the inevitable slackening of attention, I found ample opportunity to modify the Life Plan of the ageing Yvonne. It was an impulsive move, but had, as an idea, been in my mind for a long time. The team was small – three biologists and three technicians working in shifts, two nurses and the four members of the Life Plan team. It was inevitable that we should all learn to cope with the other aspects of the experiment, and I had become relatively

THE TIME BEYOND AGE

adept at the surgically precise process of removing or implanting information/ideas/events into the two subjects.

I implanted my own character, my own physical description, as one of the ghost lovers that Yvonne was taking. There was something akin to the erotic when I thought, thereafter, of what she was seeing and doing, but after a few days the futility of the action came home to me.

Nevertheless, she retained me as a lover and I never found the opportunity to remove that programme. When I heard her murmuring my name, voicing the words of her ascending passion as she went through the movements of intercourse, I felt my face burn, and my imagination stretch to its limits.

When she was with someone else I became depressed and touchy. No one in the laboratory ever found out what I had done, but they might well have gathered the truth if they had bothered to listen to the tapes of what was said in the darkness of her bedroom.

Time passed and a depression settled upon the laboratory. Perhaps the movement of Martin and Yvonne into their middle years, and into a quieter phase of their lives, reflected itself in our subdued interaction and the almost lethargic approach that we began to show towards the experiment as a whole. McCreedy, I hasten to point out, in no way suffered depression, and the technicians were, I suppose, too distant from the possibility of kudos to have any great enthusiasm at any stage of the project. But the nurses and the Life Planners, myself and Josephine all became very broody.

Josephine in particular was labouring under a black cloud. Her relationship with McCreedy was abysmal. Everything he said she disagreed with behind his back. She took her only pleasure in putting him down, contributed nothing to any discussion at which he was present, but depended on me to relay her ideas to him.

In the rapid ageing of the two subjects she saw an inevitability that frightened her.

'That's us in so very few years,' she said as she stared at the two subjects during one of their persistent rows. 'And there's nothing any of us can do about it. It's a stab at our human pride — there are some things that are inevitable, that we cannot control, and our decrepitude is one of them. And what do we do? We accept it! We are *Eos* watching the ageing of *Tithonus* and afraid to ask the great *Zeus* to add youth to immortality. *Afraid*, I said — and that's what I meant, but even so, humankind is ageing like each of us individually and our racial fear stops us asking for an injection of youth. It's so horribly ... predictable! I want to live with youth and youth's dreams ... I'm rambling, aren't I?'

I see what she meant, now, as I complete this chronicle. In the satisfaction of completion of the project there would come a rationality that I had lost during those years. At the time I didn't understand her at all.

I became infatuated with the watching of Yvonne, staring at her for endless hours, trying to find some trace of the eleven-year-old ... but all her youth and beauty were now imprisoned behind a wall of years. With each day, with each inoculation of *Chronon*, she aged before my eyes, now whiter, now more wrinkled, now a little more stooped.

She and Martin fought persistently. There was not a day passed without them shouting and swearing at each other, and ending the tussle with a cold and slippery silence, that only mellowed towards evening.

Martin spent a great deal of time alone, and the monitor reported that he indulged less and less in conversation with the ghosts around him. He retired from his work, and from his social life, whilst Yvonne remained socially active and very hostile towards her husband.

She flirted with numerous ghosts, most of them the ageing lovers she had taken during earlier years. Now, instead of the imaginary copulation that she performed before our eyes, she seemed to indulge in painfully unconcluded flirtation. When I watched her one evening, and heard her mention my name and knew what she was thinking, instead of the thrill I had felt when first I had entered her pseudo-awareness, I now felt only disgust and dismay, and I became deeply embarrassed at what I had done, but still no opportunity to remove my existence presented itself and there was nothing I could do to eliminate these scenes from my memory.

The time came when all sexual, and much social, contact ceased, and she sat and remembered, staring out from her body at the invisible monitors that brought her heartache to us as we watched from the laboratory outside the environment.

Martin, now, was alone, spending his time staring directly at the edge of the environment as if he was aware that he could not move beyond that barrier. Within his head, recorded triggers were depressing his interest in wandering beyond the confines, but it seemed to the more analytical among us that he had come to realise that there was nowhere to go anyway.

It was December of '96, and they were old people, seventy years into their lives, as healthy and sturdy as when they had been born, but old, none the less. For me, when on my shift, there was just discomfiture in administering examination to the thin torso of the woman I had once watched grow with the beating of my heart. In sleep she stirred, talked, cried. The monitors said all was well, but it was hard not to believe that she had lived too much too fast, and that all the empty days in her past were calling for fulfilment, and the brief and unsatisfactory time she had actually spent with Martin was calling for completion.

Now, however, a new sense of excitement crept into the laboratory. I felt it myself. For the subjects were at the beginning of the age barrier, and with every day took a step nearer to the figure of one hundred years, our first goal, and the age which, when reached, would be accompanied by our first report to the scientific community at large. And yet, a sort of natural caution prevailed. Within our hearts, as those weeks passed, we all began to imagine what, if anything, lay beyond the barrier of age; but within the microcosm that was our scientific community we never discussed our private fears and hopes. McCreedy talked loosely about possible regenerative processes, and we all talked among ourselves about the rationale behind thinking that age itself did not necessarily mean death. But of what was to come, there were just the imaginings and the anticipations of our scientific hearts. And, an acknowledgement to mythology, above McCreedy's desk an enormous picture of a cicada, watching us with an expression verging on amusement.

On the day that they were both ninety-nine years and eleven months old, McCreedy prepared his press statement while the rest of us accumulated the massive files of data and decided on an allotment for processing. The following day, the fifth of March '98, that momentous event occurred ... the centenary of two human beings, and there was a feeling of great relief within the whole Institute, and for the first time ever we drank openly in our laboratory, and it was not just coffee, surreptitiously sipped with backs to the health-hazard notice, but vintage champagne, eight bottles of the stuff!

I drank with restraint since it was to be my night shift, but somehow we all felt, now, that the years of narrow-minded application had been worthwhile, that there would be an end product; even Josephine seemed brighter, more cheerful.

I watched McCreedy's press conference on a small portable TV while I waited for the frail figures in the environment to sink, again, into deep slumber. There was an atmosphere of great excitement in the vast hall from which the programme was coming, and I could see McCreedy, evening-suited and proud, seated between medical experts and two politicians, confronted by a vast array of microphones, and waiting for the hubbub of human movement and whisper to die away.

The Institute itself seemed to vibrate in sympathy with that meeting of the world, away to the south, in London.

Yvonne sat for a long while that night, at the edge of the park, listening to the ghosts in her head, and staring through eyes that were as big and innocent as they had been ninety or so years back. The camera lingered on her and I returned her gaze through the monitor and I seemed to hear her laughter and her crying, and her passion, but all so far in the past, now, so long ago.

Martin was by himself beneath the oak, turning a piece of bark over and over, examining the artificial life which crawled beneath. The 'moonlight' was intense and highlighted his rigid expression, the bony crags of his face, the deepset lie of his eyes. What thoughts, I wondered, did he think at his great age? He was not senile, and Yvonne was certainly not senile, and yet there was a calmness, an abstractedness about them, that suggested mindlessness.

Did they themselves feel something significant? Were they experiencing a quieter excitement within themselves, a personal triumph? They believed themselves ordinary people, and as ordinary people they were a hundred years old. The flesh would not fall away to reveal firm skin and agile muscles and time would not fall away to reveal them in their youth and beauty, but in the mind is a store of ages and perhaps, on this night of nights, a barrier within their consciousness had dissolved for a few hours and they were living, ghostlike, as they had lived in reality, for the last seven years.

On the television screen McCreedy's angular features were emphasised by the arc lights above him as he calmly informed the conference of the progress we had made and were continuing to make. He talked about the impossibility of the experiment using ordinary human lifespans – an experiment lasting two hundred years (assuming it was successful) could be run by a computer, but not by mortal scientists. He stressed that the only purpose of the experiment at this time was to evaluate whether or not we were correct in thinking that death in old age was nonetheless a disease-caused process, taking disease to mean – at the least – the gradual failure of vital body cells due to the accumulation of the toxic by-products of mild infection throughout the life of the individual. At one hundred years of age, he said, our two subjects reared from artificial wombs, screened from all disease or body malfunction, showed all the elastic changes of age, were to all intents and purposes very old people, and yet their cellular complement was as vigorous and efficient as it had been when they had been teenagers. All the symptoms of age were built into the genetic message, he explained when prompted further, and all that had been eliminated were the non-genetically coded acquisitions of disease by-products.

The all-important questions: how long did McCreedy expect the experiment to continue for? And what did he expect to find out as the decades progressed? And was he morally justified in using human beings for experimentation outside the understanding of normal human life?

The experiment, said McCreedy, would continue for as long as circumstances permitted. He *expected* to find nothing – no scientist ever did. He hoped he would find whatever was to be found; a scientist's nightmare was to fail to observe the facts of significance in an experiment.

I could have put it better myself, but the statement was met with a respectful silence.

As to the moral question, he had a licence permitting him to work with artificially grown human beings, and he had not yet abused that privilege. Since the effective natural lifespan of the two human subjects was now ended, in a sense they were living on borrowed time, time borrowed from McCreedy himself, and they had no future, really, but to remain as a part of the experiment.

This was in March of '98, and it precipitated a phase of observation overshadowed by our burning enthusiasm. We were eager to discover what lay beyond the normal years of life, and there can be no doubt that privately we all had the wildest of visions.

Truth to tell, mine were perhaps the wildest of all. I sketched possible metamorphoses, imagined arriving at the Institute and facing subjects walking through walls, or transporting themselves instantly into the future to observe the progress of our study. I was, I confess, convinced that the apparent decay of body and – to a certain extent – mind, was a transient phenomenon, and that greater power lay at some indeterminate time in the future of our subjects.

Confiding my belief to McCreedy, I was received with hostility. He condemned me for my lack of discipline. Expect nothing, he said, because if you fervently expect anything at all, then you will tend to see what you want to see.

And then he told me of *his* secret imaginings and they so closely paralleled my own that we talked seriously, thereafter, of the possibility of such a state of existence following naturally upon a span of five or six score disease-free years.

Man had never had a chance to exploit his genetic freedom completely. He was killed, trampled, diseased so early in life that the mechanisms that might have come into operation to protect the body cells from poisoning just never came into play. What we see is man with a lifespan dictated by the length of time his body can survive an increasingly hostile microclimate. But what was his original potential? What great beings have our neotenous forms never been able to reach?

A man of religious inclination, McCreedy could not conceal from my scrutiny the fact that he believed some manifestation of godhead lay as the ultimate destiny of our two subjects.

They grew older. By day and by night they aged weeks, and the flesh sagged, their movements slowed, and the compilations of data mounted in volume, but amounted to nothing. The incidence of disease tried to rise within them, but all was monitored and prevented and they reached the middle of their second century free from infection, from tumour or other bodily breakdown.

It is impossible to chronicle those passing months and years in detail – little happened either to the subjects or to us. We talked and read, participated in any number of short-term projects, wrote papers and took long vacations, all expenses paid. Sanity was – miraculously, I sometimes think – preserved.

In retrospect I can see how, within our scientific microcosm, we became individually insulated, erected barriers behind which we guarded our memories and preserved our philosophy. Thus, I learned nothing of my companions, and – at the time – found no interest in so studying them.

At the age of one hundred and fifty-five Martin's skin seemed to regain its firmness, the loose folds tightening, and he became skeletal, gaunt. Yvonne, by contrast, sagged more, the flesh lying around her neck in three great folds, her legs becoming wrinkled and bowed.

Nothing magical or unexpected happened, however. They just became older, frailer, quieter.

The excitement of year one hundred passed into *our* distant past, and over the course of weeks, then months, the enormous ages reached by the subjects failed to arouse even the slightest whimper of joy. We worked virtually full-time countering the efforts of each of their bodies to shift into a disease condition, but all the time our eyes were watching the loose, trembling folds of skin on Yvonne and the drawn, scaling flesh of her husband. They passed towards their second century with virtually no change, virtually no movement. They were static hulks, housebound where they slept most of the time, ate slowly through tiny mouths that hardly seemed to open for the premasticated food they consumed.

Yvonne watched the monitor all the time, and when she was at her most alert, her eyes were huge, deep and penetrating, and there was a terrible sadness in them.

They passed their second century and the atmosphere in the research centre became appalling.

What was the point of it now? demanded Josephine. Why continue when all we were doing was prolonging the agony of gross body decay? There were no great secrets to be discovered. Stop the experiment. Admit defeat!

McCreedy, not surprisingly, refused. His face, these days, was showing signs of great mental strain. He was white, heavily sagging under the eyes, and he seemed ... old. He dressed in disorder, and had stopped giving press interviews. The Ministry officials who bombarded us every month were given cursory briefings and hustled away, and letters demanding that we show some results for the financial support to be proven worthwhile were answered abruptly and stingingly, and somehow – don't ask me how – those who put money into us continued to do so.

At about this time Josephine left the group. She said

goodbye to me, but there was a distance between us that made our smiles and handshakes just meaningless gestures. She never glanced at McCreedy, and McCreedy paid no attention to her.

'It's all so pointless,' she said, reiterating what she had said so many times before. 'Man's destiny was always to grow old and die, and what we're demonstrating here is that no matter how we come to terms with the forces that oppress us, our destiny will never be anything but a slow decay. What we see in a pair of individuals reflects our whole race. We have to live with our dreams, not our realities.'

She left and for a while I felt moody and listless. McCreedy, looking even older, berated her defeatist and pessimistic attitudes, and in a short time the oppressive atmosphere lifted and I felt the excitement that McCreedy felt, the sensation of hovering at the edge of something greater than imagination.

With the passing months we became a little slack again . . .

Then things began to happen and it was like an injection of life, both into us and into the hulks that peered at us from the environment.

On the morning of his two hundred and twentieth year (and three months) Martin, having remained virtually immobile for the past eighty years of his life, rose and walked swiftly – on legs that barely faltered – towards the edge of the environment. His heartbeat doubled and his blood pressure rose, and there seemed to be great surges of adrenalin passing through his body at thirty-five-second intervals.

He began to shout, in a language strange to my ears:

'Sibaraku makkura na yoru ni te de mono o saguru . . . yoo ni site . . . aruite ikimasita ga . . . tootoo hutaritomo sukkari ... tukarete nanimo iwanaide kosi o orosite ... simaimasita ...'

'My God,' shouted McCreedy, ecstatic. 'Listen to that. Listen to *that*!'

'Sosite soko ni ... taoreta ...' Martin seemed to be finding difficulty speaking these strange words, '... mama inoti ga nakunarun' d'ya nai ... ka to omou to kyuu ... ni ... taihen osorosiku natte ... simaimasita ...'

He fell silent, but continued to stand at the edge of the environment and stare through at that part that was projection.

McCreedy was shaking his head, almost in disbelief. 'The language of angels ...' he said softly. 'It has finally happened ... it has finally happened.'

'Actually it was very poorly pronounced Japanese,' said one of the technicians, a young girl and a member of the Life Plan team.

McCreedy stared at her for a moment while the rest of us tried to hide our smiles. 'The point is,' he said slowly, 'Martin never *knew* Japanese.' His face beamed again. 'He never *knew* it, don't you see? So how could he have learned it? We have our first mystery ... Lipman, we have our first mystery!' He was obviously delighted. The same technician, looking as if she hardly dared speak, said, 'Well, not exactly. We programmed him to take an elementary course in Japanese when he was thirty. The only mystery is how his pronunciation could be so bad ...'

McCreedy was completely deflated. The rest of us could hardly hide our mirth, but that was so unfair. We had all lost.

When McCreedy had gone – back to his small office to recover from his disappointment – I asked the technician what Martin had said.

'For a while we were groping our way along as if it was in the deep of night, but eventually we sat down without saying a word, completely exhausted. Then we suddenly felt . . . frightened, wondering if we were going to die, there where we had fallen.'

I looked at Martin, who was still standing at the edge of the park, staring into nowhere. 'Beautiful,' I said.

'Page 233,' she said. '*Teach Yourself Japanese*. Check it up.'

One day, when I arrived a little early for my shift, I found McCreedy seated in his small office, holding an alcohol swab to his lower left arm. An ampoule of *Chronon* lay empty on his desk. Immediately I understood why he had begun to look so old these last two years. Immediately the true dedication of the man to his own beliefs was apparent. Immediately his hypocrisy was crystal clear – expect nothing, he had said, and here he was, already modifying his own life on the basis of what he believed would occur – McCreedy, searching for a place in the kingdom of the gods, wearing his age without regret or apprehension. Was he oblivious of the fact that, having never been screened against disease, his destiny was a natural death in an unnatural period of time? I didn't ask. His dreams were his reality now, and I couldn't help but remember Josephine's parting words to me.

McCreedy just stared at me and I stared back. I left his office without saying a word.

The changes began shortly afterwards. An initial report of slight increase in girth of the crowns of their heads was followed rapidly by bizarre growth patterns in both subjects. Their heads grew to almost twice their original volumes, the increase being not in the brain but the amount of fluid in which the brain was cushioned. Their eyes became sunken and tiny. Martin's arms lengthened and the fingers stretched from his hands like tendrils, flexing and touching all that they contacted, moving almost independently.

His height increased and he began to walk with an exaggerated stoop. He found Yvonne again.

The changes that Yvonne had experienced were not the same. Her gross flabbiness became packed with fat. She became huge, a mound of flesh, and her limbs, by contrast with Martin's, shrank until they seemed mere protrusions from the bulk of her torso. Her hair fell out and the great shining dome of her head shook constantly. She remained on her bed, slightly propped up by pillows so that her tiny eyes could continue to watch the monitor. Martin fed her and cared for her, kept her covered with blankets now that she could wear no clothes.

They regained an element of their earlier sexual ability; there was a certain revulsion in watching the reconsummation of their life together, but equally there was a certain fascination about the event. We watched silently, and in great discomfort, and drew no immediate conclusions.

'We are seeing the beginning of the metamorphosis,' said McCreedy eventually. He was consumed by his dreams, and yet, as the days passed and the features of the subjects became more bizarre, and their copulation became more frequent and more incomprehensible, so we all began to wonder what was to be the end result.

The monitors filled our files with information, the rocketing, fluctuating chemical levels, the unprecedented hormonal changes, the degradation and rebuilding of body parts.

In February of '02, just seven years after the experiment had begun, Martin and Yvonne copulated for the last time, Yvonne not moving from her position, almost flowing across her bed, bearing the weight of her husband. Her great head turned to stare at the monitor and then turned back and looked at the ceiling. Martin slipped off her and crouched by her, staring into the distance. They began to tremble.

The trembling, a violent shaking of their entire bodies, persisted through the day.

McCreedy was bright eyed and full of excitement. 'It's happening,' he said. 'It may take days, but it's happening, the change, the final metamorphosis.'

He made copious notes, and in the environment the trembling persisted, a continuous whole-body muscular spasm.

After a few hours their heartbeats began to slow and the electrical output from their brains began to lessen. By evening the hearts had stopped and the brains showed no activity at all.

The monitor screens became quiet, all except one small panel, a red panel that lighted up with black words on red background. 'Subjects are dead.'

We entered the environment and approached the bodies. McCreedy stared down at the corpses for a moment. He was shaking his head. 'I can't believe this,' he said finally, thoughtfully. 'Keep a brain activity watch . . . it may be that the whole metabolic rate has slowed to a phenomenally low level. We may be witnessing some sort of stasis prior to a major change.'

I said, 'Ray – there will be no change. The subjects are dead. Completely dead.'

'Nonsense,' snapped McCreedy. 'To take that attitude at this stage would be disastrous.' He began to examine the bodies, apparently oblivious of the fact that he might be contracting or spreading disease.

I left the environment and sat, for a while, among the silent technicians who watched McCreedy on the monitors. I felt the quietness, the emptiness of the place. I stared at the white walls and the meticulously clean equipment and benches. The atmosphere was heavy, dull. One corner of the laboratory was filled with neatly stacked printouts representing the last fifty years of the subjects' lives, and staring at that pile of information I realised that nowhere in its bulk could I put my finger on a single statement of feeling, of awareness. Even the sheets on which were recorded the last living moments of Martin and Yvonne were bare, sterile accounts of failing physiology and murmurings and alpha waves; there would be no account of what they thought, what they felt as death unfurled its protective wings about them.

We had concerned ourselves with two lives and had studied everything but life itself. It had all been wasted. In the end, bizarre hormonal changes had captured our attention with their effects upon the physical forms of the two subjects, and we had sunk without trace into chemical formulae and physical law. Perhaps the inevitability of such a conclusion should have been a personal vindication, but I felt a deep sense of guilt as I left the Institute, a powerful sense of failure.

I returned five days later to collect my few belongings. I visited the laboratory and was surprised to find everything still in operation, although there was no one there. The sealed door to the environment was open and I called through. There was a peculiar smell in the air.

'Who's there?'

It was McCreedy's voice. I walked to a monitor screen and stared at him. He stared towards the camera, obviously not seeing me. 'Who's that? Lipman?'

'Yes.'

'You couldn't see it through, eh? Well . . . I can't say I blame you. But I don't give up so easily.'

He returned to the subjects, both of which were now in a bad state of decomposition. Yvonne's body had liquefied quite phenomenally and the distended, distorted bones protruded through stretched skin.

'Something will happen,' he shouted. 'This is the most abnormal decomposition I have ever seen.'

His sleeves were rolled up and a thick, green slime coated his arms – he was feeling around among the bloated viscera of the dead woman, and the body seemed to writhe beneath his touch.

I turned away. Behind me McCreedy shouted, 'Look – Lipman, look!'

I closed the door against his madness.